CRUSHED
— TO THE —
BONE

ED J. THOMPSON

Crushed to the Bone

ISBNs: 978-1-7923-7342-8 (Print)

       978-1-7923-7343-5 (Ebook)

Printed in the USA.

To my precious mother, Ola M. Henry.

Also, to the memory of my father, Harry A. Henry, who is dearly missed.

Prologue

Dale looked out the window of his truck at the pouring rain. It was like he saw on the outside exactly what was happening to him on the inside. He once heard somewhere that when it rained after someone died, it meant that God was washing their footprints off the face of the earth. To Dale, it felt like he was the one being washed out along with the rest of the snow and grime on the ground. Unfortunately, he was very much alive. The rhythm of the rain hitting the windshield matched the beat of his heart. He wasn't pained, exactly; just wounded and sore—emotionally paralyzed. Lizzie was gone, and with her went his future. Now he was truly alone.

He pulled his pickup truck into the small driveway in front of his house and ran as fast as he could onto his front porch. Just that little bit of activity left him out of breath. It was a cold winter day in Schenectady, New York. February was always one of the worst months of winter. The wind blew the door open as soon as he turned the doorknob. As he stepped inside, he immediately turned and locked the door behind him. He stood there for a few moments, lost in the silence, and cried to himself quietly, then waited for the moment to pass like it always did.

The funeral was short and quick. That was the way that she wanted it. Altogether, there were only about a hundred people in attendance. He thought there might be more, but the weather may have kept some people away. There were also a good number of people who came to the calling hours the night before at the funeral home. Many of them were present when the two uniformed correction officers brought in his son Christopher, wearing prison green with his hands cuffed in front of him. They were supposed to bring him early for a private viewing but were delayed for some reason. The fact that Dale was terribly embarrassed was probably a good sign, at least not all his feeling was gone.

Christopher was their oldest son. At thirty-six years old, he had been in and out of jail and prison since he graduated from high school. All were drug-related offenses. His parents had tried everything they could think of to help him, but nothing worked. Christopher seemed determined to ruin his life. When he wasn't locked away, Christopher only cared about scamming money from people to buy drugs. He never had a real job to speak of, at least not for more than a month or so, and he was essentially capable of doing and saying just about anything. It was truly humiliating. Schenectady is a small blue-collar town where everybody knows everybody. In many ways, Christopher was better off in prison. Drug addiction is a disease right from the pit of hell.

At least Christopher got to see his mother one last time. Thomas John, his middle son, didn't attend his mother's funeral. "TJ," as he was nicknamed, was diagnosed with bipolar I disorder when he was just twelve years old. At one point, the doctors said they had never seen anyone that young with the condition before. He now lived on his own in Albany in a supervised setting. For the most part, TJ was okay when he was on the right medication regimen, and he was compliant. Unfortunately, his past was replete with instances of hospitalizations resulting from failure to take his medication.

TJ was overcome with grief when Dale finally found him on the street in Albany two days ago and told him that his mother had passed. Dale hated to leave him there, but having TJ around was a different kind of hell that he simply didn't have the strength to endure today. TJ's mood changes tore through the family for years like the plague. Lizzie, in particular, was negatively impacted. When TJ was in one of his episodes of depression, it was like trying to pull a drowning person out of quicksand. If you got too close, you risked falling in yourself.

The house smelled like sickness. Lizzie died at home— the way she wanted. At least he could give her that. They had turned their living room into a hospital room. A guy from church came over and helped him move most of the furniture into the basement and bring in a hospital bed. A hospice aide came to the house daily for nearly two months to take care of Lizzie.

For over a year, Lizzie had denied the truth about her illness and leaned heavily on her faith. She had fought her cancer valiantly to the end. Altogether, it was eighteen months from when she was first diagnosed. At times her pain was so great that it brought Dale to his knees. Cancer comes from hell too.

He made himself a cup of coffee and sat at the kitchen table to drink it. There were so many things he needed to do that he didn't quite know where to begin. Just the thought of it all made him cringe. There was only a week before he had to go back to work, and he had no strength left to do anything. He allowed himself to dive deep into the river of self-pity for a couple of minutes; it was his right to swim there, and he had grown accustomed to the soothing motion of its waves.

Dale was still immersed in his sorrow when he heard the front door unlock and open and his youngest son, Michael, appeared. Michael was thirty-one years old and his mother's favorite. She had held him close as long as she could, which turned out to be a big mistake. Ever since he was a toddler, Michael was always attached to Lizzie's skirt. She couldn't even go to the bathroom without him being right there. They used to laugh and joke about it. Christopher and TJ would mock the way Michael whined and convulsed whenever his mother put him down. Dale regretted that he never stepped in and forced Michael to stand on his own two feet.

"Hi, Daddy," Michael said soberly as he peeked his head around the corner.

Dale hadn't seen him since the funeral. Both of them had been pretty composed throughout the service. Michael didn't show at the brunch reception at Lizzie's sister Wanda's house after the funeral, which wasn't really a surprise. His son had a habit of retreating into his own world and disappearing.

"Where were you?" Dale asked dryly without looking up.

"Nowhere, I just couldn't take it anymore," Michael mumbled. "Why? Did something happen?"

"Did you eat something?" Dale inquired, purposely ignoring Michael's question.

"No, I'm not hungry. Besides, there is nothing here to eat," Michael scoffed.

"All this food that people brought over, and you can't find anything to eat?"

"I don't want any of that," Michael whined. "I'll probably eat something later."

"Suit yourself," Dale maintained. "Do you think maybe you could help me move some of this stuff later? I have to return the hospital bed tomorrow, or they are going to charge me extra."

"I don't know, maybe if I'm here," Michael managed to say before turning and scurrying up the stairs to his room.

Dale heard the door shut and sighed heavily. He would have to figure it out like he always did. Michael was never that much help around the house—or anywhere else, for that matter. He mostly stayed in his room watching television and playing video games like a teenager.

Somehow Michael had managed to keep his job at the little convenience mart, but he couldn't be counted on to do much else. After Lizzie got sick and she could no longer wait on him hand and foot, Michael became even more of a recluse, only appearing to eat or to go to work, and he always left a mess wherever he'd been.

Dale had a lot of built-up frustration about Michael still living at home. Michael acted entitled, and the level of his selfishness was astonishing. Dale lost his temper occasionally, but he knew Lizzie hated it when he got after his son. He continued to prepare meals after she went down, but he flatly refused to do Michael's laundry or to take him to work.

Recently, however, Dale began to wonder whether there was more to Michael than he ever realized; he was always such an odd kid, like a square peg in a round hole. And he always seemed to rub his father the wrong way. As a result, Dale was more than a little surprised at Michael's hint of actual substance and depth during his mother's final days. Perhaps there was a glimmer of hope after all.

It was just 4:30 p.m. It seemed later. Lizzie was cremated, and there was no burial. Wanda was Lizzie's older sister, and she had insisted on inviting everyone to her house after the funeral. Dale made an appearance solely out of obligation, and he was determined to make a swift exit as soon as he could.

Fortunately, only a dozen or so people were there, mostly from Lizzie's family. Everyone was very kind, and he appreciated their show of support. But he was never good at these kinds of things, so being there only made him feel more pathetic than he already did. Altogether, he was only there for a little over an hour.

Wanda and Lizzie were very close. The past year had been hard on Wanda too, and Dale would not have been able to get through it had it not been for her. She had been right by her sister's side the whole time, except when she wasn't physically well herself. He had watched her earlier as she interacted with people and tended to her guests like a perfect host, and he marveled at her strength. Both she and Lizzie were exceptional black women.

Their younger brother Daniel, however, was a different story. He and Dale recently had words, and it was awkward between them now. They had only spoken twice since Lizzie died, once when Daniel called from his apartment in New Jersey to express his sympathies the morning after, and once at the funeral home.

Dale wasn't exactly angry with Daniel, just disappointed at what he considered to be a complete lack of concern on Daniel's part for his dying sister, who adored him. He didn't regret anything he had said to Daniel about it either; it was water under the bridge as far as he was concerned. Lizzie was dead.

Reverend Harris, the pastor who officiated at the funeral, arrived at Wanda's house as Dale was preparing to leave, and the two men spoke only briefly. Reverend Harris was a nice guy, but Dale didn't know him too well. He was new at the church, and they never had much contact with him prior to Lizzie being diagnosed. But Lizzie grew to love him, and he was always at the house or the hospital whenever she needed him.

The church was Grace Union Church, where they had attended as kids. It was a small southern Baptist church with approximately 250 members. Dale and Lizzie went to church every Sunday when they were first married. Lizzie was the one who got him started going to church in the first place after they began going steady in middle school. Before that, he was utterly unchurched. She had introduced him to the things of God, which was just one of several reasons why she was the best thing that ever happened to him.

Lizzie always loved everything about the Bible, and she would have gone to church more after they had the kids, but the boys made that difficult. She was always exhausted after running behind them all week, and Christopher and TJ never cooperated on Sunday mornings. Oftentimes, Dale would go to church by himself. However, after Christopher got involved in youth football, his attendance dwindled down to mostly holidays and special events.

He even stopped volunteering at the church food pantry, which he had loved doing twice a month. He now believed that that was all a mistake and that he should have set a better example for the boys. Without a doubt, he erred by not making God their priority.

Truthfully, almost nothing had turned out the way that he had hoped or planned. This wasn't the life that he had imagined that he would have or the one that he had promised Lizzie when he proposed marriage. He wasn't a bad person. He had never intentionally hurt anybody who didn't deserve it, and he was always willing to do whatever he could to help others. But it seemed like trouble regularly followed him.

Maybe he was cursed. The Bible mentions generational curses, and he came from a highly dysfunctional background. He never knew his father, and his mother was an absentee parent and alcoholic. Dale had practically raised his younger brother, Louis, when he was just a kid himself, and look at how that turned out. Maybe he was just destined to struggle and suffer great heartbreak his entire life.

He heard a preacher say once that real men get up every morning, go to work, and come home on time to the people they love. For his part, he had provided a good living for his family, and he had worshipped the ground that his wife walked on. And there was never even one night in the lives of his boys when they didn't know where their dad was.

Moreover, he had served God as best he could. Lizzie was a wonderful wife and mother and didn't deserve to die from breast cancer at the age of fifty-six. Like a small sampling of heaven, one shortened lifetime with her wasn't nearly enough. It was cruel.

Each passing day and year had been harder than the last. He could hardly remember the last time he was truly at peace. It took every ounce of strength he had just to get out of bed this morning—and tomorrow looked bleak. Loving her was the only thing he was ever good at. He was more than ready to die too.

He felt irrelevant—an afterthought. There are worse things than never having been born at all. This was one of those things. Clearly, either God couldn't help him, or he didn't want to rescue him from his grief and pain.

Regardless, Dale was very broken, and he refused to pretend otherwise or be comforted or accepting of everything as "the will of God" or as somehow being in his best interest. He was cursed; there was no doubt about it. Having taken the devil's best shot, he was crushed to the bone. This was the absolute worst day of his life.

Chapter 1

Dale Johnson was born and raised in Schenectady, New York, located in eastern New York State near the joining of the Mohawk and Hudson Rivers. Schenectady became the headquarters for the General Electric Company in 1886. It is one of the ten largest cities in New York State, having a population of approximately 80,000 people in 1962, the year that Dale was born. The city's black, or African American, population was roughly twenty percent. It is in the same metropolitan area as Albany, the state capital situated about fifteen miles southeast.

Dale had a crush on Lizzie since they were in middle school. He was a year older than her, and it took months before he could muster up enough nerve to even say hi to her. She was popular with the boys, and he wasn't in her league. He daydreamed about her all the time and watched her from afar. It was puppy love on steroids.

He nearly passed out when she walked up to him early one morning at school and tapped him on the shoulder from behind. He turned, and they were face-to-face for the very first time. She was light-skinned with piercing greyish-brown eyes. She wore her straight hair pulled back into a shoulder-length ponytail. Her skin was smooth and glowed, and her smile took his breath away. She was perfect!

"Are you ever going to talk to me?" she asked pointedly.

"Uh...what?" he heard himself say in falsetto.

"You heard me. You like me, don't you?"

"Uh...I don't know...I mean, yeah...I mean, you wanna talk to me?"

"Look, I'm just saying that it's okay if you want to call me sometime."

"Okay," was all he said.

His throat felt like it was closing. She handed him a piece of paper, smiled, and walked away. Dale was in a haze. His heart was pounding in his chest, and his thoughts were racing. He never imagined that she had given him a second thought.

Just then, his friend Jim started laughing and pointing at him. He had forgotten that Jim was standing right there and witnessed the whole thing. Now he was really embarrassed.

"Smooth, lover boy!" Jim mocked.

He put both of his hands around his own neck and acted like he was choking.

"Shut up!" Dale shouted and shoved him hard.

Undeterred, Jim started blinking his eyes excessively and swaying his hips.

"I mean it. I'll kick your butt," Dale threatened.

Jim toned down his laughing a little. Dale was bigger and stronger than him.

"Well, that couldn't have gone worse," Jim pointed out.

"Drop it! I mean it!" Dale demanded.

"Okay, Romeo, cool your jets," Jim said. "At least now you know she likes you...but I can't for the life of me figure out why."

It was a week before he called her; he didn't know what to say. Somehow, Lizzie forgave this breach in dating etiquette, and they quickly became a couple. She was enchanting, and together they were Romeo and Juliet. He couldn't believe his good fortune.

Lizzie was the one who talked him into trying out for football. She had a way of making him feel like he could do anything. He had never played organized football before, but he was strong and fast. He also loved the game. He grew five inches his sophomore year in high school to six foot four inches. He made the varsity team in eleventh grade and was the starting wide receiver his senior year and team co-captain.

He felt like he was on top of the world. Suddenly everybody wanted to be his friend, and his name was in the Daily Gazette every week. He and Lizzie were the golden couple. Other girls would occasionally flirt with him, but he barely noticed. He only had eyes for the most beautiful girl in the world.

Sometimes when they were close, he stopped listening because he experienced sensory overload. He knew that he was "punking out," but he couldn't help it. He came to life the day she smiled at him, and now his heart was wide open.

His family struggled for everything. His mother was a part-time hairdresser and a lover of the nightlife. There were many early mornings when he and his brother Louis had to peel her off the couch and carry her to bed. Just seventeen years old when Dale was born, she never married, and they never knew their fathers. She had several live-in boyfriends over the years, each one worse than the last.

The one exception was Arturo Perez. Arturo was a good man—better than she deserved. She was a hard woman and a mean drunk. Most people have good days and bad days, but his mother had bad ones and worse ones. She was a lost soul who vomited out her inner pain on everyone like a colicky baby. She disappeared for a week, and that was the last straw. Arturo moved out and got his own place, leaving Dale alone to care for both his mother and brother—again.

Louis was just eighteen months younger than Dale, but the age difference seemed greater. Dale was physically so much bigger than his brother, who was exceptionally short for his age at just five foot four inches. Dale was very protective of Louis, who looked up to his older brother in almost every way. There was a secret understanding between them, and they were their own family.

Two grades separated them in school, and Louis was the better student. Sometimes he would wait after school in the bleachers for Dale to finish football practice, and they would walk home together. That was better for him than risking being alone in the apartment with their mother. Louis lacked the wherewithal to stand up to her, and Dale always kept her in check.

They had no extended family that they knew of since their mother grew up in foster care. They didn't know how she ended up in the system because she always avoided talking about it. Apparently, she had relatives in Albany, but they never came around. Her only friends were several women she had befriended at the beauty shop. Some were okay, but most

17

were ruffians like her. Dale often dreamed of the day when he would have a normal family.

He never brought Lizzie to their apartment because he was always concerned about how his mother would behave. Outside of school, the lovebirds mostly hung out on the weekends at her house. Dale would do whatever she wanted, even go to church. Her father was a deacon, and her mother sang in the choir. They were always nice to him. Her little brother, Daniel, treated him like a celebrity.

One afternoon he was talking with Lizzie in front of her house when her father came out and asked to speak to him. Dale was immediately taken back, and he looked at Lizzie for a clue. She just shrugged her shoulders and looked perplexed. He had a bad feeling as he followed Mr. Lawson into the house.

It was a small, white two-story cape cod. The wood siding was peeling in places, and the house needed to be painted. Out front, on one side, was a narrow driveway leading to a detached garage that was too full of junk to fit a car. They walked through the front door into a small foyer and then into the living room. The two sat down on opposite sides of the sofa. The room was neat and clean, with a television in the corner that had a bunch of wires bundled together and coming out the back of the cable box sitting on top of it. Mr. Lawson seemed nervous, which made Dale even more worried. He was in his mid-forties, brown-skinned, and slightly overweight. He was also a policeman for the city of Schenectady.

"See here, Dale, I have been meaning to talk to you about this for a while," he began. "See, Lizzie is a good girl, a really good girl. And I know you two like each other and all…and nothing against you, but she is young, and I don't want to see my daughter get hurt."

"Did I do something?" Dale asked meekly.

"No, no. That's not it at all," Mr. Lawson expressed. "See, it's my job to look after her, and I wanted to ask you, man to man, you know, to promise me before this goes any further that you will not take advantage of her. You seem like a nice enough guy, but I used to be young once myself, and—"

"I would never do anything to hurt Lizzie," Dale interrupted.

"I know you say that now, but you're graduating this year, and she still has another year of school," he explained. "What happens then? Do you have any idea?"

"Well, no...not exactly. But..." Dale blurted out.

He didn't know what to say. He was thinking quickly aloud.

"Look, I probably should have said something before. It's been on my mind for some time. But I can't let you come in here and break her heart all apart and then move on with some college cheerleader or somebody. Please understand that it's nothing personal against you."

Dale could feel the weight of every word coming at him.

He sat straight up and pleaded, "No, it won't be like that. It won't be! I couldn't do anything like that! I will do anything you say, but please don't take her away from me!"

"It's not that I don't believe you, but you don't even know who or what you want at this point," Mr. Lawson explained. "I just want you to be careful with my girl's heart. It's different for boys. I know that. I just need you to look me in my eye and promise me that you will always do right by her. Because if you can't, then we are going to have to figure something else out. I need to hear you say it."

Mr. Lawson suddenly looked like a trapped animal. His eyes were big and darting, and the veins on the sides of his neck were bulging out. He clearly wasn't enjoying having this conversation any more than Dale was, and Dale wondered whether his wife had put him up to it.

"I promise on my life! Lizzie means more to me than anything! I love her!" Dale declared and choked up.

The tension in the air was suffocating.

"Okay then, we've got a deal," the older man said.

Lizzie's dad stood up and extended his right hand. Dale bolted to his feet, and they shook hands. He was sweating profusely like he did when he ran sprints at practice. His insides were still shaking when he walked outside to a waiting Lizzie.

"What happened? Is everything okay?" she asked.

"Nothing…it's okay; he just wanted to talk."

"Are you sure? Do you want me to talk to him?" she solicited.

"No, please don't," he insisted. "He just wanted to talk to me man to man. I get it. I told him that I love you."

Her eyes grew big as saucers.

"You did? What did he say?"

"He didn't say anything," Dale recounted. "I'm just glad he knows how I feel now."

"You are? So now what?"

"Now I'm going to prove to everyone how much I love you," he committed.

"You don't have to prove anything to anyone. I know how we feel about each other."

She reached out her arms, and they held each other as close as they could. Pressing into him, she began nibbling on his neck, something he had come to enjoy. This felt perfect to him. He could feel himself calming down. But he wasn't at all convinced that she had any idea just how much she meant to him.

However, that "little talk" with Mr. Lawson changed his life forever. He was now intent on proving himself worthy of Lizzie. Dale had never thought much about his future beyond high school. His grades were just average, and he didn't want to go to college. Despite making the all-sectional team, he wasn't recruited by any schools for football, and he couldn't afford to pay for college. Besides, there was just no way he was going to leave Lizzie behind—or Louis for that matter.

He needed a job. His guidance counselor suggested that he learn a trade or start taking civil service exams and try to get something with the state. There were plenty of state jobs in Albany for people who wanted to work, or so he had heard. He thought he might be good with his hands, but he didn't really care what kind of job it was as long as he could eventually make a decent living at it.

When football season ended, Dale suddenly had much more free time on his hands to be with his friends and worry about things with Lizzie. Both Lizzie and Louis were a lot more serious about school than he ever was, and they were always busy with homework. In contrast, Dale rarely studied anything. He pretty much just did what he needed to do to get by to be able to play football.

At the year-end football banquet, one of his teammate's dads walked up to him and offered him a job working at his automotive garage located downtown. The offer came out of nowhere as Dale wasn't good friends with his son Chris Carbone or anything. But Dale readily accepted because he needed the money. He figured if it didn't work out, he could always quit and look for another job.

However, Mr. Carbone was very good to him. He was tall with dark hair that he wore slicked back. He was forty-five years old, loud, and opinionated. For some reason, he took to Dale right away and asked a lot of questions about his personal life. Dale wasn't used to talking about himself with anyone other than Lizzie and Louis, so it was a little offsetting at first. But he gradually grew more comfortable.

Dale worked from 3:00 p.m. to 6:00 p.m. on weekdays and 9:00 a.m. to noon on Saturdays. It was a small garage, but it was very busy. In the beginning, Dale mostly just cleaned. But occasionally, one of the mechanics taught him how to do something, like oil changes or tire rotations. He was really interested in how cars worked, a fact that had somehow escaped him before he started working at the garage.

He was a fast learner too. He made it a point to always be on time, and he did whatever anybody asked him to do. He also asked a lot of questions. It wasn't long before Dale preferred being at the garage much more than going to school. Work made him feel like a man and not like a punk kid.

Not only did Mr. Carbone teach Dale about cars, but he also taught him basic life skills. For instance, he taught Dale how to drive and took him to his road test to get a driver's license. He also made Dale get checking and savings accounts. A couple of times, he insisted that Dale listen in when he had to deal with a difficult customer, and they talked about it afterward.

Dale wanted to save enough to go to the senior prom and maybe buy a car. He decided that he should not let his mother know how much money he made. Whenever she asked him for money, he just gave it to her. She never asked for much anyway, twenty or thirty dollars here and there, but only because she thought he was making less than he did. If she knew that he had more, then she would have asked for more for sure. She wasn't good with money because she never had any. Her job at the beauty shop was off the books, and they lived off public assistance.

Dale's friends nicknamed him "old man" because they said that he was always so serious. He couldn't help it. Although he had a good sense of humor, he was never one much for buffoonery—especially now because he was so far behind others in many areas and desperately wanted to catch up. There was simply no time for foolishness, and he refused to pretend otherwise.

Dale liked to have a good time just as much as his friends did, but there was a line that he refused to cross. He hated alcohol and drugs for obvious reasons. When it turned into that kind of party, he tried to find his way home. He had never once tasted beer, even though it was often the only thing in the refrigerator at home. Just the smell of it made him gag.

He started going to church every Sunday with Lizzie. That he felt like a fish out of water was an understatement. Eventually, he dragged Louis along too, who wasn't keen on the idea at first. But the message of everyone being a part of the family of God resonated a lot with them both.

To his surprise, Louis bought a Bible and started studying it on his own. Almost overnight, he became obsessed with the desire to know everything he could about the Jesus they were talking and singing about. And he kept discovering these "amazing" truths in "the Word" that went over Dale's head when Louis tried to share them with him. When Louis foolishly allowed his mother to learn of his developing spiritual awakening, she began teasing him and started referring to him sarcastically as her "little manger boy."

Unlike his brother, however, Dale was only there for the girl. He wasn't overly impressed with the church's teachings because they seemed a little unrealistic to him. Some of the people seemed weird too, but they were all nice enough. Sometimes he felt more than a little inspired by the sermon and the singing, but that didn't mean anything. He couldn't see himself ever taking this stuff too seriously.

Of course, Lizzie was caught up in it all. But she didn't really understand what it was like to be him—to have absolutely nothing at all. Her mother and father loved her and took care of her. There was food in their refrigerator, and she got Christmas and birthday presents every year. People told her that she was special and beautiful. She felt secure and could easily imagine an all-loving God and perfect heaven where every day was sunshine. But from where he stood, it hardly seemed possible.

There were plenty of late-night conversations on the phone with Lizzie before they went to bed. He loved listening to her share her secrets. She possessed an innocence that struck a chord in him and left him undone. He wanted to tell her everything about himself, but there was a wall he had built around his heart to protect it from predators. As a result, he still needed to keep some things to himself, which meant she told him everything, and he only told her what he thought she could handle knowing.

Oftentimes when they were together, he would pretend they were a married couple living a wonderful life together, just the two of them. Dale wanted badly to be someone that she could respect and of whom she could be proud. He wanted to be able to take her places and buy her things. And he wanted to feel worthy of her affections. His big fear was that he would never be able to do any of those things, and that she would come to her senses and realize that it was a big mistake to go out with him.

Sometimes he would take her hand and gently squeeze it to make sure she wasn't a dream. In response, the way that she would look up at him with that breathtaking smile on her face was all the heaven he would ever need. If nothing else, he was convinced that only a divine mastermind could have created someone this incredible for him to love.

Dale kept his promise and was very respectful toward Lizzie. He knew about sex. One of his mother's friends had taught him about it when he was very young. Even when Lizzie wanted to, he never would let himself go all the way. Once, he came close to losing himself in the moment when they were alone in the basement at a friend's house after the homecoming dance.

"What's wrong?" she asked as he pulled away.

"No, I can't do this."

"Why not? It's okay. Don't you want to?" she pouted.

"That's not it; you know that."

"Then what is it?"

"I want it to be right between us."

"It is right," she protested.

"You know what I mean. Not like this. You deserve better."

"Better than what?" she demanded. "Sometimes you treat me like a delicate piece of glass or something. You know that I am not perfect, right?"

"I think you are."

"That's what I mean," she maintained. "It makes me feel…I don't know…like a fake."

"I know you're real," he asserted.

"But do you see me?" she provoked. "Because if you don't, then what we have isn't really real."

"How can you say that?" he was hurt and pulled away.

His shirt was completely open, and he started buttoning up. He hated these moments between them.

"I am not a fake person. I love you," he maintained.

"I know that. Nobody is as loving as you. But, Dale, how come you can't see yourself the way that everybody else sees you? The way I see you. Then maybe everything wouldn't be so hard for you all the time," she argued.

"I'm just trying to love you the best way that I know how. Why is that so wrong?" he questioned and looked away.

He was confused and started to shut down. He wanted to leave. They never had any disagreements to speak of, partly because he was always so amenable when it came to her. The only time he ever pushed back was when she questioned some part of their relationship.

"Are you sure?" she asked. "That's all it is?"

"Listen to me, I'm sure…me and you're a promise made in heaven before there was even time," he whispered. "There has never been anything like this before."

Chapter 2

Although Dale did not fully recognize it at the time, Mr. Carbone and the two other guys at the garage were a gift from God to him. He learned much more than auto mechanics from them. They shared their personal lives, the things that they had experienced, and their current problems.

At first, Dale was hesitant about confiding in them. But they liked kidding him and offering him advice. Gradually, he began talking freely, and they became an active part of his life. Mr. Carbone even took him to get fitted for a tuxedo for the prom and arranged for Dale to be part of the group of kids who rented limos together for the event.

"Hey Dale, did you ever talk to your counselor about Delhi?" Mr. Carbone shouted. He was working on a car, his head under the hood.

"No, I tried, but she wasn't there when I went to see her."

"Well, you need to go back. I tell my son the same thing all the time. You can't just expect things to just fall in your lap."

"I probably can't get into that school anyway," Dale said under his breath.

"What? What did you say?" his boss challenged.

Dale was nervous.

"He said that he doesn't want to leave his girlfriend." Joey jumped in and grinned.

Joey Simon was only three years older than Dale, and he was already married with a baby on the way. Joey was six feet tall with an athletic build. He wore his dark hair in a crew cut. Joey graduated from Schenectady High School, but Dale never knew him before he was hired at the garage. Joey was working in the other stall on a black jeep.

Annoyed, Dale protested, "I never said that!"

"You didn't have to," Joey insisted. "Girl's got you whipped."

"What do you know about it?" Dale shot back and glared at Joey from the back corner where he was cleaning tools.

The two were kindred spirits and had developed a relationship where they enjoyed baiting each other.

"I know all you ever think about is the love of your life. Lizzie this, Lizzie that. Kiss, kiss, kiss. Say I'm lying," Joey taunted.

"Like you're any different. We hear you on the phone with Tracy. She tells you to jump and—"

"Cut it out the both of you," Mr. Carbone interjected. "Before you put the girl on her back, you better make sure that you can put her on yours. Dale, how many times have I told you that you need to be thinking about more than this minute. Mark my words, one day you will regret not taking advantage of your opportunities to better yourself. Once you get settled down, it's a different story. Isn't that right, Joey? Tell him, old boy! I don't hear you talking now. Life is hard. Same rules for everybody. You have to plan for the future you want."

"I told you, I went to see my counselor," Dale defended. "She wasn't there. What else am I supposed to do?"

"Then go back, Einstein!" his boss ordered. "Do it tomorrow, and I don't what to hear no more about it."

Dale felt trapped. Joey was right. He didn't want to talk to his counselor. Delhi State University was located about seventy-five miles southeast of Schenectady. Mr. Carbone had gone there and thought it was the perfect school for Dale. It had a two-year automotive technology program. Dale appreciated that Mr. Carbone showed so much interest in him, but there was no chance in hell that he was going to move away. He just had to find a way to tell him.

The next morning, he went to see Mrs. Arnold, his counselor. She was a grey-haired woman nearing retirement age who had a physical disability and walked with a brace and a cane. In all, Dale had only spoken to her a few times over the years. He needed to be able to tell his boss that at least he talked to her.

Her office was small, and her desk cluttered. She was on the phone when he walked up to the door, and she gestured for him to come in and sit down. As soon as she finished with her call, she looked up.

"Hi. What can I do for you, Mr. Johnson?"

"I was wondering if...if you knew anything about Delhi college?

"Why do you ask? Are you thinking about applying there?"

Dale wasn't sure how to answer and hesitated slightly before responding, "I heard that they have an automotive mechanics program."

"Yes, that's true. But I didn't think that you were interested in going to college," she said pointedly.

"I'm probably not, really," Dale needed to say. "My boss at my job wanted me to ask."

"Well, I think that it might be a good program for a guy like you. Would you live on campus or commute?"

"Commute?" he asked.

"Yes, it's only a little over an hour from here. Lots of kids commute from home. I bet you can do it, if you want to. Look let me put together a packet for you. I would have made something up for you already had I known that you were interested. But there still might be time. I know people there. Delhi is a state college, so it is affordable, and we can definitely get you some financial aid. Would that work?"

Dale shook his head and said, "Yes, but do you think I can get in? I mean, with my grades and all?"

"You didn't take the SAT, as I recall, but as I said, let me see what I can find out. Fair enough?"

"Yes, thank you very much."

"Oh, you're very welcome. Give me a week. Okay?"

Dale was more than a little stunned by the way that conversation had gone. He half-expected Mrs. Arnold to laugh in his face. He never seriously thought about college. Also, no one ever told him anything about commuting. He wasn't exactly sure how that would work, but if he could somehow manage it, then Lizzie's dad would see that he was serious about her because he would stay local. He knew that it was a long shot, but the very idea was enticing. Maybe he could find a life that mattered after all.

As soon as he walked into the garage that afternoon, Mr. Carbone followed him out back into the bathroom and asked about it.

"Hey, did you go see the counselor like I told you?"

"Yeah."

"So…what did she say?"

Dale sat down on a small bench there and started to change into his work clothes.

"She said that she would look into it for me. She said I should have said something to her earlier."

"What?"

His boss raised his eyebrows in utter amazement and leaned on the door frame.

"Tell me this, isn't that supposed to be *her* job?" he asked. "These people never cease to amaze me."

"She said to give her a week," Dale reported.

"Good. See, I told you. Was that so hard?"

Mr. Carbone was clearly satisfied with himself, and he wasn't going to lose the chance to rub it in.

Dale walked over to the toilet and began to relieve himself.

"I still probably can't get in anyway," he maintained. "I didn't even take the SAT. Don't get your hopes up. I only went to see her because you made me."

"What you mean is that you don't want to get your hopes up," Mr. Carbone argued. "It doesn't matter what I think, buddy boy. Only what you think. It's your life; only you can live it."

Dale didn't say anything. He just walked to the sink and washed his hands. He had no idea why Mr. Carbone cared so much when he had his own son to worry about. Sometimes it was annoying.

Lizzie absolutely loved the idea. She said that this was the first time that she had seen him excited about something that didn't involve football. While he didn't think that was the case, he didn't say anything. All that mattered was that she was excited for him, which meant somewhere inside, she believed that he could succeed at college. That meant everything to him. But he still wondered if maybe he should have kept the whole thing to himself—just for now.

It turns out he was right. It was too late, and he didn't meet the minimum requirement for admission to Delhi. Mrs. Arnold knew it all along. She had a different idea—SUNY Schenectady County Community College. He could start taking classes in the summer. They had a program with Delhi, so he could possibly begin taking automotive classes at Delhi by winter. She said he qualified for financial aid and could probably graduate owing little or nothing in student loans. Dale was disappointed. All he heard was that he wasn't ready for college.

"This is good news. Why do you look so glum?" she asked and began nibbling on her bottom lip.

"I know. I'm okay," he said.

"Dale, I am really proud of you," she said. "This is a big step. You were so dead set against going to college when we talked before. Something changed. *You* changed. I can see it. Good for you...a lot of kids here don't have a clue about what they want...about who they are or what's important. But you do. That puts you ahead of the game, in my book.

Come on; this isn't bad news—none of it. You can do it! You really can!"

"Thank you for helping me," he said sincerely.

He knew that she was right. He never even tried to put his best foot forward academically. He needed to catch up—and he would do it all for Lizzie.

The remainder of the school year was probably the beginning of the best period of Dale's life. Once he got his head around the idea of going to summer school, he started to feel better about everything. Being a graduating senior was exciting. There were parties and special moments with Lizzie. Everyone was congratulating him and seemed impressed when he told them his plans.

Dale and Lizzie slept together for the first time on graduation night. Initially, he resisted again, but it felt right this time. He never knew that he could ever love another person this much. They fell asleep in each other's arms afterward, and he was afraid that her father had half of the police force out looking for them. But it was quiet when they walked into her house around 1:30 a.m. He danced in the street all the way home.

***

Chris Carbone also graduated, and they took a few pictures together at graduation, at his father's insistence. Dale was finishing up his shift at the garage the day after graduation when his boss called out to him to move the white pickup truck in the back lot into the first stall. Dale did as he was told and put the keys on the rack where they kept the customer's keys.

"What are you doing?" Mr. Carbone asked and stared at Dale.

"What?

"With the truck?"

"You said to move the white truck?" Dale responded.

"But did I tell you to put the keys over there?"

Dale was confused.

"Joe, did you hear me tell him to put the keys in the rack?" Mr. Carbone asked snidely.

"Nope, you never said that," Joey replied.

"Steve, what did I tell this guy to do?"

"I heard you say move it. That's all I heard," Steve answered.

"Dale, ask me what I want you to do with the keys," he demanded.

"Okay...okay. Look, I don't know what's going on, but what do you want me to do with the keys?"

"Listen closely this time, hot shot," Mr. Carbone instructed. "We want you to take those keys...and use them to drive your graduation present home."

There was a moment of silence while they waited for Dale to figure it out.

"Wait...what? I don't understand," he maintained.

No one said anything or moved.

Dale stood there thinking, searching.

Suddenly he jerked his head and looked hard at the Chevy truck. Then he lowered his head, put his face in his hands, and began to sob. He didn't want to and was trying hard to fight it. But it came like waves running through him. Shocked and embarrassed, he didn't want to look any of them in the eyes.

He had never been so sweetly honored before. For the very first time, he felt the love of God deep down in his soul. Love that didn't make sense—that he didn't deserve. Louis tried to tell him about it once, but he just didn't get it. While people had done nice things for him before, there was never anything quite like this. Just then, he felt his hardened heart being changed from the inside out.

The three men rushed him, and they laughed and cried together.

Chapter 3

Dale began seeing in color. His heart had been almost as callous as his mother's heart; he just hid it better. Now everything was different. School was different, and his relationships were different. He always knew that he had learned not to trust anyone fully. But it was much more than that. He was so angry about his life that he was secretly waiting for his opportunity to get back at a world that had turned its back on him from the second he was born.

The change taking place within him was monumental. He was no longer plotting and biding his time. No eye for an eye; the feeling disappeared in an instant. And while he still felt unworthy of Lizzie, he didn't feel empty anymore.

He had two summer classes: English and math. Dale liked math more than reading and writing. But he attacked both with the same intensity. Louis helped him write his papers, and he studied almost every night. His efforts bore fruit, and he did very well in both classes.

Dale worshipped his truck. It had 89,000 miles on it when he got it, but the body was in great shape. He was always working on it and buying something new for it. Joey joked that Dale washed his truck more than he washed his own backside.

The truth is that having his own transportation immediately raised their standard of living because being mobile meant that doing things like going to the supermarket, the laundromat or a doctor's appointment didn't have to take all day. They no longer had to take the bus.

Moreover, he and Lizzie started going on real dates by themselves. They went to the movies and to the mall in Albany. Sometimes they just drove to the park and talked. She acted like it was no big deal to her, but he could tell that she welcomed the upgrade. His self-esteem was sky-high. There's nothing like laughing from your heart for the first time. He felt like he was living somebody else's life.

The one constant negative in his world, however, remained his mother. Louis was evolving rapidly as his growing faith anchored him. He kept trying with their mother, and she kept disappointing him. One night she threw a tantrum about nothing in particular and slammed the door to her bedroom behind her. They just looked at each other and sat there together in the living room, listening while the demons inside her howled at the moon. Dale just shook his head and turned up the sound on the television. Louis, however, looked seriously dejected.

"You're joking, right?" Dale exclaimed.

Louis didn't respond.

Dale continued, "How many times are you going to do this? You know that she's never going to change."

"You don't know that!" Louis shouted.

"The hell I don't," Dale argued. "You're crazy, and the sooner you stop beating your head against the wall, the better. She's a monster, period. Get over it!"

"She just needs help." Louis countered. "We need to find someone. Maybe a counselor or somebody. I don't think anyone has ever really tried to help her."

"All of the counselors in the world can't save someone who doesn't want to be saved."

"God can do it!" Louis pressed. "I've been praying, and I know that he can. You don't know what you're talking about. Don't forget she's our mother!"

Dale's blood came to a rushing boil.

"Say what?" he fumed. "Don't forget she's our mother? Is that what you just said to me? Because I wish that there was a way I could somehow forget that that mess in there is our mother. I am finally starting to find my way out of this hell hole that she keeps trying to bury us in. And you better find your way out, too, before it's too late"

"Addicted people can recover," Louis refuted. "We can't just give up on her. It's our job to help her!"

"You're a fool if you believe that," Dale countered. "Leave her be. I'm not telling you again!"

Dale stared angrily at Louis for a couple of seconds before getting up and storming out of the room. His brother had a weakness for their mother that made no sense to him. LaToya Johnson was pure evil, and she didn't care anything about her children. She treated Louis bad especially—like something she found on the bottom of her shoe.

The only reason they were still with her and not in the system themselves was because Dale had covered for her all these years. He cooked and cleaned while she sat on her butt or ran the streets. He was the one who made sure Louis got to school every day and had what he needed. She would probably be in jail now if it weren't for him. Whenever the social workers from the county had come to the apartment for a surprise inspection, he had lied for her. She had walked away from any parental concern or responsibility long ago.

But he hated fighting with his brother. Louis was the only one in the world who shared his pain. He stayed in his room the rest of the night. The next morning was Sunday. Service was at 11:00 a.m. He woke up at 9:15 a.m. and jumped in the shower. He opened the door to his brother's room, turned on the light, and without saying a word, he headed toward the small kitchen to start breakfast. Dale was just finishing cooking the eggs, bacon, grits, and toast breakfast when Louis walked in.

As usual, they didn't speak or acknowledge one another. Louis went to the refrigerator, took out the orange juice, poured a little into two glasses, and sat down. Dale set the plates of food on the table before sitting down.

"Uh, Dale...I'm really—" Louis began.

"I know, man. Me too," Dale interrupted.

The brothers typically didn't sit together in church. Dale always sat closer to the front with Lizzie. Louis sat in the back with the teenagers, who were trying to stay out of the eyesight of their parents.

Dale liked being there now more than before, and he could pretty much pay attention throughout the entire sermon without fixating on his girlfriend. He didn't understand everything the way that Louis did but was trying to get as much out of the messages as he could. Dale could taste the promise of a better life that was being taught, and he was starting to believe that maybe God did have a plan for his life after all.

Typically, if Lizzie had time for him after church, they would hang out. If not, he went back home with Louis and wasted the rest of the day away. His mother always slept well into the afternoon and stayed in her room the rest of the time. She was never a big eater, but she would call out to them if she wanted something. Unless the weather was bad or she didn't feel well, she almost always had someplace that she needed to be in the evenings. She would occasionally bring a guy home, which Dale hated because her room was next to his and the walls were paper thin.

Every so often, Dale met up with Joey at night. Joey wasn't a homebody, and he had a hard time being cooped up in the house with a new baby for long. They would go to a pizza place or to a bar and just talk or play pool. Joey hated that Dale didn't drink beer, and sometimes Dale would nurse one just to appease him. But he never actually swallowed any of it.

However, their conversations were good because they gave Dale insight into what it was like to be young and married. Dale didn't personally know any other guys his age who were married. Joey was honest about his struggles, and they talked about everything. Dale listened intently, but he rarely offered Joey any advice because he was pretty much clueless when it came to relationships and family matters.

***

His high school counselor was right. By January, he was commuting to the Delhi campus. He liked his automotive classes, although he was surprised at how hard some of them were. It was Lizzie's senior year, and they were looking forward to her graduating in the spring. She wasn't exactly sure what she wanted to do after high school, but her parents were pressuring her to go to college. She was thinking about maybe nursing as a career path.

The subject of marriage came up between them on occasion. Obviously, Dale wanted to marry her as soon as possible. But he didn't think her father would be onboard with that, and he really wanted her father's blessing. He surmised that he needed to graduate from his program and have a full-time job with benefits before approaching her dad. With this plan, they were at least two years away.

***

There was a slight hiccup in Dale's trek along the road to validation that spring. He was sitting alone at the kitchen table one afternoon, getting ready to go to work at the garage, when Louis walked through the door. Dale took one look at him and jumped to his feet.

"What happened to you?" Dale yelled as he rushed toward his brother. He grabbed Louis by the shoulders.

"Nothing. I'm okay," Louis responded as he pulled angrily away from Dale and tried to hurry past.

Dale grabbed him again and pulled him close so he could see his face clearly. There was blood coming from a cut under his right eye, one nostril, and the middle of his lip. The other eye was badly swollen, and it looked like one of his front teeth was chipped. There was also blood and grass stains on the front of his t-shirt, which was ripped at the neck.

"Tell me what happened!" Dale demanded again.

Their mother heard the commotion and opened her bedroom door, took one look at Louis, and started screaming.

Dale turned and glared at her.

"Shut up!" he shouted.

She complied immediately.

"I'm not asking you again. Who did this to you?"

Crying now, Louis muttered, "Ray J and that dude with the braids asked me for money and—"

Just that quick, Dale contorted his body in such a way that he made a complete revolution in the air, and he reached the front door in one giant leap. He turned back again momentarily to face his mother.

"Clean him up!" he barked. "Do you think that you can do that?"

She nodded but didn't say a word.

Dale ran to his truck and headed toward the school. Two blocks down, he saw a small group of kids standing at the corner. He stopped and rolled down his window.

"Where is Ray J?" he demanded.

They all looked at each other.

"He's at the court," a young girl responded.

Dale hit the gas pedal, and the tires on the truck squealed loudly as he raced away. He made a right turn toward the city park. Just before he arrived, he saw people on the playground and a group of boys playing basketball in the distance. He parked about a hundred yards away from them and walked the rest of the way. Just as he reached the playground, he recognized Ray J standing in a circle of boys just off the right side of the basketball court.

As soon as Dale saw him, a surge of emotion swelled up in him like he had never felt before. He would later have almost no recollection of what happened after that. He just remembered pouncing like a lion and punching Ray J in the face repeatedly. Someone had tried to intercede by jumping on Dale's back, and he threw the kid something like ten feet in the air in one smooth motion. The sound of a girl screaming and shouting brought him to his senses, and he stopped swinging his arms.

Exhausted, Dale was sweating and salivating. But he was also still drunk with anger, and he wanted to fight some more. The people there all jumped back in unison when he stood to his feet and hovered over his prey, who was curled up in a fetal position. They all just watched in amazement as Dale turned and walked slowly in the direction of his truck.

When Dale arrived back home, his mother was sitting at the kitchen table, eating something out of a bowl. He was still a little dazed, and his right hand hurt. Without saying anything to her, he walked directly into his brother's room and found Louis lying on his back on the bed, holding a plastic bag with ice in it on the side of his face.

"You okay?" he asked, still a little out of breath.

"Yes, I think so. Where'd you go?"

"It doesn't matter," Dale responded. "Tell me the truth, do you need to go to the emergency room?"

"No, I threw up after you left."

"Okay, you rest," Dale directed. "I will be right out here if you need me."

"Okay."

Dale called the garage and told Mr. Carbone that his brother had gotten beaten up and that he couldn't work today. It wasn't a problem. Obviously, Dale didn't come clean with the rest of it. He checked on Louis several times during the rest of the evening. His face was badly swollen, but he seemed to be sleeping soundly.

Surprisingly, his mother had done a pretty good job of cleaning him up. She even managed to change his clothes and to give him some aspirin. Louis didn't have a fever when Dale checked on him before he went to bed around 11:00 p.m., about two hours after his mother had flown out into the night to meet up with the other vampires.

Lizzie was horrified when he told her what he had done. He had considered not telling her about it at all, but then he had the problem of having to explain Louis's bruises without lying. Dale had never intentionally lied to her before. He wasn't sure what to do, which is why he didn't call her until the day after.

"I don't know what you were thinking," she declared. "You could be in jail right now!"

"I was thinking about my brother," he insisted.

"I know, but where would Louis be if you went to jail?" she argued.

"You don't understand. Nobody touches my brother!"

"Yes, but you could have called the police," she pointed out. "You could have called my Dad."

"Call your father? Dale asked in disbelief. "Are you kidding?" He started to laugh, but he caught himself. "I did what I had to do," he maintained.

"And what if you killed that boy?" she suggested. "What about Louis? What about me? I have to be honest; this side of you scares me."

"You don't ever have to be afraid of me," Dale asserted. "I'm not like that."

"That's not what I mean, and you know it," she argued. "You hold so much stuff inside all the time that you can explode at any moment. I know you try, but I worry about losing you to something crazy like this."

"Look, I'm sorry. I messed up. You're right. I know. I know..." he trailed off.

"What if those guys try to retaliate against you?" she raised. "Or Louis? Oh, my God! Should we tell somebody?"

"No, please don't say anything," he begged. "That's not the way it works around here. They get that I didn't start this. Nothing else is gonna happen."

"Okay, but I am not sure about any of this," she responded.

"I got it covered. I promise...I promise."

His words hung in the air like a thick blanket.

Dale was truly sorry for what he had done. Not for going after Ray J—the little punk deserved it. But for taking a chance of losing Lizzie. However, she wasn't right about everything. Calling the police was weak. He was a man and needed to protect his family. But he knew he also needed to be smarter about it. Although he wasn't overly concerned about anything happening to him, now he was worried about his brother being targeted at school.

Louis was out of commission for a week while he recovered. After that, Dale drove him to school and picked him up every day those first couple of days back. Louis thought it was embarrassing, and he insisted on being dropped off behind the building where no one could see him get out of the truck. Eventually, he begged Dale off completely. There was never any retaliation.

Chapter 4

Dale had a hairline fracture on his right hand near his thumb that needed a cast. He only went to the emergency room at Lizzie's insistence when the pain was still there after a week. He was concerned at first that the cast would be a problem at work. Mr. Carbone had just started letting him do a little work on cars now, and he loved it. Dale ended up telling his boss that he got mad and struck his hand on something. He didn't elaborate further. But he told Joey everything because he mistakenly believed that his friend would understand.

"Dude, I think you're sick," Joey said without much hesitation.

"Sick how? Like you wouldn't have done the same thing," Dale defended.

Joey laughed and said, "No way. Besides, Tracy would tear a new hole in me. You ever think that you might have a problem with anger?"

"I don't have no anger problem," Dale blurted out. "I keep to myself. I don't have problems with anyone. Guys talk smack all the time, and I let it go."

"Still waters run deep," Joey insisted. "You could have killed him, Apollo Creed."

"But I didn't," Dale protested and tried to hide his dismay.

Joey wasn't convinced, and the scowl on his face spoke volumes.

"You don't even remember half the stuff you did," he continued.

"Give me a break! All the stupid crap that you do," Dale maintained. "You didn't see him. You didn't see my brother's face!"

"True; but, dude, you seriously blacked out," he chuckled. "You said it yourself. That's pretty intense."

Dale was more than a little irritated, but he refused to give Joey the benefit of knowing that he had struck a nerve.

"So, what do you think I should have done? Gone to the school the next day and reported that piece of garbage to the principal?" Dale asked sarcastically.

"I think you should have called the police," he said and laughed under his breath.

"Right…you don't know what you're talking about," Dale replied dryly.

"Okay, if you say so, brother," Joey said, intending to sound skeptical.

They were both momentarily silent.

"Listen, I'm not just breaking your balls," Joey continued. "I remember watching you play football. You always played angry with a chip on your shoulders. Don't get me wrong, that's one of the things that made you a helluva player. But it's just that…it's almost like you were born ready to fight."

Dale had always been particularly sensitive to criticism of any kind. He tended to internalize it and brood over it for long periods of time afterward. He also struggled with an inner belief that everybody else did things perfectly, or at least better than he did. In real-time, it looked like he was overly defensive and dismissive of others.

He was almost as good at defending himself with his words as he was with his fists. He had learned how to use his quick wit as a weapon, and he never backed down from an argument. Moreover, Dale definitely had a mean streak. Lizzie and Joey were right; he was reckless when he went into attack mode.

***

Dale got to interact with Lizzie's entire family at her graduation and see firsthand what it was like to have a lot of people celebrate someone's success. Her graduation party was at a restaurant downtown where he was introduced to her grandfather, both grandmothers, several aunts and uncles, and a host of cousins.

Dale sat right next to Lizzie at the head table with her parents and her sister and brother. Her dad was in a good mood and went out of his way to include Dale. It was a grand time all around—definitely one of his favorite memories.

Lizzie decided to go to community college. She still wasn't sure what she wanted to study, and it made sense to take some time to figure it out. Dale was supportive and told her to do whatever she wanted to do. He knew better than to put undue pressure on her.

But he was more than a little relieved when she decided to stay close to home. He didn't want her to go away like her sister, Wanda, who was at SUNY Brockport. She made it sound exciting, and Dale was secretly concerned that Lizzie would go there too, and that he wouldn't see her much. Also, it occurred to him that she might get there and find herself a superstar basketball player to date.

The summer after Lizzie's graduation was idyllic. He didn't have to go to summer school, and he still only worked part-time at the garage, allowing them to go on picnics and hikes and to concerts in Albany and Saratoga Springs. Her parents were even okay with them taking a day trip all the way to Niagara Falls. Dale had never really been anywhere before, so every excursion was a special treat. Sometimes they brought Louis or Wanda along, but it was usually just the two of them. He hated when the summer ended, and they had to go back to school.

***

After giving it considerable thought, Dale concluded that God is real. But that was as far as he was willing to go. There simply was too much evidence to the contrary to believe that God is truly in control of the universe. If the Bible was correct and God is limitless in power, then it doesn't make sense that he has the ability to change lives and circumstances and doesn't do it for the innocent and the faithful.

If nothing else, it appeared that God's hands were tied in terms of what he can do in people's lives—almost like he made a deal with the devil or something. Most of the black people Dale knew were living hand-to-mouth and struggling to survive their whole lives. And yet, they were talking about the goodness of God all the time. Clearly, God was not good all the time.

Nevertheless, this was a huge leap forward for him. Dale simply kept his reservations about God to himself. There was no denying that both Louis and Lizzie were completely sold out for Jesus, which wasn't necessarily a bad thing. Louis, for one, saw good in everybody. He had a heart of gold, and was determined to do whatever he could do to make the world a better place. Still, Dale didn't exactly envy his brother's idealism. Where they lived, people regularly mistook kindness for weakness. Although Louis understood that, he also didn't care. He was a much better person than Dale was, no doubt about it.

Chapter 5

Louis got a job at Burger King, and he loved it. However, he smelled like grease all the time, which made Dale sick to his stomach. As a senior in high school, Louis was already accepted at SUNY at Buffalo with early admission.

Dale was very proud of his brother. All the other kids on their block seemed content to repeat the mistakes of past generations, but something inside of both he and Louis made them imagine a life beyond their present circumstances. He was especially grateful to God for that.

On the other hand, their mother was mostly concerned with how Louis' leaving home and going to school would affect her monthly government check. She didn't seem too happy for her son; never congratulated him or even acknowledged his accomplishment. Unlike Dale, however, Louis never held it against her.

Dale knew that his total disdain for her was going to be a problem for him in the future. Sometimes he could barely stand being in the same room with her too long. He was ashamed of her, and the way he dealt with it was to never talk about her to anyone. He said as little as possible to the outside world about what went on at home, and forbade Louis from talking about her too. She was their not-so-little secret.

Lizzie had long stopped asking him questions about his mother, and he appreciated the fact that she did not press the issue. She obviously noticed early on that when she raised the subject, he became tense and would immediately shut down. But he also understood that she was curious. The only thing he did disclose to her about his mother was that she was an alcoholic who had trouble being around people.

Time flew by, and things were falling into place. Lizzie was happy with her classes, and she found a little part-time job at the YMCA. Her parents bought her a small car, and she loved the freedom that came with it. Their relationship was in a good place, and they were pretty much on the same page about everything. Nothing was forced between them. Everyone around them could tell they were in love. They were electric.

Unexpectedly, Louis received a small scholarship from a local African American woman's group. His name was listed in the graduation program along with all the other scholarship winners. Dale sat with Lizzie, Wanda, and his mother at graduation. He made his mother come too because he knew Louis really wanted her there. But he was nervous the whole time while waiting for the sky to fall in.

To her credit, she was on her very best behavior and somehow managed to only swear about five times, which was a record for her. They went out to lunch afterward to celebrate. It turned out okay. His mother barely spoke, but Louis was very happy—and that was the most important thing.

After lunch, Lizzie announced that she had a surprise for Louis. She seemed excited and wanted Dale to take them somewhere. After he dropped his mother off at home, he followed her directions, and they ended up at the church. Dale just looked at her.

"Come on!" she insisted and jumped out of the truck.

She and Wanda were giggling.

There were several cars in the parking lot, so they could tell that the church was open. The four of them walked inside. Lizzie led them downstairs to the community room. As they opened the door, about fifty people began to applaud, and a huge congratulatory banner was hung with Louis's name on it. Balloons were everywhere.

Louis was at a complete loss and just stood there with a surprised look on his face. Then music began to play, and Rita Johnson stepped forward. She was a young, pretty girl from the choir with an amazing voice. She began to sing a song that Dale had never heard before. It was beautiful. The refrain was, "Even angels envy the way God loves you."

Louis was obviously moved by the show of affection. Neither one of them had ever had a birthday party before. Louis looked around and noticed the tables set up all around, laden with drinks and deserts, and then at Dale for a moment in amazement before hugging Lizzie and Wanda. Then Louis turned and walked in the direction of his friends and disappeared into a haze of youthful exuberance. Dale glanced back at Lizzie, and his heart just about burst with joy when she raised her eyebrows and blew him a kiss.

He had never seen his brother so happy before. He watched as Louis laughed and engaged with people. Louis was never as guarded as Dale was, and was much more likely to show his emotions, whether joy or pain, on his face. Dale considered that to be a weakness, which meant that Louis was one of his weaknesses.

Their mother had made him responsible for his brother very early on. There was a time when he actually thought that

Louis was his baby. Before Lizzie, Louis was the only one he cared anything about.

Lizzie had really outdone herself. She said that she wanted Louis to have a day he would always remember. Although Dale didn't see her at first, Lizzie's mother was also at the party with her little brother Daniel. Apparently, she had helped pull everything together, and Dale made sure Louis thanked her too.

It never occurred to Dale to throw Louis a graduation party. His mind didn't work that way. He was always on top of the essentials but rarely thought beyond that.

Indeed, Dale was always more than willing to help anyone in need if he was able to do so, but that person needed to ask him directly for assistance. For some reason, it typically wouldn't ever occur to him to just volunteer to help. That was something he was never taught and was still learning to do. Lizzie had to remind him to get Louis a graduation present, which he had waiting at home.

People had brought gifts and cards for Louis, and Dale loaded all those things in the back of his truck. He ended up driving home alone because Louis wanted to go out with his friends, and Lizzie needed to stay at the church to help with the cleanup. At 7:00 p.m., she kissed him warmly before he left and asked him to call her later.

His mother was home when he got there and came out of her room when she heard all the commotion he was making while attempting to carry all the gifts into the house in one trip.

"What's all that?" she asked.

"There was a graduation party for Louis at the church. He got a lot of gifts."

He noticed that she had changed her clothes from earlier and she wore a t-shirt and shorts now.

"That's nice. Is it stuff for college?" she wondered and walked closer to get a better look.

"I don't know. He didn't open anything. There was no time," Dale explained.

Dale dropped everything on the living room floor. He would take them into Louis' room later. He started to walk away.

"I like your girl," she said.

"Thanks."

"They both seemed nice. What's her name again? Lizzie?"

"Um, yes...Lizzie."

"She's very pretty," she reflected. "I really liked her dress."

Dale acknowledged the compliment by looking directly at her, but he didn't say anything.

He was more than a little suspicious. His history with her was devoid of many tender moments. When he was younger, she would bully him to get her way. He was never afraid of her, but her words hurt just the same. Over time, he had grown more and more indifferent to her, and now he towered over her physically, so she wasn't a threat.

These days, their personal interactions were minimal because he paid for the things that they needed out of his own money, except for the food stamps that she still left for him on the counter every month. He was a grown man now who no longer needed his mother. Who said there is no God?

"Um, are you gonna move in with her after Louis leaves?" she finally asked.

"Nope, I wasn't planning on it," he said. "Why do you ask? Do you want me to move out?" He was annoyed already.

"Hell, no! That's not it at all. I was just...you know... wondering," she offered.

"Well, no then," he replied sharply. "Louis is just going to school. He'll be home a lot for breaks and summers. He is not ready to be out on his own."

"I know," she agreed. "I notice how much you do for him."

They were both silent for a moment.

"Did your girlfriend say anything about me?" her voice was just slightly above a whisper.

"No. Nothing," was his cold response.

He walked to his room and shut the door.

***

Neither one of the Johnson boys knew what Louis needed to bring with him to school. Thus, Lizzie and Wanda did most of the shopping for him throughout the summer. Dale barely saw him, as Louis was off doing his own thing. But they continued to go to church together every week. Lizzie took one class in the summer, but Dale just worked full-time. There were more good times and laughter together. In the end, he knew that time with her was all that he would ever need.

The trip to Buffalo to drop Louis off at college was unexpectedly emotional. Nobody had prepared him beforehand, and Dale felt like he had been ambushed. They had somehow managed to cram all of Louis' stuff into the truck. Lizzie would have come too, but there was no room for her to sit during the seven-hour drive. They left Schenectady around 6:00 a.m.

Their mother didn't get up to see them off, not that he expected her to. Perhaps she and Louis said their goodbyes the night before. He never asked Louis about it.

Louis was excited. He talked pretty much the whole way to Buffalo, mostly about things he had read in the school catalog about student life. He wanted to be active in student government and join several clubs and organizations. He was active in a few during high school, such as the black student's action group and the key club. Dale was certain that Louis' college experience was going to be very different from his own.

The college campus was a zoo. Louis' dorm room was on the ninth floor of a huge building. Getting an elevator was nearly impossible, and the whole affair was stressful. Louis was in a tiny suite with three other guys, two of whom were already there by the time they arrived. Louis looked nervous, and Dale tried to reassure him. Lizzie had given Dale a list of information to bring back, such as Louis's full address and a contact person at the dorm. Once he was set up, Louis walked Dale back to the truck to say goodbye. They embraced briefly, and Dale slipped some folded money in Louis' front pocket.

"What's that?" Louis asked, reaching into his pocket. "You don't have to do that. I got money."

"You take it. And call me if you need more. You hear?" Dale encouraged.

Louis looked down at the ground, trying hard to keep his composure.

"Yeah, okay," he managed to say.

"Okay then," Dale said. "Let me go; I have a long drive."

"Thank you for bringing me." Louis was clearly fighting back the tears.

"You're welcome. Have fun, and I'll see you."

Dale got in the truck and turned on the ignition. He looked back at his brother, smiled, and waved his hand.

Just as he began to pull away, Louis stepped forward and gestured for him to roll down the window.

Dale complied.

"I put something in the glove compartment for you," Louis said.

"For me? What is it?"

Louis smiled through his tears, turned, and headed toward his dorm. He never looked back.

Dale drove away. Traffic was heavy, and he really had to concentrate on what he was doing. For the moment, it took his mind off the wellspring of emotion rising inside of him. He had started to feel it the moment that they left the dorm room, but he somehow had managed to push it down, but now it was pushing back with great force—and it hurt.

His heart was racing too, and he took a couple of swallows of cold coffee that he had in a thermos. He suddenly remembered that he needed to gas up before he got back on the thruway for home, so he got off the next exit and drove to the nearest gas station. He began to shake as he pulled into the parking lot and immediately turned off the ignition. Dale lowered his head and cried there for a few minutes before getting out of the truck.

The fresh air felt good. After clearing his head, he pulled up to one of the pumps, went inside the store to pay, and filled his tank. He was just pulling away when he remembered what Louis had told him. Stuffed inside the glove compartment was a square box. When he opened it, he observed a black leather-bonded Bible with his name engraved on the cover. There was a note too. He slowly opened it.

> Dale,
> There's something I have wanted to say to you for a long time, but I have been afraid to. There is absolutely no way that I would be here today if it wasn't for you. You're my hero, and I thank God every day for you. My biggest fear is disappointing you. I know you're still struggling inside to know God, and I feel bad because you made it easy for me to experience Him. You gave to me what nobody ever gave you—a father who is good. Ironically, I know that the angels envy the way that God loves you.
> Louis

It was almost fifteen minutes before he was able to drive; he was so overcome. He was so glad that Lizzie hadn't accompanied him on this trip after all because he cried off and on for seven hours straight along Interstate 90 East.

He only told Lizzie that Louis had written him a nice note, but he didn't tell her how it impacted him when he read it. The truth is that Dale was still not fully comfortable sharing his feelings with her. When they first started dating, there was a strange combination of excitement and fear coexisting inside him. Never having experienced real affection before, he really struggled with being himself around her—much more than the average guy. It only worked out in the end because she seemed to somehow understand that he was broken and needed time to figure out how to process all the different emotions taking hold of him.

Once he got settled into college life, Louis almost never called home. Dale was annoyed with him that first month after he left, but after talking with him a few times, he realized that no news was good news. He was also starting to see that Louis was stronger than he ever knew—a thought that was very compelling to him.

The Bible that Louis gave him immediately became his prized possession, along with his truck. It was a men's study Bible which had a lot of commentaries that explained scripture in a way that made it easier to understand. Louis had chosen well. Dale brought it with him to church every week, and he regularly read it at home when time permitted. He was desperately seeking truth.

Chapter 6

His mother found herself a new boyfriend, and Dale hated him at first sight. It goes without saying that anyone attracted to her had to have serious issues. Trent Dawkins was his name. Everyone on the street knew the Dawkins family. They were always in trouble, fighting, and getting arrested, or otherwise wreaking havoc at every turn. Dale only saw him a couple of times, and his mother never really introduced them. Just one more in a long line of losers was the way he saw it.

He was still in bed one cool fall morning when the phone rang. It was Lizzie letting him know that his mother was in jail. Her father had called her and told her to reach out to him. Dale wasn't too surprised. He knew something like this was bound to happen sooner or later. She played with fire every second of every day, so she was overdue for a good burn.

Dale got dressed and drove downtown to the police station. The woman there directed him across the street to Schenectady city court. After emptying his pockets, he had to walk through a metal detector. He was then directed to courtroom number one. There were a lot of people mingling in the hall outside of the courtroom. Dale just pushed his way through the crowd and walked inside. The room was almost full. Interestingly, there were wooded pews on both sides of a middle aisle, like in a church. The alter was an elevated desk surrounded by several flags, including the American flag and a New York State seal on the wall above. He found an open seat in the back and sat down.

The room was bright from all the overhead lights. The court was called to order, and everyone stood when the judge came in. He was a greying white man in his late fifties wearing a black robe. A uniformed man in the front started calling different cases, and one by one, people in custody were led in through a side door. The acoustics in the room were bad, and it was hard to hear from where he sat. But Dale could follow what was going on for the most part.

He had been there for about an hour when the officer called the case of "People versus LaToya Johnson," and his mother was brought in through the door. She looked like a hot mess. Her hair was mussed, and her clothes disheveled. Both hands were handcuffed in front of her.

The charge was assault in the first degree for the stabbing of Trenton Dawkins. The public defender was assigned to represent her, and a man stood up and entered a plea of not guilty for her. Bail was set at $50,000, and the judge encouraged her lawyer to make a bail reduction application. The whole thing lasted no more than five minutes. She didn't say a word to anyone except a few whispers to her lawyer.

He had no idea what to do next. Obviously, he didn't have $50,000 to bail her out, not that he would have forked it over if he had the money. Dale was both angry and embarrassed, but what else was new? Lizzie's father knew all about this before he did. It was almost eleven o'clock when he left the courtroom, and he had a one p.m. class on campus, which meant that he needed to leave right away if he was going to make it on time. He would worry about his mother's situation later.

The car radio reported that Trent Dawkins was in the hospital with two stab wounds to the chest and was in critical condition. Dale knew that this was bad, and a feeling of dread came over him. He couldn't really focus during class, and he called Lizzie as soon as he got out. She told him that her dad said that he should go see his mother's public defender. He immediately made an appointment for 9:30 a.m. the next morning.

The public defender's office was located downtown in a government building on State Street. Dale arrived on time and entered a small waiting room with about ten empty chairs crammed together. A receptionist sat behind a window and told him to have a seat. By the time the receptionist opened the door next to her desk and called his name, several people had come in and occupied the other chairs.

The whole office seemed cramped. He was led down the hall to a small conference room and was instructed to have a seat. Dale was slightly nervous, although he was not quite sure why. He wasn't worried about his mother—he knew she would survive whatever happened, but she still had the power to bring them down with her. That was true whether he liked it or not.

Dale was lost in his thoughts, somewhere between discomfort and confusion, when the lawyer he saw in court yesterday walked in the room. He was a tall, thin guy with round glasses and dark brown hair that was parted on the side and neatly slicked back. He carried a small, thin yellow folder under his arm.

"Hello, my name is Jeff Stone," the man extended his right hand, which was boney and cold.

"Hi, I'm Dale Johnson."

After sitting down on the chair directly across from Dale, the lawyer put the folder on the table and opened it. "How are you related to LaToya?" Mr. Stone asked and cleared his throat.

"She's my mother," Dale answered.

"Does she have any other children?" he asked and lifted his pen.

"Yeah, my brother, Louis."

"How old are you?"

"I'm twenty years old. Louis is eighteen," Dale replied.

"Do you both live with her?"

"Yes, but my brother is away at college in Buffalo."

"Is your mother employed?"

"No," was all Dale said.

"Do you know if LaToya has a criminal record?"

"Not that I know of."

"Any medical or mental health conditions that you know of?" Mr. Stone asked.

"No, but…she drinks a lot, if that counts."

"Did she ever…go to an alcohol program?" the lawyer asked.

"No, not that I am aware."

"I see. Well, do you have any questions for me?" Mr. Stone inquired.

"Yeah, what is happening with her?" Dale mumbled.

"Right now, your mother is charged with felony assault. Apparently, she got into an argument with the victim last night." He paused as he looked at his notes. Suddenly looking up, he said, "Trenton Dawkins is his name. Do you know him?"

"No," Dale replied.

"He's in serious condition now," Mr. Stone announced. "He was stabbed in the chest twice. They think that the knife might have nicked a vital organ. If he dies, then she will probably be charged with murder. Hopefully, he will survive."

"Murder?" Dale repeated in sheer amazement.

"We just have to wait and see," Mr. Stone offered. "She will be back in court on Thursday for a felony exam. But that's really just a technicality in this case. LaToya signed a statement where she admitted to stabbing him. So there's no question that they have the right person."

"What about her bail?" Dale wondered.

"It is set at fifty thousand for now. That is cash or bond," the lawyer explained. "Of course, that will go up if the victim dies."

"Can I see her?"

"Yes, you can visit her at the jail," Mr. Stone said.

"Okay."

"Let's just pray that he survives," Mr. Stone asserted. "Since she doesn't have a criminal record to speak of, she could still make out okay."

His mother's lawyer tried to sound optimistic, but it came off as disinterested.

Dale was silent.

"Oh…did she say why she stabbed him?" Dale wondered. "I thought that they were dating."

"She said that they were drinking, and he got mad about something and slapped her. They began physically fighting, and he tried to choke her. There were some bruises on her neck and face that I saw. She says it was self-defense. There were supposedly witnesses, but I have not seen any of their statements yet."

"Is there anything I can do to help her?" Dale asked.

"No, I'm sorry. Let's just hope for the best. That's about it," Mr. Stone concluded.

Dale walked to his truck while shaking his head in disbelief. There was no way he was going to the jail to visit her. He wasn't even sure why he had asked that question. Everybody they knew was probably talking about this and laughing. He needed to call Louis and let him know before someone else did. He also needed to tell his boss, but the very thought of having to do that made him cringe. Other than that, he decided that he was just going to lay low and grin and bear it.

The phone rang just as he was getting home. It was Lizzie.

"How is your mother doing?" she asked.

"I don't know for sure, but she's pretty tough. I'm not worried about her."

"Do you know what happened?"

"Just that she stabbed him after he slapped her," Dale replied. "The public defender said it was self-defense."

"Will she have to stay in jail?"

"Yeah, I think so," Dale said.

"Is there anything I can do to help?" Lizzie questioned.

"No, not that I can think of. Just pray that the dude doesn't die."

"Aww, I feel so bad for you," she said. "You sure you're okay?"

"Yes, I'm sure," he said, trying to convince himself. "Just talking to you helps. Please don't worry about me."

"That's impossible. I love you."

Typically, hearing her say that would have warmed his heart, but not so much this time.

"What did your father say?" he wondered.

"About what?" she asked.

"About all of this? Is he mad?" Dale probed.

"Why would he be mad at you?" she asked.

"I don't know. I bet he wishes you weren't with me."

"He's not like that," she disputed. "Anyway, it doesn't matter what anybody thinks."

"Thanks for saying that," he said.

"It's true," she maintained.

Of course, by the time he got to work, the guys already knew about his mother, but they didn't say anything to him about it. In Dale's mind, he was struggling to find the words to tell his boss. He was thinking about it during the whole shift. He knew he had to say something but just couldn't bring himself to do it.

"Hey Dale, can you go and see if that Mazda part came in?" Joey asked at one point just before closing.

Dale walked out and returned with the box and handed it to Joey. As soon as their eyes met, Dale knew that Joey knew. He felt the support and was immediately comforted. He turned and walked directly into the office and told Mr. Carbone everything.

It was easy, and his boss was better than great. He shook Dale on the shoulder with one hand and made Dale promise to let him know if there was anything he could do to help.

Dale called Louis that night. It wasn't that hard to tell his brother the news because they were used to their mother's drama. Louis didn't say a word at first. Then he asked if he needed to come home. Dale advised that he didn't think it was necessary and promised to keep Louis informed of any developments in her case. Louis seemed relieved.

He couldn't decide if it made sense for him to go to court to witness everything firsthand or not. The hearing was already scheduled for the next day. While there wasn't anything he could do to help her, there is something to be said about providing moral support to our loved ones and to the people in our lives when they are down. She fit the bill of someone in his life, so he figured he might regret it later if he left her out to dry.

***

Dale was eating dinner and watching television alone in the apartment when the phone rang. It was his mother calling collect from jail. He accepted the charges.

"Hello," he said.

"Dale, it's me."

"How are you?" he asked, monotoned.

"I'm in jail and going crazy," she complained.

"I know."

"I shouldn't be here. I didn't do anything," she argued in rapid-fire.

69

"You stabbed somebody," he pointed out. He was agitated already.

"It was self-defense, and everybody knows it," she stressed. "I told that old fool not to put his hands on me. He's lucky I didn't kill him."

"You might have!" he exclaimed, struggling to maintain his composure. "He's in the hospital in serious condition. What do you think is going to happen to you if he dies?"

He didn't want to make things worse for her by kicking her when she was down, especially since she wasn't going to listen to anything he said anyway. But he always hated the way that she rationalized her behavior. She acted like she was justified in doing whatever she wanted to do in response to anything that caused her angst.

"He ain't gonna die. I don't believe that," she protested.

"Doesn't matter what you believe. Why did you call…is there something you want?" he redirected.

"Yeah, the social worker from the county came to see me. I can't remember her name. She said you have to call her. Something about my check and all…I don't know."

"Okay, I'll call her."

"Good, cause I don't want them messing around with my money."

Dale could hardly believe what he was hearing. "Um…I was in court yesterday when they brought you in. I saw you," he stated point blank.

"Really?" she sounded surprised. "I didn't know you were there." She sounded embarrassed too.

"I wanted to make sure you were okay," he confessed.

"Listen, I appreciate you coming and all, but you don't have to come to court," she commented. "I know you got stuff to do. I'm okay. I probably won't be in here much longer anyway. Like I said, it's all a big mistake."

There was an awkward silence.

"Can you call out anytime you want, or how does that work?" Dale wondered.

"There are hours when we can use the phone," she explained. "So I can call you to let you know what's going on with my case."

"Okay. Anything else?" he heard himself ask.

"No, but please don't forget to call the social worker lady for me, okay?"

"I won't," he promised.

"Alright, I'll talk to you later."

She hung up first.

Dale had so many mixed emotions that he could hardly think straight. One thing was for certain: his mother lacked any ability whatsoever to fully appreciate just how much of a jam she was in. She had no experience with normalcy and, therefore, she didn't react to events and circumstances the way the average person would. Perhaps that was a good thing in this instance.

He rarely felt sorry for her because she courted trouble just for sport. However, there's no denying that she wasn't dealt a fair hand in life, and now she was as broken as a person could be. But he also recognized that she was his family and she had feelings, too; that should matter to somebody. Louis was right about that part of it.

Fortunately for her, Trent Dawkins didn't die. His recovery, combined with conflicting eyewitness accounts, meant that the charge against the defendant was eventually reduced to a class A misdemeanor crime of assault. Upon her plea of guilty to that charge, she was sentenced to one year in the county jail with mandatory drug and alcohol treatment. Dale read all about it in the newspaper, just like everyone else. She never called him.

***

The first time Louis came home from college was for thanksgiving. He didn't seem that happy to be there. Apparently, he had a lot of new friends in school and couldn't wait to get back to them. He was different; not necessarily in a bad way, but he had changed somehow, which meant that they were different now. But Dale had been looking forward to Louis' homecoming and spending time with the old Louis.

They were invited to dinner at Lizzie's house. He'd never had Thanksgiving dinner with the Lawsons before. Usually he just stopped by after dinner for dessert because he always made dinner for him and Louis at home. But Lizzie had insisted that he eat with them this year. She directed him to bring flowers for her mother. Dale wasn't exactly sure why it was so important to her that he be there, but he thought it best not to ask her outright.

It turned out that Wanda brought a guy home with her from college. It was the first time she had done so, and the family was all abuzz. The new guy ended up being the focus of attention throughout dinner, which clearly didn't sit well with Lizzie. Dale had never really seen that side of her before and he thought it was amusing. Overall, it was a very low-key event, and he appreciated the way the Larsons' treated him and Louis like family.

Louis wanted to go and visit their mother at the jail before he went back to school. Dale flatly refused to go with him, so Louis went alone the day after thanksgiving. When Dale later asked him how it went, Louis related that he tried to witness to her about Jesus, but she wasn't interested. Dale was flabbergasted. He wanted to laugh, but it was sadder than funny. He couldn't believe Louis even considered doing that, but he didn't say anything. Apparently, all she wanted was for Louis to put some money in her inmate account so she could buy cigarettes.

Nothing really changed for them with their mother being in jail. Louis went back to Buffalo. Dale returned to his normal routine as if nothing had happened. When he called the social worker, she said he could stay in the apartment and continue to receive support in his mother's name if she was confined locally.

Dale also called the public defender after his mother was sentenced to see what the alcohol and drug treatment was about. He said that they were county-run programs for inmates that were mandatory and that she could possibly get out of jail after just nine months, depending upon her completion of the programs and based upon her behavior in jail.

Dale was doing well in his classes. Lizzie, however, did not like community college. She said that she was bored most of the time. He encouraged her to explore her options and maybe look at some other programs. The real problem was that she had no idea what she truly wanted to do with her life, and she knew that her dad would flip out if she didn't get a degree.

Louis only came home for Christmas for one week of his month-long school break. He spent the rest of the time at a friend's house in Lima, Ohio. During that time, Lizzie started spending more time with Dale at the apartment. She never stayed the night, but she hadn't even been inside before when his mother was there. He was enjoying having the place to himself.

Chapter 7

Lizzie loved Valentine's Day. In the past, she always planned their entire evening, and Dale was always more than willing to do whatever she thought up. This year she wanted to meet up with some of her friends at a nice restaurant. He didn't really like places that were too fancy, but he pretended to be excited. She was easy and never needed grand displays of affection. As long as he made some small gesture of some kind, like flowers and candy, she was happy.

Valentine's Day was on a Friday this year, which meant he had to work at the garage. He never liked to take any time off, but he asked Mr. Carbone if he could leave early that day because he was afraid he wasn't going to be able to get showered and changed in time. They had a 7:00 p.m. reservation at a restaurant near Albany.

They managed to get there on time. The restaurant was bustling, and the ambiance was very romantic. Altogether, there were four couples. Dale knew everybody except for one guy. They had a nice table near a fireplace. He could see why she chose it.

Lizzie looked beautiful, and he was proud to be there with her. He tried to pay attention to the conversation, but his mind kept drifting. The ladies were doing most of the talking. The food wasn't that good, in Dale's opinion, but he wasn't really that hungry.

At one point, just after dinner, their waiter came over and whispered in Dale's ear, and his face dropped a little.

"Is something wrong?" Lizzie whispered.

He stood up. He looked unnerved.

"I don't know. Maybe. I'll be right back."

Dale marched out of the restaurant. He was only gone a few minutes. He slowly walked back in and stood behind her.

"Dale, what's wrong?"

"There's something I need to tell you...but I can't," he muttered. He looked dejected.

"What is it?"

Her eyes were big and her brows raised.

"Um...There is some guy here to tell you something," he whispered.

"Who? Where?" she asked in a panic.

At just that moment, the music that had been playing in the background stopped abruptly. Lizzie's little brother Daniel walked in and stood in the middle of the room. He had on a suit and tie and looked like the world's smallest funeral home director. He smiled at his sister through his obvious nerves, looked down at a piece of paper, and began to read aloud before the entire room.

> Lizzie,
> There is no verse that does you justice.
> No song that captures the essence of what you
> mean to me or how you make me feel.

No dance more stirring than the way that you have
reset the rhythm of my heart.
I know, because I looked everywhere to find them.
I wake up every morning desperate for you.
My prayer every night is in gratitude of the gift that
is you.
I hold my breath every time you reach out and
touch my hand or kiss my face.
No man could love you better than I can.
I know, because I have struggled to hide my soul's
obsession with yours.
There are much better men than me, for sure.
Stronger, wiser, worthier; it's true.
But only I can hear your heartbeat in the wind.
And see your beauty in a rose.
God exhaled, and I breathed you in.
I vow to war even against death just to stay by your
side.
Our love is heavenly divine.

Dale took the small box containing the ring out of his pocket and dropped to one knee. The sound of the people in the room gasping in unison rang out like a symphony of church bells.

"Elizabeth Christina Larson, will you marry me?"

She looked stunned.

"Oh my God, yes!" she tearfully exclaimed.

He put the ring on her trembling finger.

The people in the restaurant began to clap and cheer. Lizzie helped Dale to his feet, and the two kissed tenderly.

She never saw the rest of her family—her mother, father, and sister—walk in. They were all crying and laughing. Her friends had left their seats at the table and were surrounding them. Everyone was excited, hugging one another and talking at the same time. The people working in the kitchen had all come out to watch too. It was a big deal for the whole restaurant. Dale wasn't expecting that.

The waiter brought over champagne that he said was on the house. The noise level in the restaurant had risen considerably. In all the commotion, Dale watched as Lizzie stole a moment to herself to examine her ring closer and then shimmer in delight. He was blinded by her radiance even as time stood still for him. He never imagined that it could be like this. The power of their love was burning brighter than he ever dreamed.

Lizzie's mom insisted that they both come back to the house. It took thirty minutes just to get out of the restaurant because everyone there wanted to congratulate them. He felt like a celebrity! As soon as they got into Dale's truck, she turned and punched him in the arm. He threw his body against the driver-side door with exaggerated force.

"Ouch! What'cha do that for?"

"You almost scared me to death, you idiot!" she cried out. "You know my dad is on the police force. I thought something must have happened to him."

"Gotcha," he said with a smirk.

"I swear, I don't know about you sometimes. Alright, tell me the truth, who helped you with all this? I know you. There's no way that you came up with this on your own. No way. Tell me…who?" she insisted.

He turned up his nose and wiped away an imaginary tear. "Ye of little faith," he kidded.

"Who?" she demanded. "Dale, stop playing around and tell me the truth."

"Your mom, mostly," he revealed. "But everyone helped. Even your dad."

"My dad?"

"I asked him for your hand in marriage on Thanksgiving. I almost had a heart attack. Your father is a seriously scary dude, by the way. But he said yes, so here we are," Dale explained.

"Really? You asked him?"

"Wanda helped me pick out the ring," he volunteered.

"It's perfect!" she squealed. "You guys did a fantastic job! I love it!"

"It was mostly me," he teased.

"Wait a minute…you're telling me that my whole family knew for three months?"

He could hear her thinking.

"And who wrote the poem?" she asked.

"I did," he joked.

"Who wrote it, Dale?" she pressed.

Her tone sounded serious again. She clearly wanted straight answers and he was bothering her.

"Well, if you must know, Louis wrote it technically, but I told him what to say."

"You're so full of it. It's beautiful."

"You're beautiful," he said.

True to form, she didn't respond to his compliment.

"Oh my God! Wasn't Danny adorable?" she proclaimed. "When I first saw him, I was like…okay, something isn't right. But I couldn't figure it out. How did you get him to do it?"

"He wanted to. That kid is a rock star."

She giggled and squeezed his forearm as he drove.

Lizzie talked the whole drive to her house. Dale mostly just listened and reveled in her excitement. They sat in the truck in the front of the house for several minutes before going in. She was giddy, like a little girl on Christmas morning. They just needed a moment alone with their dreams.

All day he had been a nervous wreck. He kept thinking that he was never going to be able to pull this off and that foolishly he had let Lizzie's mom talk him into biting off more than he could possibly chew. He had felt queasy all through dinner and had to fight to hide it. But now, with Lizzie here in his arms, all was right with the world.

Chapter 8

Everybody knows that weddings are for the bride and her mother. And Dale was more than willing to leave all the planning to them; the getting engaged part alone almost killed him. Moreover, he had never even been to a wedding in his whole life and really didn't know very much about them. Lizzie became immediately obsessed with the planning, and he initially enjoyed seeing her excitement.

They decided to get married one year to the day that they became engaged, on Valentine's Day. Honestly, he was hoping for a wedding date a little sooner, but he was soundly rebuked when he suggested it. For one thing, his mother could be getting out of jail by early summer, and he didn't want to live with her ever again. Also, he was on track to graduate from his program in a couple of months. The pieces were all coming together quite nicely, although he still needed to find a full-time job. He was ready now to begin a new life—and he didn't want to have to wait another year to do it.

Joey laughed wildly when Dale announced that he was getting married. Dale expected as much from him and let him have his fun. With a toddler and another baby on the way now, Joey was overwhelmed. He often vented about his growing distress and said that he wished that he had waited before marrying. Dale wasn't bothered in the least by Joey's juvenile behavior.

On the other hand, Mr. Carbone couldn't have been happier for him. He hugged Dale when he first heard the news and kept patting Dale on the back all shift. He seemed proud. It spoke volumes that Mr. Carbone was so impacted by events in Dale's life. Dale knew that his co-workers really cared about him and only wanted the best for him. He felt safe with them, which was monumental growth for him.

***

Louis came home for spring break. He seemed happy. They were able to catch up on what was going on with each other. Louis was still undecided in his course of study and talked about maybe pursuing counseling as a career. Clearly, he had given it a lot of thought and was excited by the possibilities. Dale was happy for him.

"I feel like I missed out on a lot of things because we weren't exposed to a lot," Louis articulated.

Nodding his head in agreement, Dale responded, "I know. I feel the same way, too, sometimes. But you're a smart dude; you'll figure it out."

"I hope so. But I'm not so sure. The best part about being at a school where no one knows me is that I can kind of pretend to be someone else, you know," Louis explained.

"What are you talking about?" Dale asked. "You just turned nineteen years old. Nobody our age has a clue about anything. It doesn't have anything to do with how we were raised."

"I know, but I just want to be normal," Louis persisted.

"Yeah, I get it," Dale conceded. "But I'm not sure that it's a good idea to completely forget who you really are or how you got here."

"No, I know that. But like...there are so many people around campus, and I feel like I can be exactly who I am without anybody judging me."

"Really?" Dale asked in a tone that revealed his skepticism.

"Yeah, here people had a problem with me even being a Christian," Louis continued. "They made fun of me, and I never felt like I fit in. I wasn't a jock like you, with muscles and a fine girlfriend and everything. I've always been Dale Johnson's little brother. At UB, nobody sees me that way or cares who my brother is."

Dale sat straight up in his seat and jerked his head back. He had an uneasy feeling in his gut.

"Wait a minute. Are you saying you needed to get away from me?" he asked directly. "Is that what this is about?"

"No, no; not at all," Louis defended. "I'll carry you with me wherever I go. I still hear the stuff that you used to say to me in my head all the time. I need you in my corner. I always will. But now I have to go out and fight my own fight. Don't you see?"

There was an intensity on his face and a sense of urgency in his voice. He sounded like he was pleading for his life, and Dale took a couple of seconds to process what he had just heard. Slowly, his demeanor softened.

"Yeah, I think I get it. I'm with ya. You go out and do you. How did you get so wise?" Dale questioned with a slight smile.

"I learned it from you. You taught me everything I know," Louis spoke clearly.

"I don't think so. Not all that," Dale acknowledged.

Louis met up with his friends all week, but Dale felt that the time that he spent with his brother was important for their future. They were both changing and needed to stay connected on some level.

But now that Dale had a better idea of how Louis was feeling and thinking, he determined in his heart to change his expectations concerning his brother. They both desperately needed to find their way out of the dark past, but their paths weren't the same. Louis caught a ride back to school with someone from Schenectady. Dale wasn't surprised that he didn't go to the jail to visit their mother this time.

***

Lizzie reported that they were not going to get married at the church. To relieve their guests from the hassle of having to shuffle around in the cold of winter, she wanted the ceremony and the reception to be in the same place. Accordingly, she dragged him all over the county to look at venues.

However, he literally was just the chauffeur because he didn't have an opinion on anything—not that she bothered to ask for it anyway; he just wanted them to make up their minds. Mercifully, she and her mother settled on a country club on State Route 5, just outside of the city of Schenectady.

Mr. Carbone told him that he could have a full-time job at the garage once he graduated if he wanted it. But Dale wasn't sure about that because there already wasn't enough work to go around when they were all there. Joey was full-time, and the other guy, Chip, was part-time. The last thing that Dale wanted to do was to make it harder for his boss to run his business and make a profit.

Apparently, there were a lot of jobs in the capital region for mechanics. He needed to explore his options. It was important to him that he presented right on his wedding day—he needed to show the world that he could provide for his wife and family.

His relationship with Lizzie's father remained a work in progress. Ever since their first talk, Dale wasn't fully comfortable around Mr. Larson. He had been so nervous on Thanksgiving when he had to ask his girlfriend's dad for permission to marry her. Louis was the only person Dale told beforehand that he was planning to propose, and they had tossed around some ideas of what Dale should say to her father.

When the moment came, however, he could barely put two sentences together. Somehow, he had managed to get his question out; he knew that he sounded pathetic and was more than a little embarrassed. In response, Mr. Lawson showed almost no expression when he gave them his blessing, but he thanked Dale for being a man and asking him first, which was nice.

Dale never thought that there would ever come a time when he needed a break from Lizzie. But she was consumed with "the wedding," and there was only so much of it he could take. He simply couldn't wait for everything to be over. To him, it was like focusing on the wrapping paper rather than on the gift inside.

One Sunday afternoon, he found himself at the Lawson's house alone with Lizzie and her mother when they apparently decided to gang up on him. He was watching a football game in the living room when they came in from the kitchen and sat down on both sides of him.

"Dale, can we ask you a question?" Lizzie asked.

"Sure, what is it?"

"How come black men aren't romantic?" she asked pointedly.

"Excuse me?" he remarked.

"You heard me; how come black men aren't romantic?" she goaded.

"Who said that black men aren't romantic?" he rebuked.

The two women laughed.

"Come on, be serious," his future mother-in-law scolded. "Just answer the question because we really want to know."

She was an attractive woman who obviously took care of herself. However, Lizzie looked more like her father, although she clearly inherited her cheekbones and copper skin tone from her mother.

"Well, I don't agree with the question," Dale replied.

He redirected his attention to the game.

"But that's the question on the table," Lizzie persisted. "So answer honestly, please, because we're trying to learn your species."

They were staring at him intently, but he refused to look at them.

"My what? Go away, please," he pleaded.

"C'mon, we won't tell anybody how we found out," Mrs. Lawson egged on.

"I already answered you." He was still focusing on the television.

"No, you didn't. You think that it's because of slavery?" Lizzie's mom suggested.

"Slavery? What?" Dale remarked. "You guys, this isn't funny."

"Is it because working in the hot sun all day destroyed the romantic gene somehow?" Lizzie harassed. "It's a fair question, you gotta admit. So, just tell us, and we will leave."

She tried to rub his shoulder, but he shook her off.

"Look, I'm not playing this game," he contended. "Lizzie, please."

He attempted to stand up, but they both pushed him down.

"It's not a game," Mrs. Lawson persisted. "If not slavery, then what? Tell us your theory. What have you heard?"

"Please leave me alone," Dale insisted. "Just go have your 'I-am-woman, hear-me-complain' moment somewhere else."

"Why are you getting so nervous?" Lizzie asked.

"I'm not nervous."

"Yes, you are," Mrs. Lawson refuted. "You're sweating. What are you trying to hide, Mr. Man? Just tell us the truth!"

"C'mon on, Lizzie, I'm serious," Dale appealed.

"No, we are not going," she pressured. "We're just trying to get to the root of the problem so we can help you."

"The root of the problem is you—the both of you," he declared. "How's that for getting to the root?"

"Now you're talking foolishness. See, I told you he didn't know," Lizzie said over Dale's shoulder.

"Girl, you sure you want to marry him?" her mother asked. "I thought I always told you to go for the money, not the muscles. You should've picked the bachelor behind door number two."

The two women erupted in laughter, jumped to their feet, and headed back to the kitchen.

Dale wasn't a complete idiot. He could take a joke. He fully understood that Lizzie and her mother were just having a little fun at his expense. However, sometimes the things that make a joke funny is the underlying truth contained within, and he couldn't help but wonder if his fiancé was trying to tell him something. Nonetheless, he promised himself that if ever the opportunity was presented to him when he might return the favor, he wasn't going to pass it up.

***

Lizzie told him that she wanted her brother to be a groomsman and that he needed to choose a best man and another groomsman. He picked Joey and Louis. The guest list included 120 people. It was a little embarrassing that he could only think of ten people he wanted to invite. He got to choose where they went on their honeymoon, as long as he chose someplace warm. Joey suggested that he look into the Caribbean, and Dale called a travel agent. Other than that, his responsibilities were mercifully limited.

However, he still needed to figure out the role his mother would play at the wedding. At this point, she didn't even know that he was engaged. He hadn't spoken to her since she called him after she was arrested. He just figured that he would tell her when she got out of jail. He seriously doubted that she would have much interest in his plans anyway, which would have been okay with him. He really didn't want her involved at all; she was too much of a wild card and would just end up embarrassing him.

But what son doesn't invite his own mother to his wedding? That would look too weird. This wasn't the kind of issue normal people typically faced. Hopefully, it would all work itself out in the end.

A letter arrived addressed to Dale and Louis. It was written on jail stationery and the handwritten name printed on the top left-hand side of the envelope was "LaToya Johnson, #82001354." He didn't open it immediately; rather, he placed it in a pile on the kitchen counter with all the bills and junk mail that he had yet to sort through. Most likely, it was just a solicitation for money for cigarettes. A couple of hours later, he grabbed the envelope, sat down, swallowed hard, and open it.

> Dear Dale and Louis,
> How are you? I am fine. I am hoping to come home soon. As part of my progrom, they want us to write a letter to someone who we have hurt, so I am writing to you guys. I know that I am not a good mother to you both. But I want to be. Some really bad stuff happened to me that I never told you about and messed me up bad. I am going to stop drinking and try to act better. I am very sorry, and I hope that you both can give me a secund chance.
> Your loving mother,
> LaToya Johnson

Dale got up, put the letter back in the envelope, and returned it to the top of the pile. The clock read 8:40 p.m. He needed to hurry. He was supposed to pick Lizzie up at her job because she didn't have her car. She got off work at 9:00 p.m., and she was waiting for him in the doorway when he pulled up in front. He drove her home and pulled into the driveway. He parked, and they sat there in the darkened truck like they had so many times before.

"Is something wrong, Dale?" She wondered.

"No, why do you ask?"

"Because you're so quiet. You haven't said a word."

"No, I am just tired," he responded.

"You seem sad."

"I'm not sad. I'm really glad to see you," he sidetracked. He moved closer and kissed her on the cheek.

"Are you sure?" she asked. "Did something happen?"

"I'm sure. Nothing happened!" he said emphatically."

"Okay, I just want you to be okay."

After she left and he was driving home alone with his thoughts, he planned to come clean with her later. He just wasn't prepared to talk about it with her at that moment. As soon as he got to the apartment, he called Louis' dorm and left a message for him to call home. The phone rang fifteen minutes later.

Dale read the letter to his brother.

"Do you know what she's talking about?" Louis asked.

"What do you mean?"

"The bad stuff that happened to her," Louis emphasized. "You think she was molested or something?"

"I don't know. Maybe," Dale conceded.

"Because if she was, it would explain a lot."

"Explain a lot about what?" Dale questioned.

"Why she is the way that she is. It can take a lifetime for people to overcome trauma from their childhood," Louis preached.

"I don't know anything about her childhood trauma. At this point, I don't care either. All I know is that I'm getting married in six months, and I'm terrified that this woman is going to show up drunk at my wedding, cuss out the preacher in the middle of the ceremony, and challenge one of the guests to a wrestling match at the reception."

"No...I know. I get it," Louis acknowledged.

"You want to start a new life?" Dale railed. "Well, I want to start a new life too."

"Maybe it won't be that bad," Louis countered. "I think there's a good chance that she'll behave herself at the wedding. I really do. If for no other reason than she knows you would probably kill her if she acted out. You're the only person in the world she's even a little afraid of."

"That's because she knows I know how low she can go," Dale growled. "And that's why I'm worried about what she'll do."

"Maybe if you just talk to her before? Explain everything," Louis offered.

"Talking things out never worked with her in the past," Dale positioned.

"Maybe she changed?" Louis suggested. "She was never locked up before."

"There's going to be a bar at the reception with free beer," Dale said without any inflection in his voice.

"Oh…so what's the plan….maybe…maybe we drug her? I know a guy," Louis spoke in a hushed tone.

"I already thought about that," Dale played along. "But I don't think drugs work on the undead."

Chapter 9

Dale was more than a little concerned when Lizzie's dad called him out of the blue. He felt his body immediately tense up. Mr. Lawson seemed to be warming up to him more since the engagement, but the two had never spoken on the phone before, and it was a bit of a jolt to his system when Dale realized who was calling him.

"Dale I was wondering if you had made any decisions about what you're going to do after graduation. You graduate in a couple of months, right?"

"Ah…in May, right."

"Do you know what you're going to do after?" Mr. Lawson asked.

"Well…I—"

"The reason that I ask is that I know that there's an opening down here at the police garage," Mr. Lawson explained. "Somebody just quit, and they're looking for someone. If you're interested, I could talk to the foreman for you. It's a city job with benefits and a pension. I can ask more about it if you want. But I didn't want to say anything to anybody without checking with you first. It's up to you; I'm not trying to tell you what to do."

"Yeah, I know…but do you think they would hire me after all the stuff that went down with my mother?" Dale asked.

"What does your mother have to do with you?"

"Well, I think she has a felony or something," Dale related.

"That doesn't matter," Mr. Lawson replied. "There's a reason why they cut the cord at birth."

Dale felt foolish.

"Right. Well, yes, Sir…I think that I'm interested," Dale hedged.

"Good then. Sit tight and let me see what else I can find out."

"Thank you, Sir," Dale said. "I really appreciate it."

"You don't have to thank me. You're going to be my son-in-law. That makes us family…understand?"

"Yes, I understand."

Dale was ecstatic. Not just about the job prospect, which sounded great, by the way, but also about the fact that apparently, Mr. Lawson was willing to go out of his way to help him. Yes, he probably was doing it mostly for his daughter, but Dale felt good when Mr. Lawson called him "family." The gesture meant a lot because Dale desperately wanted to be a part of Lizzie's family, an association where everybody loved and cared about each other.

The interview went well. Applicants for the position were required to possess two years' experience in addition to having an associate's degree. Obviously, Dale didn't have the work experience, but the foreman said that his time at Carbone's Automotive Repair might suffice. He would also have to take civil service exams if he wanted to be promoted past entry-level.

The interview included a tour of the police garage, and he was introduced to some of the mechanics. He really liked what he saw, but he told himself not to get his hopes up, as there were several other people who had applied for the job—more qualified people.

Dale didn't want a big deal made about his graduation. At first, he wasn't even planning to go to the ceremony at all because it was the same weekend that he needed to go to Buffalo to pick up Louis. But Lizzie insisted that he get his degree with his class. She said that he needed to learn how to be proud of his accomplishments.

It was a nice day with some sun and temperatures in the mid-70s. Lizzie's mother and father came, along with Daniel. Louis was there too, but he didn't sit with the Lawsons. After the ceremony, they went back to Lizzie's house, and her father cooked barbeque on the grill. Dale always liked how the Lawson family said grace and thanked God for his goodness before every meal. Everybody was in a good mood, and there wasn't too much discussion about the wedding. From Dale's perspective, it was a near-perfect day with family.

***

Dale woke up the next morning to the sound of his mother coming in. At first, he thought he was dreaming. It also occurred to him that it might be Louis leaving for his first day of work back at Burger King, but it didn't sound like Louis. She was always so loud. Besides, he recognized the spirit she carried without seeing her.

It was 8:45 a.m. The only reason he wasn't at work already was that he had a physical that morning. He slowly rolled out of bed and put on a pair of sweatpants. He opened his bedroom door and went directly to the bathroom. When he came out, she was in her room with the door open.

"Hi," he said, standing in the doorframe.

"Well, hello to you, stranger. How ya been?" she asked.

"I'm good. You should have called me. I could've picked you up," he said.

"No need. I walked. It felt good being in the fresh air."

"You have to call your social worker so they can start sending you checks again," he advised.

"I don't know where that number is."

"It's on the refrigerator," he answered.

"Oh, okay."

"Look, I have to hurry. I have to go take a physical and get to work. Do you need anything?" he asked.

"No, I'm just so glad not to be locked up no more," she explained. "I can't tell you. Do you have a couple of dollars I can have? I need to get my hair done."

"Yeah, sure."

Dale walked to his room and took forty dollars out of his wallet. He handed it to her and turned away.

"Louis is in there sleeping," he said. "He should be getting up soon for work."

"How's he doing?" she asked.

"I just picked him up from school on Friday," Dale said. "He's doing good."

"Good, glad to hear it…Oh, we need more beer. I just took the last two."

Dale took a quick shower. He didn't want to be late for his appointment. Before leaving, he went into Louis's room and told him the exciting news. Louis just looked straight ahead in a sleep trance with no expression on his face and rolled over without saying a word.

The city of Schenectady required all potential hires in the garage to take a physical. He hadn't been offered the job yet, but Dale thought that this was promising. Mr. Carbone was genuinely happy for him when he told him that he had applied for the position. He went on and on about everyone he knew there and the things that he had heard. He said that he would put in a good word with his contacts.

Now that his mother had resurrected, he knew he needed to talk to Lizzie about his concerns as soon as possible. He really didn't want to be the bearer of bad news, but he knew that the longer that he waited to talk to her, the worse it would be. So that night after his mother had flown out into the evening air, he called his fiancé.

"I think there could be a problem with my mother and the wedding," he said.

"What kind of problem?" she asked.

"Well, she is not used to that kind of thing, and I'm worried that she might not know how to act right. Especially if she's drinking."

"What if we talk to her about it?" Lizzie innocently asked.

"That's like talking to a wall," he replied. "I told you she is not good with people. It could be really embarrassing for us."

"What did she say when you told her we're getting married?"

"I didn't tell her yet," he confessed. "I only saw her for a minute this morning. Who can say when I'll see her again? She's got a whole lot of trouble to catch up on."

"Are you afraid to tell her? Is that why you haven't told her yet?" she wondered.

"No, the only thing that I am afraid of is her embarrassing me and ruining the wedding."

"You gotta tell her."

"I know," he acknowledged.

They were silently thinking together.

"Maybe we could just elope," Dale jokingly suggested.

"That's not funny. We're *not* eloping," she stated emphatically.

"Yeah, well, we'll see what you think when she starts pole dancing in the middle of the reception," he offered.

"Pole dancing?" Lizzie reacted. "She's not a stripper... is she?"

He laughed. "I don't know what she is," he said bluntly.

"She's not a stripper!" Lizzie said definitively.

"Okay, if you say so," Dale replied.

"Oh my, honey. Is this what has been bothering you?" Lizzie questioned. "I knew there something going on in that head of yours."

"I know it's a bad thing to say, but I've been dreading the day she got out of jail," Dale spoke out.

"Okay. Well, don't say anything to her yet. Let me talk to my mom."

"I am really sorry about all of this," he said.

"You don't have to be sorry. I'm just glad you told me."

Louis came home that night just before midnight. Their mother got in when Dale was in the shower the next morning at 6:15 a.m. When he came out of the bathroom, she was in her room with the door closed, presumably passed out. He wanted out. There was absolutely no way he was going to live there with her for another nine months until his wedding—he couldn't do it anymore. He decided at that moment that he was going to find his own apartment. This is why they cut the cord.

Lizzie thought it was a good idea when he told her. She said that she'd been meaning to talk to him about the possibility of looking for a place now, and she would move in with him after the wedding. She was hesitant to bring it up because she didn't want to put extra pressure on him. But she made a good point, he could use his upcoming nuptials as the reason why he was moving out, which was important if they didn't want her to get angry or offended enough to trash their wedding.

Their target was September. They would look for a two-bedroom apartment so Louis could have a place to come home to during school breaks. But that meant they had to stay there with her in the apartment through the summer. Even though their interactions with her were quite limited, living with her was no small feat. Everything she did got under his skin—now more than ever before.

Lizzie and her mother came up with the game plan for the wedding. Lizzie's Aunt Gloria would be assigned to help with his mother. Lizzie said that her Aunt Gloria was a sergeant in the United States Army and was tough as nails. "Operation LaToya" essentially entailed constant surveillance and total take down if necessary. No mercy. Dale liked it, but in the back of his mind, he feared that Aunt Gloria was about to meet her match.

It was nearly a week before his mother was awake and sober in the daylight hours so he could talk to her. He and Louis had just returned from church on a Sunday, and she was sitting in the living room watching television and smoking a cigarette when they walked in. After greeting her, Louis went into the kitchen and began preparing lunch for them. Dale sat down on the opposite end of the sofa from her.

"I have some news I've been meaning to tell you," he began.

"News? What kind of news?" she asked.

"Good news. I just got a new job, and I am getting married," Dale announced.

"Married? To who? Is this the same girl you were with before?" she wondered.

"Yes, Lizzie," he said.

"Her daddy knows? He gonna let her marry you?"

"Yes, he is," Dale related. He was slightly offended.

"She ain't pregnant, is she?" she questioned and took a puff of her cigarette.

"No, she isn't pregnant," Dale scoffed.

"Well, when is this wedding?" she asked.

"In February."

"Oh," was all she said.

"Her dad actually helped me get a job at the police garage," Dale volunteered.

"You working with the police?"

"Not working with them, just fixing police cars," he explained.

"You gonna be police?" she asked and laughed to herself.

"No, I will work for the city. I'll be a mechanic working mostly on city-owned vehicles," he reiterated.

She took a moment to think it through. He waited.

"Look at that, you getting married before me," she said. "Well, I wish you all the best. I really do," she said as she narrowed one of her eyes and took another drag of nicotine. "I don't know too much about being married, but you'll probably be good at it."

"Thank you," he commented. "We have a lot of things to do between now and February, including finding a place of our own."

"Is this gonna be a church-wedding kinda thing? Cause I don't know about me walkin' up in some church. Hell might freeze over," she said and chuckled.

"No, it's not going to be at the church," he responded. "But it is going to be pretty big because Lizzie has a pretty big family. But I will let you know as we go along."

He stood, picked up his Bible and notebook, and walked to his room. He was proud of himself. That had gone pretty much exactly the way that he had planned it in his head. He just hoped that the rest of it worked out as well.

At some point, she was going to realize that his moving out meant that she would be in the apartment by herself with no one there to do for her. Over the years, he had been made to feel like her personal slave. She clearly didn't know how to run a household, which meant that she was eventually going to make more bad choices. Case in point, she never called her social worker like he told her to do, yet she was fit to be tied when she didn't get a check at the beginning of the month. There simply was no winning with her.

***

Dale was scheduled to start his new job on July 5, the day after the holiday weekend. He was very excited. Mr. Lawson seemed pleased when Dale called him and told him that he had gotten the job. Dale thanked him profusely for his help. He warned Dale that there was a lot of politics to deal with when working for the city. His advice was to play it straight and not get caught up in the different cliques.

For her part, Lizzie was running full force. She was taking a summer class along with working full time. Her preoccupation with the wedding waned a little as her to-do list dwindled down, but her overall anxiety level remained high. There were two bridal showers being planned. Also, something bad happened with her wedding dress that caused a meltdown. They had started looking at apartments but hadn't found anything yet. Mr. Lawson warned that it was all going to get worse before it got better.

Joey wanted to throw Dale a bachelor party, which Dale graciously declined. While he appreciated the sentiment, he was not going to a strip club. However, Joey wouldn't take no for an answer. After some back and forth, Dale agreed to an overnight trip to Philadelphia for a Philadelphia Eagles football game in November. It was perfect because the Eagles played the New York Giants, and Dale was an Eagles fan while Joey loved the Giants. Dale had never been to an NFL game before.

***

Several times during the summer, Dale and Louis found themselves discussing their divergent beliefs about God and the Bible. For one thing, Louis believed that the Bible was the actual Word of God and that it was without any errors. In contrast, Dale figured that even if the Bible was inspired by God, it was written by human hands and therefore had to contain a ton of mistakes.

"I don't see how anyone today can say that everything in the Bible is true," Dale postured.

"Jesus said that his Word is truth," Louis pointed out.

"But that's not the same thing as saying that every single word printed in the Bible is true," Dale commented.

"Yes, it does," Louis argued. "Otherwise, how do we know what is true and what are the mistakes?"

"The parts about who God is are true. Some of the other stuff about the people and places in the Bible are not necessarily true. Period." Dale said forcefully.

"Everything we know about God is based upon his interactions with the people in the Bible," Louis countered. "It's not enough to just believe God exists; we also have to believe that he interacts with his people, both yesterday and today."

"I don't buy that for one second," Dale expressed.

"Then the problem you're going to have is that it really isn't possible to please God without faith in both who he is and what he does," Louis preached. "In other words, God demands that we trust that he is on our side even when it doesn't look or feel like he is. We can trust that he is there because we know who he is, and we know what he does. That's really why people of strong faith can sing praises to his name, even when they're going through hell on earth."

The summer was over in a flash. Dale was busy with the new job and wasn't that focused on too much else. But he liked it. The people were okay, and there were a lot of new things to learn. He worked the day shift and had all his evenings and weekends free. It was the perfect setup for him.

Whether he spent time with Lizzie depended more on her schedule than on his own because she was much busier than he was. He was still hanging out from time to time with Joey, who now preferred to be called "Joe" since his wife had a baby boy in August nicknamed Joey. Dale really missed Mr. Carbone and not being at the garage. He felt a little lost without them.

Lizzie managed to find them the perfect apartment not far from where her parents lived. It had two bedrooms and a small room that could be used as an office or another bedroom. Due to needed renovations, however, it wasn't available until November. Dale decided that he would bring all of Louis' stuff with him when he moved into the new place because he knew that anything he left behind would eventually turn up missing. His mother's friends could not be trusted.

Dale almost had a heart attack when Lizzie's mother announced that she wanted to meet with his mother about the wedding.

"I don't understand why you need to meet her," he protested. "She doesn't care about this wedding or me."

"Well, we want her to feel included," Mrs. Lawson said. "Women don't think like men. It's the right thing to do."

"You don't know her," Dale resisted. "It is better just to let sleeping dogs lie."

Mrs. Lawson laughed at that before she knew it.

"Listen," she began, "I understand how you feel. I really do. But trust me, Dale, I know what I'm doing."

"I don't know..." Dale trailed off.

"You're her son. She must be wondering. This is a way to smooth things over, so she doesn't feel put out. I'm asking you to do this as a favor to me."

Dale sighed heavily and voiced, "Okay, I'll do it, but I make no promises."

He thought it best that the meeting take place at their apartment so his mother would feel less intimidated. He didn't mention it to her in advance to make sure she didn't have much time to think about it beforehand. He just casually told her one afternoon that Lizzie and her mom were on their way over to talk about the wedding and that he wanted her to meet Lizzie's mother.

"Why I gotta meet her?" she asked.

"Because we're going to be family, and it's the right thing to do," he insisted.

"They might be your family, but they surely ain't mine."

"Can you just be nice, please?" he begged. "Is it going to kill you to try?"

She was in her room when his fiancé arrived with her mother. He seated them in the living room, and they chatted for a moment. Mostly, they just tried to reassure him that everything would be alright. He knocked on his mother's door and asked if she could come out and meet Lizzie's mom.

"I'll be right there," she shouted through the door.

A couple of minutes later, she walked into the living room. She had changed her clothes and combed her hair. Dale stood and introduced her.

"This is my mother, LaToya Johnson. This is Lizzie's mom, Cheryl Lawson."

"Please call me Cheryl," Mrs. Lawson spoke as she stood to her feet. "It's so nice to finally meet you."

"It's nice to meet you too," his mother replied. "Please have a seat. Can I offer you anything to drink?"

"No, thank you. I just wanted to meet you and talk to you about the 'big wedding' coming up," Mrs. Lawson said. "I have to say, my husband and I just love your son to death. You must be very proud of him. You have done a terrific job with him."

"Thank you," she answered and shot a quick glance in Dale's direction.

"Well, both of your sons, actually. Louis is such a sweetheart too."

"Thank you kindly," LaToya replied.

Mrs. Lawson began, "I was wondering if there was anything special that you wanted at the wedding. Or someone you wanted us to invite?"

"Not...not that I can think of offhand," LaToya replied. "But can I think about it and let you know?"

She appeared to be a little apprehensive.

"Yes, of course," Mrs. Lawson agreed. "There's still some time before the invitations have to go out. Just let me know. We're thinking that there will be about 120 people there. That's the most the room holds." Mrs. Lawson offered.

"Um…do I have to do anything at this wedding?" LaToya asked timidly.

"No, not if you don't want to. It is going to be a really simple ceremony. Lizzie's colors are…what Lizzie?"

"Rose," replied Lizzie.

"That's right, rose," Mrs. Lawson stressed. "She wants you and me to wear dresses with colors in the rose family. So we need to order our dresses together. I have some ideas I can send over for you to look at, if that's okay with you."

"I never had a fancy dress before, "LaToya confessed. "I don't even know my size."

"We can figure all that out," Mrs. Lawson said measuredly. "Every girl needs a fancy dress, I say. I think you're going to look beautiful!"

"Thank you," LaToya said and blushed.

The rest of the discussion was about the favors and stuff. His mother listened politely, and Dale was bored. Altogether they were only there about thirty minutes before they said their goodbyes, hugged, and shuffled out the door. Dale was really pleased with how well his mother handled herself. He could see that she was trying—which is something that she almost never did. He was relieved that he had jumped that hurdle.

Shortly after, the phone rang.

"How do you think it went?" Lizzie asked.

"Great, "Dale admitted. "Your mom was amazing. What did you think?"

"We thought she was sweet," Lizzie stated.

"Yeah, well, that sweet thing almost stabbed a man to death."

"Yeah, I know," Lizzie conceded. "But I couldn't help but feel a little sorry for her."

"Sorry for her? I don't feel sorry for her at all," Dale insisted.

"I don't believe that," Lizzie contested. "You just don't want to say."

"Nope, you're wrong," he asserted. "Only a fool feels sorry for the snake that bit him."

"I think that she really loves you in her own way," Lizzie offered.

"Lucky me," Dale sighed.

"You're so angry with her, and I think she knows that," his fiancé opined. "Somewhere along the way, you got the upper hand—and you know that."

"It's hard to explain," he replied.

It turned out that Lizzie was good with his mother. They seemed to have connected on some level. Over the next several weeks, Mrs. Lawson picked his mother up twice and took her dress shopping. Dale didn't much like the idea of not being there to supervise, but they didn't want him there. Lizzie said it was fun spending time with her, about which he was extremely skeptical. When he asked his mother how things were going, she only said that Lizzie and her mom were "good people."

All the wedding planning made Dale realize just how much of a worrier he was at heart. He was regularly having nightmares. Once he dreamed that his pants fell down in the middle of the ceremony. His recurring dream, however, was about him being late for the wedding and trying to get to the country club, but he couldn't remember where it was. There were many nights when he woke up sweating and his heart felt like it was going to jump out of his chest.

Everyone said what he was experiencing was normal. However, Dale knew he wasn't just having "cold feet" like Joe suggested. He adored Lizzie, so that wasn't it. She was his forever love. However, try as hard as he might, he simply couldn't get out from underneath his own personal cloud of self-doubt and insecurity.

***

The football trip to Philadelphia was awesome and helped to settle him. It was just him, Joe, Louis, and Daniel. Lizzie's father said that it was too cold for him. They went down the night before, checked into the hotel, and had dinner at a sports bar with a ton of Eagles fans. Joe almost got in a fight with several of them because he insisted on wearing his Giant's jacket, which immediately drew the ire of the entire bar, including a group of drunk guys at the next table.

The game-time temperature was twenty-two degrees Fahrenheit, with a wind chill of minus ten degrees Fahrenheit. They froze their butts off. Daniel had so many layers on that he could barely bend his body enough to sit. But it was fun, and the Eagles won 25-22, which made it all worth it, as far as Dale was concerned.

One night right after Christmas, Joe dragged Dale to a bar downtown on the pretense of needing to talk to him about something. When they arrived, there were a bunch of guys he knew waiting there, including Mr. Carbone and several of his co-workers. Lizzie's dad was there too. It was a special surprise, and Dale was truly touched that people showed up to celebrate him. Even some guys he played football with in high school made an appearance. Everyone kept buying him drinks, which he felt obligated to accept. However, he refused to drink beer. Nevertheless, it was the first time—and the last time—in Dale's life when he was intoxicated.

***

It turns out that Louis didn't much like the idea of leaving their mother by herself in the apartment. The two brothers had words about it. In the end, Dale told him he had no choice. Officially, Louis's legal address would remain with their mother so she could continue to get state assistance for him. But Dale rejected the idea of Louis being alone with her during school breaks.

Dale barked, "I don't think that you'll be happy until she stabs you in the heart!"

Although Dale understood on some levels why Louis was worried about their mother, he still couldn't fully grasp the apparent need his brother had to save her at every turn. Maybe Louis was too young to remember how she would leave them for hours—and in some instances, for days—with people of dubious character. Dale recalled a couple of times when he had refused to stay with some people.

Moreover, as neglectful as she had been of them both, it was always very easy for her to overlook Louis completely. And Dale knew how much her rejection affected his kid brother. They had talked about it numerous times, and yet here they were, having the same argument once again.

Louis was obviously overcompensating. Maybe he just couldn't help himself. It was almost like he had added pressure on him all the time to get her to love him before it was too late.

In the end, it was unlikely that there was much Dale could do to deter him from trying.

Regardless, Dale was determined not to dwell on the past. For some reason, God had given him this incredible opportunity to be happy, and he was taking it. He didn't believe that everyone was created entirely equal. Some people were born victims. He would obviously help his mother out when he could, but he would do it on his own terms. The new life he envisioned with Lizzie didn't include images of him waiting hand-and-foot on his mother, further enabling her demons. He simply refused to let her hold him down any longer.

The final days leading up to his wedding were all a haze. Lizzie and her mother kept adding to his list of things to do, and he just did everything they asked him to do without grumbling or complaining. He was stressed, and there were so many different feelings flowing together through him that he welcomed the distraction. But he was also determined to be bold and fearless. So, with eyes wide open, he dove headfirst into his river of dreams and rode its strong current into his destiny.

Chapter 10

Dale instantly understood just how much God loves him. The revelation erupted in his heart like a tidal wave. No doubt, like most grooms, Dale's lasting impression from his wedding will always be of his bride waking down the aisle coming toward him while looking more beautiful than he ever thought possible. After all the preparations, he was still caught completely off guard by her splendor and left breathless.

However, it turned out that it was much bigger than that for him. Inside, there was a stirring in his soul that he had never felt before. For the very first time, his focus wasn't solely on how much he loved Lizzie but rather on the God who had created someone this perfect, especially for him to have and to hold for a lifetime. During the ceremony, the pastor spoke about how marriage wasn't just an expression of the bride and groom's love for each other, but it is also represented the way that Christ loves his people.

"Can you feel it?" he asked while looking directly at Dale. "Can you feel the spirit of the almighty God moving on the altar of your heart?"

Those words found their intended mark in his soul as he stood there before all creation and pledged his life and undying devotion to his beloved. So amazed and caught up, however, he also simultaneously made a holy vow to God, the creator, that he would serve him for the rest of his life. Both were promises freely made.

His heart was so full of thanksgiving and praise to God for saving him and bringing him to this place in time. Nobody knew the expressions of his spirit or the inner cry of his heart. That is, not one person in the capacity-filled room was aware of the sweet surrender taking place inside of him—not even Lizzie.

Dale had charged himself beforehand to maintain his composure throughout the ceremony. But he also hadn't anticipated standing there in the presence of the Lord in such a real and tangible manner. Nobody could have. Although he never shed a tear, he could feel himself being changed from the inside out. He felt himself being reborn!

Louis recited the poem that he wrote for Dale's proposal in the ceremony, and Rita Johnson sang an emotionally charged love ballad that Dale felt down to his toes. Lizzie was crying and shaking for much of it, and Dale had to resist the temptation to take her in his arms right then and there and comfort her. When he was finally able to kiss and touch his wife, it was like heaven and earth coming together. He remembered thinking at that moment that, at the very least, he would always have this day—no matter what.

The wedding went right into the reception, which was held in an adjoining room with large open windows. The view of the snow on the rolling hills was spectacular. It was Valentine's Day, and it seemed like everyone was in the mood for romance. The band played mostly R&B ballads, with a few dance tunes thrown in there. Their first dance was to a Teddy Pendergrass song that Dale had selected. When Lizzie danced with her dad, they both cried all the way through it.

She also danced with Daniel to Michael Jackson, and he caused quite a stir when he spontaneously began to moonwalk. The entire scene was magic.

Dale was particularly touched by Joe's best man toast, which he read from a wrinkled piece of paper that he had problems pulling from his pants pocket:

> "Lizzie, I hope you know you have got yourself a good man. An old soul in a young man's body. I have never seen anybody love anyone the way Dale loves you. He literally carries your heart in his heart, so tender, so right. And you know that his heart is raw too. This is a man who you will be able to count on day in and day out. This is a man who inspires even me to love deeper and harder, to hold on tighter, and who I am proud to call my best friend."

As soon as he finished, Dale walked up to him, pulled him close, and whispered in his ear,

"Great speech! Where did you find it? In a fortune cookie at Ling Ling's?"

"No, actually it's from my daughter's Beauty and the Beast wedding book. I figured that if it was good enough for the beast," Joe joked.

The two men grabbed at each other and laughed hard.

Dale only spoke to his mother briefly the entire day. He just asked her how she was doing, to which she responded that she was good. Lizzie's dad had picked her up early for the wedding so everyone in the bridal party could get dressed together. She looked good; actually, he had never seen her look better. They put makeup on her, and somebody did her hair in a sophisticated style. The dress she wore suited her. Lizzie said she was a perfect size two.

He was watching from the back when she walked down the aisle at the beginning of the wedding, and she looked very nervous. She seemed so determined not to make a mistake. She knew that she was out of her element, and it was obvious that it was important to her to make a good impression. She had never acted like she cared in the least about what anyone thought about her before this. He later learned that she and Lizzie's Aunt Gloria were good friends by the end of the night

It was a perfect wedding! Dale had somehow managed to be on time and keep his pants up. However, both the bride and groom were exhausted by the time that they left the reception at 9:00 p.m. They had to change their clothes, and it took quite a while just to say goodbye to everyone. Louis drove their mother home in Dale's truck. The limousine driver drove them to a hotel in Albany near the airport. They had an early flight to New York City and then on to Jamaica for a week of fun in the sun.

Still overjoyed by the events that made up the best day in his life, Dale was in a playful mood as they walked into the hotel. When they reached the door to their room, he put down their bags and he picked her up in one quick swoop, and carried her inside. The room was softly lit, an Anita Baker song filled the air, champagne was on ice, and rose petals were everywhere.

"Oh my God!" Lizzie exclaimed. "Did you do this?"

"Like I said before, the brothers invented the romance game, baby," he whispered in her ear.

Their wedding night was magical, everything he imagined it would be. It felt like they were in a fairy tale, and it was the most beautiful love story ever written. He knew in his heart that this was just the beginning of their happily ever after.

Unfortunately, the honeymoon didn't go exactly as planned. It started out great. Dale had never been on a plane before and he had never been out of the country, not even to Canada. He was excited. Their beach view room at the all-inclusive resort that he chose was very romantic. It was like they were in heaven.

However, a few days in, Lizzie got sick and couldn't get out of bed. They thought it was food poisoning because she was experiencing stomach issues. The nurse who examined her from the resort said she had a low-grade fever and that it was probably just a virus that needed to run its course. Dale had dinner alone the last two nights that they were in paradise. He couldn't wait to go home.

Chapter 11

I t turned out that his mother was right. Lizzie was six weeks pregnant on their wedding day. She said that she was late all the time and that she had been so stressed with all the wedding preparations that it never occurred to her that something was off with her body. Needless to say, they weren't particularly happy about the news.

Neither were her parents. They came home to an apartment with almost no furniture, an empty refrigerator and pantry, and shower and wedding gifts everywhere that needed to be opened, recorded, and organized. Dale had hoped that everything would settle down once the wedding was over, but clearly, that wasn't even a possibility now.

Mrs. Lawson decided that Lizzie was coming back home until she felt better. Dale's assignment was to set up the apartment. Using their wedding gift money, they bought a new bedroom set, a sofa set, and a television. The rest was supplemented with things people gave them. When she felt up to it, Lizzie and her mother came over to the apartment and worked on things. It was two months before she physically moved in with him.

Dale was starting to hate his job. A co-worker who didn't care much care for Dale was promoted to shift supervisor. A little guy, he was nasty and condescending. It seemed racial, but Dale couldn't prove that. He put up with it because he was the new guy, and he felt that he didn't have a choice, but he didn't need the added pressure.

Dale went to church every Sunday, even when Lizzie was too tired to go. After his experience during the wedding, he was more interested in the God of the Bible than ever before. He paid attention to everything with added purpose. It was like he was hungry for something, but he wasn't sure what he wanted. The food pantry at the church was open every other Saturday, and he decided to volunteer there.

Lizzie must have noticed that he seemed different. One night in bed, she asked, "How come you decided to volunteer at the church now?"

"No reason. I've always wanted to do something," he replied.

"Does it have anything to do with the baby?" she wondered. "Some guys go through changes, too, when their wives are expecting."

"I don't think so. Maybe. I just want to get more grounded. I feel like I have more direction now or something; like I am just coming out of the dark about a lot of things," he admitted.

"You're always so hard on yourself, she commented. "You're not in the dark any more than anybody else."

Dale had to go to his mother's apartment several times to pick up things that he'd left behind. He didn't call her when they returned from Jamaica. She wasn't there the first few times he stopped by. He made it a point to knock before entering because he didn't want to walk in on her and see something that he couldn't get out of his head later. He eventually called her and was surprised when she answered.

"Hi, this is Dale," he said.

"Hey, how are you?" she asked.

"I'm good. How are you?"

"I'm doing pretty good," she related. "Yeah, I'm doing pretty good. Can't complain, you know. How was your trip?"

"It was hot there. It felt good to get out of the cold. Lizzie got a little sick there at the end."

"Sick, how?" she questioned.

"Her stomach was bothering her a lot, and at first, we thought it food poisoning. Turns out she's pregnant."

"Pregnant already. Boy, you don't waste no time, do ya?"

"We didn't do it on purpose," he said defensively.

"It doesn't matter whether you did it on purpose or not. Babies don't need your permission to come."

"Some people love being with their kids," he replied.

"Well, you know I don't babysit," she said jokingly.

"Tell me about it," he responded under his breath.

"Tell her to drink a lot of ginger ale. It will help settle her stomach and keep her strength up."

"Okay, I'll tell her. You set? Do you need anything?" he asked.

"Well, I don't know…if you think about it, you think that maybe you can get me some orange juice and some of that lotion you buy for me?" she solicited.

"Yeah, okay," he replied.

"And some beer too," she added.

"Okay. I'll drop it by when I can."

"Thank you," she said.

Dale told Joe over the phone that Lizzie was pregnant because he was too afraid to tell him face-to-face. To Joe's credit, he didn't rub it in, at least not as much as Dale had anticipated.

"Welcome to my world, old man. Let's see how you like it," he resolved.

Although it got a little better for her, Lizzie was sick for nearly the entire pregnancy. She never went back to school. She was also very fragile and emotional and would cry at the drop of a dime. He felt both guilty and overwhelmed; of course, he never told Joe that.

Exactly one week before the baby was born, Dale was in the shower when Lizzie said that Joe was on the phone. Dale knew immediately that something was wrong. Joe was a night owl and he never did anything in the morning of his own accord. Dressed only in a towel, Dale took the phone and braced himself for the punch. It came in one swift motion and left him completely stunned. Mr. Carbone had a heart attack in his sleep last night. He was dead.

Dale bent over and was struggling to breathe. No one close to him had ever died before, and grief was yet another new experience for him. He was having trouble processing this information. Mr. Carbone looked fine the last time that he stopped by the garage. He was in good shape for his age and was never sick. This was unbelievable.

"Is everything okay?" Lizzie asked.

"No," he said and began shaking inside.

"What happened?" she demanded.

Dale tried to respond to her, but the words didn't come.

"Dale, tell me!" she shouted.

He somehow managed to put enough words together for her to get the gist of it.

"Oh, Dale, I'm so sorry. I know how much he meant to you."

She put her arms around her husband and held him close. He just stared ahead.

The next few days were dreadful. Lizzie went with him to the calling hours. She was wearing one of those big-tent maternity dresses, and she waddled when she walked. They were one of the first ones there so Lizzie didn't have to stand in line. Mrs. Carbone, who was standing next to her son, Chris, and her two teenage daughters, smiled when she saw him and kissed them both.

"Oh, look at you, honey," she said to Lizzie. "How are you feeling?"

"Fat," Lizzie replied with a smile.

"How much longer?"

"Any day now."

"Well, that's exciting. Be sure that you let me know when the baby is born."

"We are so very sorry for your loss," Lizzie lamented.

"Thank you both. I must say that I feel like I am living a nightmare. I can't believe he's really gone," she bemoaned.

"Please let us know if there's anything we can do to help," Lizzie said.

"Thank you. That's very kind," Mrs. Carbone acknowledged. "Dale, we need you at the church tomorrow at 9:00 o'clock, okay?"

He just nodded without saying a word.

Mrs. Carbone stepped forward and cupped his face with one of her hands.

"Ahh, honey, look at you... I know, it's awful...Christopher loved you like another son. He was so proud of you. He cried at your wedding, and I'm so glad he got to see that," she said.

Dale couldn't contain himself any longer, and he wept openly. Both women reached out and did what they could to console him.

A Mass of Christian Burial was held at the large Catholic church downtown. Both Dale and Joe were pallbearers. The eulogies were short and touching. Dale heard several things about his former boss that he didn't know. For instance, he didn't know that Mr. Carbone was recruited by a couple of division I schools for football, but he injured his right knee his senior year and was unable to continue playing. Obviously, even with all his pushing and prodding, Mr. Carbone was not a braggart. Dale left the funeral feeling like he had missed out on so many opportunities to really get to know one of the few people in the world who had invested selflessly in his life.

He couldn't comprehend just what made Mr. Carbone want to take him under his wing in the first place. He had a son and a family that loved him. Dale was just another city kid who was destined to amount to next to nothing. Out of nowhere, a white man who he didn't even know reached out and lifted him up.

Dale never had a chance to ask him why he did it, and now he desperately needed to know the answer to that question.

Worst yet, he never had a chance to say what was in his heart to properly thank him, assuming that he had plenty of time to do so. He was more than lost in his grief.

Mrs. Carbone was approached by someone about buying the business, and she decided to take the offer. Although Dale understood why she was selling the garage, it bothered him just the same. Everything was just happening so fast, and he was barely holding on as it was. He heard that the buyers were going to tear down the building and replace it with a fast-food franchise.

Lizzie went into labor just as Dale was getting off from work. She didn't appear to be in too much distress when he arrived home just ten minutes after she had called him. He had ignored every speed limit sign that he came upon in route to the house, but he only pushed it slightly while transporting her to the hospital. He didn't want to be reckless.

Her parents were waiting for them at Bellevue Woman's Center when they walked in the main entrance. Lizzie's water broke while sitting in the waiting room, and they were in an examining room when Dale witnessed her first really bad contraction. Suddenly, he was gripped in fear—they both were. None of the classes they had taken had effectively prepared him for this. The terror inside told him that Lizzie was going to die just like his mentor.

It's a good thing that his mother-in-law was in the delivery room with them because there was no way that Dale would have survived on his own. Lizzie cried incessantly between contractions, and when they came, she screamed for bloody murder. He prayed in that room more than he had ever prayed in his life. He begged God to spare her and made promises that no man could possibly keep. They were there all night, and after nineteen hours of labor, Lizzie gave birth to a healthy baby boy.

Later that day, he called Mrs. Carbone, who answered on the first ring.

"Hello."

"Uh, Mrs. Carbone. This is Dale."

"Oh, hi, honey, how are you? Is everything okay?" she asked.

"Yes, I just wanted to tell you that Lizzie just had the baby."

"Really? Is she okay?"

"Yes, it was a long labor," he said. "She's very tired, and she's sleeping now."

"What did she have, a boy or a girl?" she wondered.

"A boy. He weighed almost ten pounds," Dale said proudly.

"Oh, my word, that's a big baby! I am so happy for the two of you. What's his name?" she asked.

"We named him Christopher, after the man I loved like a father."

Chapter 12

Christopher Paul Johnson was a beautiful baby. And he was a good baby. He slept through the night almost from the beginning. His father was beside himself. In the course of a week, Dale's emotions traversed from the depths of despair to feeling like he was on top of the world. However, the abrupt change of events was very hard on him, and he was sorely wounded. In response, he decided to focus on satisfying his own expectations of who he wanted to be. Lizzie needed him, and his son needed a father. This was his chance for validation as a man, and he embraced it.

Once they settled into a routine, however, life with an infant was doable. Because Lizzie had the baby all day, Dale took the night shift. He fed the baby breast milk from a bottle and held him until he went back to sleep, which usually didn't take more than a few minutes. He really wanted the time alone so he could bond with his son on his own. There were only a few times when Dale couldn't get him to go back to sleep, and Lizzie had to get up and do it.

Christopher was about three months old the first time he met his other grandmother. That wasn't intentional, at least not on Dale's part. He called her a couple of days after the baby was born. She didn't express any desire to see her grandson, and her interest seemed to be only cursory. Dale continued to run a few errands for her upon request, but he never took the baby over to her apartment.

Louis came home for thanksgiving and stayed in his room at Dale and Lizzie's apartment. He immediately loved being with the baby, and Dale enjoyed watching the two of them interact. It was Louis who got their mother to come over for dinner one night when he was home for Christmas break. However, she did not engage her grandson much.

Dale was still having problems at work with his supervisor, who seemed to be stuck on stupid. The guy's name was Geoff Tanner, and Dale had grown to despise him. He mostly just avoided Tanner as much as he could. Joe found a new job with the New York State Department of Transportation, and he really liked it. Dale was considering whether he should start looking for another job, too, although he didn't like the idea of giving Tanner the satisfaction of knowing that he had run him away.

One morning at the beginning of the shift, Tanner approached Dale in front of two other guys and accused him of botching up a job.

"If you don't know what you're doing, then you need to ask someone. You can't just pretend that you completed a job that you didn't." Tanner reprimanded.

"I don't know what you're talking about. I didn't pretend to do anything," Dale refuted.

"Well, the car you worked on two days ago is back with the same problem, the same brake problem!" Tanner shrieked.

"Sorry to hear that, but it wasn't me. I haven't done a brake job in over two weeks. You got the wrong guy," Dale maintained.

"No, I don't. I checked the log, and it was you. Don't try to lie your way out of it. That's the problem with you people. You don't want to pull your own weight."

"Excuse me? Who are you calling 'you people'?" Dale objected.

"Oh, did I offend you?" Tanner ridiculed. "Cause I'm standing right in front of you, letting you know that I am not going to put up with this crap from you. Do you understand?"

At that moment, Tanner stepped closer and was standing directly in front of Dale, face-to-face.

"I understand that you need to get out of my face!" Dale roared.

"Or what?" Tanner dared.

Dale didn't say anything. He turned angrily and started to walk away.

"That's what I thought," Tanner goaded. "You're all talk. I should write you up. I don't take lightly to being threatened by the likes of you—"

Before he knew it, Dale had pivoted and shoved Tanner up against the wall with one hand and was holding him there by the neck.

"No, Dale, let him go! Let him go!" someone shouted from behind.

He immediately released his grip, and Tanner slid down the wall and instantly started coughing and gasping for air. Dale turned and stormed away. He knew right away that he had made a mistake and was embarrassed. He was approached an hour later by the receptionist, who told him he needed to go to personnel.

Dale was very angry with himself for letting Tanner get to him. Personnel was near City Hall, and he had to drive there. He figured that he was probably going to get fired and was already dreading having to tell his wife. When he arrived at the personnel office, he was instructed to take a seat, someone would be with him momentarily.

A tall woman with blond hair called his name and led him to a small office. Inside was a white man with a round, chubby face sitting at a desk. He stood up and introduced himself as Tim Ross. He told Dale to take a seat and explained that he was a union representative.

"I understand that there was some kind of altercation with another employee this morning at the police garage. Is that correct?

"Yes," Dale replied.

"Can you tell me what happened?"

Dale told him everything as best he remembered. Mr. Ross listened carefully without expression.

"If you were having problems with this guy, why didn't you report him?"

"Because I didn't know I could. I'm still on probation. I didn't want any problems," Dale explained.

"Okay, I get it, but it would have been better if you reported it. He filed a complaint against you for assault. You've been suspended with pay. I will represent you. There will be an investigation and possibly a hearing. You could be terminated."

"I see," Dale said. "How long will this all take?"

"Shouldn't take that long initially. I will know in a week or so if the city is going to formally charge you," Mr. Ross explained.

"Do I need a lawyer?"

"No, not at this time. Maybe later if criminal charges are filed."

"Okay, good," Dale replied. "Should I be worried?"

"Hard to say. It's too early to tell. Any other questions?"

"So, you will call me in a week?" Dale asked.

"Yes, possibly sooner," Mr. Ross stated. "Here's my card. You can call me anytime if you have more questions."

"Thank you," Dale said and walked out of the office feeling very dejected.

Lizzie was sitting on the couch breastfeeding the baby when he walked in. He told her what happened. She looked worried but didn't say anything. Dale went into the bedroom and lay down on the bed. He just kept going over what had happened in his head. Eventually, he fell asleep and was awakened when Lizzie came in and gave him the phone.

"Who is it?"

"It's my Dad," she said. "He wants to talk to you."

Dale sat up and cleared his head before conversing. He spoke to his father-in-law for only a few minutes, explaining what happened at the garage and what Mr. Ross had said. Mr. Lawson tried to sound encouraging and told Dale to try not to worry about it too much.

"Sounds to me like the guy had it coming," Mr. Lawson said.

Dale thanked him and hung up. Lizzie was standing at the kitchen counter preparing dinner when he came out of the bedroom.

"Did you call your father and tell him what happened?" he asked in a normal voice.

"Yes, I did. I thought maybe he could help in some way."

"Well, do me a favor and never do that again," he said.

"Why? What did he say?" she inquired. "I was only trying to help."

"I know you were, and he was fine. But never again, please," he asked firmly.

He went back into the bedroom and shut the door.

Dale brooded throughout the evening. He was feeling sorry for himself and needed some time to work things through. The thought entered his mind to call Joe and talk to him about it, but he decided against it. He wasn't sure Joe would understand, and the last thing that he wanted was to fight with him. His biggest concern was how he was going to provide for his family if he lost his job. It seemed like the blueprint for his life was always going to be two steps forward and one step back.

Later that night in bed, Lizzie snuggled up close to him.

"Are you still mad at me?" she asked.

"I don't even know how to be mad at you," he admitted.

"I was only trying to help, you know," she explained. "I thought my Dad could maybe call somebody or something."

"I know what you were trying to do," he replied. "But you should have asked me. We can't go running to your father every time something happens. I need to figure out how to stand on my own two feet."

"It doesn't mean that you're weak just because you ask someone for help," she said cautiously.

"Sometimes it does make you look weak," Dale replied. "Not everything I learned growing up on the block was bad. Guys who didn't stand up for themselves got eaten alive. Maybe I could've handled this thing with idiot Tanner differently; I really don't know. I tried to walk away, and he saw that as weakness. More than anything, I need you to trust that I can take care of us."

"I do trust you. Everybody knows how strong you are," she whispered.

"I feel like I can do anything if you're in my corner."

"You're my man," she uttered. "Where else would I ever be?"

Dale was very worried, but he would never admit that to Lizzie. They didn't have much money in the bank, and he was against any kind of handout. He might start calling around to see if any place needed some extra help, even on a temporary basis. Auto shops were always looking for mechanics, although many of them didn't pay well. He was just going to have to trust that God would protect them.

Two days later, Mr. Ross called him.

"I am happy to report that the city has decided not to proceed with any formal charges against you," he said. "You need to report to work on Friday, tomorrow like normal."

"That was quick," Dale asserted. "I thought you said that it would take a week."

"You were very fortunate. The eye witnesses supported your version of the events."

131

"They did?" Dale asked.

"Yes. Also, you were right, and you weren't the one who worked on the unit with the brake problem."

"So, what now?" Dale wondered. "We go back like this never happened, or is there going to be something in my file."

"No, nothing in your file. I'm not at liberty to say too much more, but there's a new supervisor on the day shift starting tomorrow," Mr. Ross said.

"Really? That's a relief. I was very concerned that Tanner would be gunning for me now more than before."

"Like I said, you were very fortunate," Mr. Ross spoke. "If it was just your word against his, then it might not have ended this way. You really should have reported the harassment as soon as it started. We have a very aggressive anti-discrimination policy here in the city of Schenectady, and people would have believed you, had you reported it."

"You say that now, but I'm not so sure. It still would've been my word against his. I just wasn't sure what to do," Dale explained.

"I understand, but please remember what I said," Mr. Ross advised.

"Um, excuse me for asking, and I understand if you can't say, but I was wondering if my father-in-law had anything to do with how this turned out?" Dale blurted out.

"Who is your father-in-law?"

"Sergeant Lawson in special investigations."

"Sergeant Lawson," Mr. Ross repeated. "No, we never reached out to him. There's nothing that he could have done for you anyway. I'm very sorry any of this happened."

"Thank you. I really appreciate it."

"Oh, Mr. Johnson, I also wanted to let you know that a lot of folks you work with have a really high opinion of you. When you get off probation, I think you should seriously consider taking the promotional exams when they come up. We need good men like you."

"I will. Thank you again."

Dale was relieved. He knew an answered prayer when he saw one. The fact that Mr. Lawson wasn't the one who bailed him out meant that he could continue to look at himself in the mirror. When relaying what Mr. Ross had said to Lizzie later, Dale omitted what he had said about his father-in-law not being involved. Dale wasn't competing against her dad. Rather, he only desired to attain the same level of respect in her eyes.

He appreciated his job now more than ever. The truth is that he always liked the work. Men need work that is personally rewarding because, without it, they cannot feel truly respected. Work is how men judge each other. God himself commanded men to work in the beginning in the book of Genesis. Mr. Carbone once told him that his son hated the idea of working on cars, which really bothered him at one point. Dale couldn't help but wonder where he would be if Mr. Carbone had not pushed him into this direction.

***

They really had their hands full when Christopher became a toddler. He had so much energy that Lizzie could barely keep up with him. The kid was a bruiser and would run nonstop from one end of the apartment to the other end. Some afternoons, Dale would take him to the park and just chase him around in circles to tire him out.

Christopher was strong too, and he kept jumping on and off the furniture. When he was two years old, Christopher threw a tennis ball so hard against the front picture window of his grandparent's house that it completely shattered. It was clear from the very beginning that he was going to be an athlete of some kind.

Lizzie's second pregnancy was entirely unplanned, just like the first one, and was greeted with the same apprehension. They knew they wanted more children, but the plan was to wait until they were more established financially. Christopher was eating regular food now, and they no longer had to buy baby food, but he still was wearing plastic diapers at night. They were very expensive, and Dale was still in an entry-level position with the city. They were basically living hand-to-mouth, and a second child would pretty much prevent Lizzie from going back to school or working out of the house.

Fortunately, the pregnancy itself wasn't that bad. Lizzie was mostly good until the very end when she developed gestational diabetes and had to be put on bedrest. There were days when it was overwhelming, but they managed. Lizzie's mother watched Christopher during the day at her house, and Dale picked him up on his way home from work. He did the cooking and cleaning and took care of Christopher until he went down for the night. It was a full day.

The baby was born healthy and without complications. He weighed just under nine pounds. They named him Thomas John after Lizzie's dad, but Dale wanted to call him "TJ." He was much fussier than Christopher had been, and there were many sleepless nights for them both.

Dale was embarrassed at work one day when he sat down for a break and fell asleep. Everyone thought that it was funny because they all knew what he was going through at home. Although Lizzie felt better after giving birth, she continued to struggle with handling all that was coming at her, and she was anxious a lot. Dale did everything that he could to support her. He just put his head down and kept plowing along.

Chapter 13

Louis found a girlfriend. Her name was Desiree Sally. Dale hated her. Louis brought her home with him for Thanksgiving, and Dale couldn't wait for them to leave. Not exactly a beauty, she was earthy and wore her hair in a short, natural afro style. She was also slightly overweight, wore no makeup, and had an affinity for wearing sandals, even in the cold weather months.

A conservative Christian from Lima, Ohio, Desiree was fortunate enough to have already figured out everything that was wrong in the world at the tender age of twenty-one. She was convinced that most people were going straight to hell. Dale was mostly bothered by the fact that Louis seemed content to let Desiree tell him what to do and what to think. He thought the plan was for Louis to take this time to find his own place in the world. Instead, it seemed he had opted to find someone else to ascertain his rightful place for him.

Louis was in his senior year, and both he and his girlfriend were going to graduate in May with degrees in social work. The topic of life after college naturally came up over dinner one night.

"So, Louis, have you decided what you will do after you graduate?" Dale asked.

"No, I'm still not sure."

"Maybe you should look into taking some civil service exams," Dale suggested. "A lot of them are offered in the spring."

"I'm not sure that government is the right route to go," Desiree interjected.

"What do you mean?" Dale wondered.

"We want to really impact people's lives. The government generally treats the symptoms and not the diseases in society," Desiree responded.

"What diseases?"

"Social injustice caused by racism, sexism, and corporate greed," she explained.

"I don't know much about any of those things," Dale expressed. "But government-secured student loans don't pay themselves back. At this point, the important thing is to get the best paying job you can find and worry about equality later."

"I'm not sure we agree," she offered. "We think it's more important to seek to discover your God-ordained purpose in life."

"And how do you do that?" Dale asked.

"By rejecting anything and everything that doesn't line up with your core values."

"Core values?" he asked and grimaced.

"Yes, things like truth and justice. The things that truly make us happy. Money isn't important. At least, it isn't to us," she spoke defiantly.

"Is eating a core value?" Dale questioned. "Because you need money for food. Even Jesus had a regular job."

"Maybe so, but it wasn't a government job," Desiree countered.

Dale was offended. He wasn't sure if she was aware that the food that she ate all weekend was paid for by someone who worked for the city government.

Lizzie's advice to Dale later was to take the high road and just keep his mouth shut so as not to offend Louis. He knew she was probably right. He also knew he wasn't about to keep quiet. The first chance he got to talk to Louis alone, he jumped in headfirst.

"So, are you serious about this girl?" Dale asked.

"Serious, how?" Louis answered.

"Are you planning to be with her after graduation? Or are you just friends?"

"We are more than friends," Louis replied.

"You never mentioned her before," Dale complained. "You aren't planning to marry her?"

"I don't know," Louis responded. "Why? You don't like her, do you?"

"She's like the only girlfriend you've ever had," Dale pointed out. "Do you think you're ready to get married?"

"I don't know," Louis replied. "Besides, we are both as old as you were when you got married. And Lizzie is the only girlfriend you ever had."

"I've known Lizzie since seventh grade," Dale argued. "It's not the same, and you know it."

"What I know is that you don't get to tell me who I should be with!" Louis shouted.

"I am not telling you who to be with; I'm just trying to figure out where you are in all of this. If you want to marry her that bad, go ahead!"

"See, I knew it," Louis fretted. "I knew you didn't like her. I could see it on your face. You just don't like the fact that she's strong and speaks her mind!"

"Your mother is strong and speaks her mind," Dale rebutted.

"That's not fair!" Louis erupted.

"Really, well, I want to be a fly on the wall when you introduce that flower child you brought home to the night queen."

"Why can't you just be happy that I met someone who cares about me?" Louis hollered.

"Why are you so defensive? I only want you to slow down and think about what you're doing."

"It doesn't matter what you want; I never asked for your opinion."

"You're right," Dale acknowledged. "You two have it all figured out. I'm not the one who has to live with her. Good luck with that."

Dale walked away. Apparently, the only person in the entire world who Louis was capable of standing up to was his brother. Dale had watched them closely, and Louis wasn't himself around his girlfriend. Maybe it had something to do with his problems with their mother. There was really no way of knowing for sure. But he really needed to snap out of it before he did something stupid.

Louis was quiet the rest of the weekend and left to go back to school without barely a word to Dale. But Dale didn't care because everything he said was the truth. He knew Louis well enough to know he would eventually come around once he had time to fully think things through. He wasn't overly concerned.

Louis didn't come home for Christmas or for spring break. Lizzie thought that was odd. Dale just figured that he was just enjoying his last year. Dale had spoken to him a few times on the phone, and he seemed okay, a little distant maybe.

One call from him was just to wish Dale a happy birthday. When asked about graduation weekend plans, Louis just said that he didn't know any specifics yet. Dale intentionally avoided asking him about Desiree or his future job prospects.

One spring evening, Dale was putting Christopher down for the night when the phone rang. It was Louis. After some small talk, he managed to get to the point of the call.

"I have something to tell you, and I know you're not going to like it."

"Yeah, what is it?" Dale asked tentatively.

"First, I need you to hear me out. Just let me say this, please." Louis pleaded.

"Okay," Dale agreed.

"Desiree and I got married over spring break," Louis announced in a rush, followed by a big sigh.

"Really?" Dale muttered.

"Yeah, we just went, the two of us, to the courthouse here in Buffalo and had a judge perform the ceremony. Neither one of us wanted any fuss," he explained.

"I see," Dale said.

"We are moving to Kenya in a couple of weeks after graduation to do missions work. We have hooked up with an organization that is doing great work with women and children in crises. It's a shelter that provides services and helps to facilitate the healing process. It's God's work! Some of the things these women have been through are unimaginable. It is a great opportunity for us, and we are really excited."

"Are they going to pay you?"

"It's not really about the money," Louis deflected.

"Well, I don't know what you want me to say," Dale said while struggling to suppress his outrage.

"You could be happy for us," Louis suggested mildly.

"Happy? You want me to be happy that you decided all this behind my back?" Dale fumed.

"I swear that I was going to tell you over Thanksgiving, but then—"

Dale interrupted, "You were planning to do all this before Thanksgiving, and you didn't say anything?"

"I wanted to tell you, but you wouldn't let me," Louis said.

"Exactly how did I stop you, Louis?" Dale questioned. "I asked you point-blank what was going on with this girl, and you lied to me."

"You gave me no choice," Louis argued. "I really wanted you to like her, but you didn't even give her a chance. Tell me, what was I supposed to do?" Louis sounded desperate.

"You should've been a man about it!" Dale declared. "You should've told me what was in your heart. If you love her, then say you love her. I don't care anything about this girl. But I do care about you and what happens to you. But apparently, you don't care what I think. So why did you call me? Why are you telling me this now?"

"Because you're my brother!" Louis yelled. "Because I didn't want to leave the country without telling you."

"Well, thank you for filling me in," Dale stated snidely. "You two lovebirds, be sure to stop by and see us if you're ever in town."

"Dale, please don't do this," Louis begged. "It doesn't have to be like this!"

"You know, for as long as I can remember, nobody ever gave a damn about you or me," Dale unleashed. "Not even our piece of a mother. I was just a kid myself, and here I was taking care of you. I put you first, and I was always ready to fight if anyone even looked at you sideways. But I never thought in a million years that you..." Dale choked up. He lost his thought along with his voice.

"I'm only trying to do what's right for me," Louis contended. "I'm not rejecting you."

"Then you should do that," Dale conceded. "Yup, you should definitely do that."

"Please try to understand," Louis cried. "I never meant to hurt you."

"Good to know," Dale said using a dismissive tone.

They were both quiet and silence hung in the air.

"Goodbye, Louis," Dale pronounced and hung up the phone.

He just sat there for several minutes. He wasn't really thinking about anything. There was a burning inside, and he was just trying to wait until it subsided. Lizzie, who had been in their bedroom with the baby, walked in and sat down beside him.

"What happened?" she asked.

"Louis is moving to Africa with his new wife, the lovely Desiree, and they are going to work in a women's home or shelter or something."

"When?" she wondered.

"After they graduate."

"Is he coming home before?" she wondered.

"I don't think so."

"So, wow...they're married, huh?"

"Yup," Dale said.

"When?"

"Spring break, some justice of the peace."

"I heard you fighting with him, and I knew that it wasn't good. How did you leave it with him?"

"I told him to go to Africa. I'm done."

"Well, you can't just write him off, you know," she pointed out. "He's your brother?"

"He wrote me off."

"No, he didn't," she said. "You know he loves you. And you love him too. Neither one of you are completely right here, in my opinion."

"What did I do?" Dale pressed.

"You have to let him make his own decisions and his own mistakes," she maintained.

"You really think I don't know that!" he shouted. "He is a grown man. I feel like everyone thinks I just go around telling him what to do all the time. Well, that's not true, okay? He picked his own college, his own major, his own everything. I hardly ever talk to him anymore. I've always supported him in whatever he wanted to do. But all this Africa stuff is Desiree. I know it because I know Louis. You watch and see. He's going to let this girl suck the life out of him."

Dale was out of breath, and he sat there rubbing his forehead just above his eyebrows with one hand.

"But that's his choice," Lizzie contended.

"Yes, it is," Dale agreed. "But I don't have to like it or agree with his decision to let her lead him around by his you know what. And that's my choice."

"I just feel bad for Louis," she articulated. "You're all he has."

"Nope, he has a wife." Dale rebutted.

Dale and Lizzie didn't go to Louis' graduation; they weren't invited. Dale was hurt even more by the added slight. In the back of his mind, he was hoping that Louis would have invited them despite their differences. But it would have been awkward anyway, so it was probably for the best. Dale decided to put it all aside. It wasn't like his life wasn't already filled to the brim. He trusted that they would come together at some point and figure it out.

Apparently, Louis called his mother to say goodbye. Dale was dropping off some things for her when she casually brought up the subject.

"Have you heard from Louis?" she asked

"No, I haven't," Dale replied. "You know that he got married?"

"Yeah, he called me and said that they got jobs in Africa."

"That's right."

"Is she a nice girl?"

He shrugged his shoulders, and she asked for more information with only a blank look.

"I don't know," Dale replied. "I only met her once."

"Do you know how long he's going to stay there?"

"I have no idea."

"I must say that I am surprised that he would move all the way to another country," LaToya said. "I always thought that he would always be where you are."

Dale did not respond.

"When he was a kid, he wouldn't let you out of his sight," she continued.

"Well, he's not a kid anymore," Dale said definitively.

"You sound mad."

"Nope, I'm way past mad."

"Oh!"

It was two months before Dale heard from Louis. They got a postcard. It read:

> Hello Dale and Lizzie,
> I just wanted to drop a line and let you know that we are doing fine. We love this country and the people already. We are doing great work at the shelter too. Kiss the boys for us!
> Louis and Desiree

There was no return address. But it was a nice card. It had giraffes on the front.

Chapter 14

I t was discovered that Lizzie's dad had been cheating on her mother for years. Mrs. Lawson received a phone call from a woman who gave her name and said that she was calling to apologize for having an affair with her husband for more than a year. She said that there had been several others before her. She gave names. Being the last woman scorned, she was clearly hell-bent on getting even. It worked. And she managed to destroy an entire family in the process.

Lizzie was devastated, and her mom was inconsolable and needed to be medicated. Dale was affected too. He had made Mr. Lawson a role model. In hindsight, he probably shouldn't have been so surprised. He was around cops all the time, and Dale knew how they were. All they ever talked about were their conquests. But he naively believed his father-in-law to be the exception.

The divorce was drawn out and nasty. Lizzie was very angry with her father and refused to speak to him at all. He was vicious in his attacks on his wife. Moreover, he didn't seem to be overly concerned about his children.

Lizzie spent a lot of time commiserating with her mother and sister. She was preoccupied with every detail of what was going on with her parents and left the boys with Dale much more than before. The whole thing left her quite bitter and shaken, and Dale was very worried about her. Some of the accusations being made in the divorce were things that the children should never know about their parents.

Daniel, who was normally a good student, and a senior in high school, was really struggling because he was having problems staying focused. One night he called Dale at home.

"Hey man, what's going on?" Dale asked.

"Um, I don't know. I was hoping that I could maybe talk to you about something," Daniel replied.

"What is it?"

"I just can't take all of this drama anymore," Daniel exclaimed.

"I know," Dale sympathized. "It's been pretty bad."

"My mom is sad and cries all the time," Daniel related. "My dad tells me to stay out of it because it's none of my business. I don't know what I'm supposed to do."

"Look, I don't necessarily agree with everything your dad says, but he has a good point. None of this is your fault. You can't fix any of it."

"I know, but I live here," Daniel pointed out. "I just can't ignore the firestorm all around me!"

"Right, but what about if you try to just focus on the things you can control, like taking care of yourself and making the most out of your last year in high school," Dale suggested. "You know, only a crazy person consumes himself with other people's stuff that he can't do anything about. You're not crazy. So just try to distance yourself."

"I know, but I'm not so sure," Daniel admitted.

"People get divorced every day, Daniel. It's not the end of the world."

"Yeah. I guess that's right. Thanks."

"Anytime," Dale offered.

Dale told Lizzie about his conversation with Daniel. She missed the point entirely. She immediately zeroed in on her dad's inability to take responsibility for his actions. However, the truth was that nobody was even attempting to put Daniel first.

As a result, he had become the biggest casualty of his parent's need to make the other one pay for perceived wrongs. Wanda and Lizzie were adults, and they were having serious problems adjusting to their parents' failed marriage. But Daniel was still a kid—and he was in danger of drowning if someone didn't throw him a lifeline.

On his own, Daniel had reached out to Dale, something Dale knew he shouldn't take for granted. So he made a special effort to touch base with the poor kid on a weekly basis. It was easy for him to follow through on because it made him feel less helpless. He just needed to be careful that Daniel wasn't made to feel like some kind of a project.

After some consideration, Sunday after church became "dude's night," and Daniel regularly took advantage of a standing invitation to come over to the apartment and hang out with Dale and his nephews. Dale usually made dinner, and Lizzie went to her mother's house. They would just play with the boys and pass the time talking about anything or nothing. It worked, as Daniel clearly welcomed the time away from the girls and readily availed himself of the opportunity to safely vent. He continued to come over until he went to college in the fall.

Dale ran into his father-in-law at a retirement party for one of the police investigators. This was the first time that Dale had seen him since all the trouble began. For obvious reasons, Mr. Lawson no longer attended church. He looked different, smaller somehow. There were about 150 people at the party, and he was across the room from Dale. Although Dale wasn't intentionally avoiding him, he had no desire to talk to him either. He assumed that the feeling was mutual.

However, as Dale was heading toward the door for an early exit, Mr. Lawson intercepted him.

"Hey Dale, I was hoping you and I could speak privately before you leave."

"Yeah, okay," Dale reluctantly agreed.

The two men walked over to an empty corner just outside the banquet room.

He began slowly, "Listen, I wanted to thank you for helping my son. Daniel told me that you've made a big difference for him."

"You don't have to thank me," Dale said. "I care about him."

"Oh, I know you do. But he looks up to you, and I'm glad that you were there."

"I wasn't going to say anything, but you know he feels like he's caught in the middle between the two of you," Dale asserted. "That's a lot for a teenager to handle."

"I know it is," Mr. Lawson admitted. "I feel bad about that. I do. But everything that happened is not my fault, you know."

"But you can take responsibility for your part," Dale admonished. "How you feel is the least of it. You have three children, and they didn't do anything. What are you doing about their pain?"

His father-in-law looked confused.

"Lizzie won't even talk to me," he argued. "Wanda treats me like I'm a monster. There's nothing I can do."

Dale couldn't believe what he was hearing from someone he once looked up to. Moreover, he refused to feel sorry for a man who fathered a child with a former lover and hid it for years from his wife and family.

"Your children love you, and you know it," Dale exploded. "Lizzie is so broken up over you that she doesn't know what to do. But they don't respect you, and I don't see why you think they should. You screwed up, and you know it. You wanna know what to do? Well, for one thing, leave their mother alone! If you don't want to be married anymore, that's your business. But it's time for you to man up before you lose everything!"

"Gentlemen, you might want to keep your voices down," a uniformed officer peeked his head around the corner and whispered.

"I am not a monster, you know," Mr. Lawson replied in a hushed tone. "I sacrificed for years for my family, for my kids. Most men wouldn't have put up with what I did."

"You sound like you're proud of what you did." Dale confronted. "Are you? Is that it?"

They were both struggling to keep their voices down.

"No, I'm not proud of everything. But I'm not a bad guy either."

"Prove it!" Dale shouted. "The Bible says that women are the weaker sex, but sometimes I'm not so sure."

151

"I'm not going to stand here and listen to you judge me!"

"Trust me; I have been around enough to know how the game is played. I just didn't know you were all in, player," Dale argued.

"Well, let's see what you say after you've been married for twenty-eight years!"

"So now you want to curse my marriage to your daughter. Nice!"

Dale shook his head and walked away.

He was angry, but he mostly felt bad for Lizzie and her siblings. Their father was completely lost. Now he had to decide what he was going to tell his wife about this "special" little talk he just had with her dad.

Initially, he considered not telling her anything, but he hated the idea of keeping secrets from her. However, he also knew if he told her everything it would just add to her agony. Ultimately, he half-heartedly mentioned that he spoke briefly to her father, who basically said he was grateful to Dale for looking out for Daniel. She only asked if her dad was alone or if he was with someone.

As Dale understood it, the big stumbling block in the divorce proceedings was that her mother wanted to keep the house, and her dad wanted to sell it and split the proceeds. Just before they were about to go to a court hearing, however, her dad suddenly changed his mind and agreed that his wife could have the house. Dale had no idea if anything he had said that night had anything to do with his change of heart, but he was glad that he had the chance to speak his mind.

Chapter 15

The Bible says that children are a heritage from the Lord, meaning that within every child is a sacred promise. When Lizzie became pregnant again, they just accepted it as the will of God. First, they were never really good about birth control. The pill made her cramp, and Dale didn't much like male contraception. Secondly, they were hoping for a girl. They could have easily ended up with their own football team. They left it mostly in God's hands.

Michael David was born smaller than his brothers at barely six pounds. He was a fussy baby and wanted to be held all the time. It was hard on Lizzie because pregnancy always took its toll on her both physically and emotionally. Although her mother helped when she could, the divorce meant that her mother had to get a job and wasn't available during the day. Dale usually rushed home after work to take over and give Lizzie a break.

He was finally promoted at work to a supervisory position. He had been taking the exams for years, but there were never any available positions. Then suddenly, within the span of a month, there were two openings. The promotion meant more money, which they desperately needed, but things remained tight, and he struggled a lot to hold things together.

However, unlike Joe, who had three kids too, Dale didn't resent his life. He really did believe that it was just the stage that they were in and that they just needed to weather the storm. He loved his wife and his kids, and he was grateful for all his blessings, both big and small. It turns out that he was an optimist at heart, which is something even he would never have guessed.

Wanda got married the same year Michael was born. She met Simon Spears at work, and they were married within six months. He was divorced and about ten years older than her, but he seemed nice enough. She wanted a church wedding but didn't know how to accomplish that, considering her parent's situation. The wounds were still too fresh to try to have everyone in the same room together.

They ended up getting married in a restaurant without her father being present, although he was aware of the upcoming nuptials and had a chance to meet his new son-in-law. Daniel acted in his father's place during the ceremony. Overall, the wedding helped improve Lizzie's general outlook. She needed something to look forward to, and she looked beautiful standing up at the wedding for her sister.

***

Christopher had trouble with school almost from the very start. He was behind the other kids in development and had a hard time staying on task. Both Dale and Lizzie worked with him, but it was very frustrating for them.

His real problem was his reading. He was actually pretty good with numbers. It was hard to teach him to read in the first place because he couldn't seem to remember what sound each letter represented. His teacher said it might just be immaturity on his part because all kids are different. But he was so far behind the others that they agreed to keep him back and let him repeat kindergarten. When he continued to struggle, the school psychologist indicated that he suspected Christopher had a learning disability associated with the way that he processed language.

In third grade, Christopher was put into a special class, presumably to provide him with the additional help that he needed. But he was embarrassed by it and kept calling himself "dumb." It was heartbreaking for his parents, but they didn't know what else to do. The expectations from the special education teachers were lower, which meant Christopher was less of a problem at home. However, he had low self-esteem, and Dale feared that it would become a much bigger problem for him later.

The answer ended up being youth football. Dale was hesitant to sign him up at first because the practices were three times a week, and fitting them into an already tight schedule was a tall order. Also, the games were on Sundays, which meant they would miss church. But Christopher wanted to play so badly that Dale couldn't deny him.

Although it wasn't a shock that he was a good player, nobody could have predicted that he would dominate. He was stronger and faster than any other kid in his age group by far. When Christopher realized that he was "the man" on the field, his confidence soared, and he no longer cared what class he was in at school.

TJ played football, too, when he was old enough, but he wasn't as good as his brother. It wasn't long before he began misbehaving on the football field and at home. He also had a bad temper for a fourth-grader. But he was afraid of Dale, and at first, he would only go so far for fear that his dad would punish him.

But his behavior gradually worsened over time. He started talking really fast, as though he was trying to complete his entire thought without taking a single breath. Worse yet, he was never tired in the evenings and often stayed up all night, waking up everyone else in the process.

One night, TJ started screaming and crying for no apparent reason and was inconsolable. Eventually, Dale had to put him in a bear hug on the floor to keep him from hurting himself. It was as if he was demon-possessed. Concerned by the yelling, one of their neighbors called the police. You could tell by the look on their faces that the two officers who responded were horrified by what they found. Dale was at his wits' end. He had completely lost control of his house.

The doctors kept saying there was nothing wrong with TJ. He complained all the time that his stomach hurt, but they couldn't find anything wrong with him. They took him to several specialists, but no one made a definitive diagnosis. Their best guess was anxiety.

When he was twelve years old, there was a six-month period when he didn't act out once. Dale was hopeful that they were over the hurdle. Then one day, TJ started running in circles and giggling. He couldn't stop himself, and his breathing became loud and labored. It was difficult for them to watch. The fit of giggles went on for twenty heart-wrenching minutes. Lizzie cried while Dale held his son close and prayed.

There was a time when it was widely believed that only adults could have bipolar disorder. As it was explained to them, bipolar disorder is an illness of the brain that causes extreme changes in a person's mood and behavior. No one even mentioned the condition to Dale and Lizzie as a possibility until they asked about it. A woman at their church said that her brother was diagnosed as bipolar based upon extreme mood patterns that had existed for years. TJ's doctor thought that it was a distinct possibility, and after consulting with others, finally made the diagnosis of bipolar I disorder.

The good news was that now they knew what they were facing. The bad news was that there is no cure for pediatric bipolar disorder, and TJ was going to need long-term treatment that combined medication and therapy. His parents were both relieved and distressed. The next several years ended up being a search for the right medication. All of them came with side effects, and in some instances, the side effects were worse than the disease. The daily grind was a heavy load to carry.

Though they loved their brother, Christopher and Michael resented TJ because he demanded a lot of attention. TJ enjoyed being the focal point of the family and had gotten pretty good at manipulating them. But his disease was real and potentially life-threatening if not controlled. Sometimes he carried a sadness that was contagious. Michael was often afraid of TJ, and he would act out on his own if Lizzie wasn't there. They were advised not to leave the boys alone in the house together.

***

The three were always breaking things in the apartment. They were rough on everything—the furniture, walls, and floors.

One day, Dale received an unexpected call from Mrs. Carbone, who he hadn't spoken to in months. Mostly, they just exchanged Christmas cards. She also would send Christopher birthday cards with money in them.

"Hi Dale, how are you?"

"I'm good. How are you?" he asked.

"I can't complain. A little older, but also a little wiser, I like to say. Listen, I am calling for two reasons. First, I wanted you to know that I am retiring at the end of the school year and moving to Florida."

"Really?" Dale exclaimed.

"Yeah, with the kids all gone, I really don't have any reason to stay here. Chris lives in Florida with his wife and kids. After twenty-five years with the school district, I'm ready to kick up my feet and curl up somewhere warm with a good book," she said and laughed to herself.

"Good for you," Dale stated. "I'm really happy for you."

"Thank you. I'm excited. I get to be closer to the grandchildren and do some of the things that I have always wanted to do, like travel."

"That's so awesome," he declared.

"Yes, which brings me to my other reason for calling," she transitioned. "I was wondering if you and Lizzie might be interested in buying my house," she explained. "It needs some work, but it's in pretty good condition. It has four bedrooms and a finished basement. I would sell it to you at a good price. I'm not looking to make a profit. It would make me happy just to know that you were living here. It would be like it was still in the family."

"I don't know what to say. I really don't," Dale uttered.

"Good," she affirmed. "You come over this week sometime and look around and see what you think. And bring the boys. I want to see Christopher. I saw his picture in the paper a while back. He is so handsome. He looks like a Green Bay Packer!"

"Okay, let me talk to Lizzie, and I will get back to you. I can't tell you how much this means to me. Thank you so much!"

"Oh, it's nothing, honey," she replied. "Okay, I will wait to hear back from you."

Chapter 16

Dale hadn't heard anything from Louis since he received the postcard several years past. There were constant reminders, and he was always aware that a part of himself was missing. Louis just had a birthday, and Dale didn't even know how to contact him if he wanted to send him a card. That fact alone spoke to the depth of Louis' hurt and anger. None of this made any sense. He and Louis had disagreed before without lasting implications. Dale blamed Desiree and remained unrepentant about anything he said to Louis about her.

Likewise, Lizzie refused to forgive her father. Mr. Lawson tried talking to her several times, but she either wouldn't come to the phone or played dead while he tried to get her to contribute to the conversation. Dale stayed out of it. He knew she was trying. Both Wanda and Daniel had moved on to the new normal, but Lizzie always had been daddy's girl. She just needed time.

Unfortunately, the rift meant that the boys didn't really know their grandfather. Wanda had two children in rapid succession and they had relationships with him. Mr. Lawson came to some of Christopher's games, but he didn't sit with them. It was weird.

Once Dale ran into him in the school parking lot after a game.

"I see that Christopher is still doing his thing out there," Mr. Lawson commented.

"Yeah, he's starting to take what they give him instead of trying to run everybody over. Next year is varsity, and the competition is going to be tougher," Dale contended.

"Tell him I said he played a good game."

"I will," Dale said.

"How is Lizzie?"

"Tired. It's hard for her with three boys, you know," Dale explained.

"I heard you moved into a house."

"Yeah; trust me, we needed it bad. We were on top of each other in that apartment."

"Well, for what it's worth, I'm proud of you. You're a good man. My daughter is lucky to have you." Mr. Lawson complimented.

The boys were growing like weeds. Christopher looked exactly like his father. He was very content with being a jock and took full advantage of his popularity, especially with the girls. TJ was out of school a lot because the medications worked only some of the time. He lived mostly in Christopher's shadow and never could find his own identity.

However, he was much more sensitive than his brothers were, or so Dale believed. For instance, TJ was the one who was more likely to clean his room or help his mother with a chore without being asked. However, he went for the jugular when he was angry, which unfortunately meant he was capable of saying some of the most hurtful things to people—especially to his brothers.

Michael was simply spoiled and lazy. Lizzie got into the habit of calling him "her baby," and their son embraced the moniker. He acted entitled, which really got under Dale's skin. Not exactly a loner, Michael's friends were the misfits in the school—the ones obsessed with comic book characters and liked audio equipment way too much. He was also interested in weird stuff like wizards and demons.

Michael was of above-average intelligence but earned only average grades in school because he didn't much care to be there. Dale concentrated most of his efforts on Christopher and TJ, who were always clamoring for his attention. He left Michael in his mother's apron pocket—exactly where he wanted to be.

***

Christopher got one of his girlfriends pregnant just before the start of his senior year. Neither Dale nor Lizzie knew the girl at all. Her mother called, spoke to Lizzie, and asked for a meeting. Dale hit the roof and was furious at Christopher. He threatened to take him off the football team so he could get a job and take care of this baby.

They agreed to meet at a small café downtown the next day. The girl's father was equally incensed. Her name was Sonja Murphy. She was going into her junior year—just sixteen years old. Her father had a good job with one of the state agencies in Albany, and the meeting began with him ripping into Christopher. Everything could have gone off the rails right there, except for the keen ability of Sonja's mother to rein in her husband.

Thereafter, although the mood remained tense throughout, the discussion was productive. Sonja was being banished to her grandparent's home in Illinois after Christmas to give birth in the spring. Her parents would take primary custody of the child in Schenectady, and Christopher could have visitation. Support would be addressed at another time.

Dale took the pregnancy crisis as his own personal failure. He never had the "facts of life" talk with Christopher because he had wrongly presumed that the boys were aware of how he felt about promiscuity. Christopher had another girlfriend and wasn't even really dating Sonja. It was truly a crime of convenience.

Dale saw these events as further evidence of his shortcomings as a father. Neither one of his boys had a genuine interest in their spiritual growth; it was their father's responsibility to train them in that area, and Dale couldn't remember the last time they had stepped foot in a church. Michael knew more about the underworld than he did about the things of God.

Despite his pending fatherhood, Christopher had an outstanding senior year on the football field. As the starting running back, he was an all-conference selection after rushing for 1,234 yards with 19 touchdowns while leading the team to a 9-1 season. There were several small colleges that expressed interest in him, but he didn't have the grades or desire to go to college. He basically peaked in high school.

***

Dale invited a guest for Thanksgiving dinner. He intentionally didn't tell Lizzie until that morning. She didn't press too much when he mentioned it, probably because he had done all the work, including preparing the entire dinner, except for the deserts. Even though the boys ate like bears coming out of hibernation, there was plenty of food. He prayed that he was doing the right thing and waited until the very last moment before telling her that her father was on his way.

"Who? You're kidding, right?" she protested.

"No, I ran into him, and he said he was alone, so I invited him," Dale explained.

She walked out of the kitchen and proceeded up the stairs to their bedroom. He heard the door slam. He thought it best to let her cool down while he finished setting the table.

Mr. Lawson arrived ten minutes later. He brought flowers for his daughter. Dale invited him to have a seat in the family room where Christopher and TJ were watching a football game. Then Dale walked up the stairs, took a deep breath, and opened the door. Lizzie was lying on the bed.

"Dinner is ready. Your dad is here."

"I'm not eating," she snapped.

"Oh, yes, you are," he countered. "We're not going to be rude to anyone in this house, especially not to family."

"No, I'm not. I can't believe you did this."

"I did it for the boys. They don't even know their grandfather, who lives twenty minutes away. It's not fair to them."

"They don't really know your mother either," she resisted.

"Which is a good thing, believe me. Besides, my mother is not interested in a relationship with our kids. That's on her. But I did it for you too," he maintained.

"You don't understand. I can't," she asserted.

"Yes, you can. You have to forgive him at some point. It doesn't have to go back to the way that it used to be between the two of you, but you have to move on. C'mon, Lizzie, aren't you tired of being mad at him? It's Thanksgiving. Please? For me?"

"I don't really see what choice I have," she complained. "You made sure of that. Thank you very much for ruining Thanksgiving for me!"

"You love me. I know you do. Go ahead and tell me you don't."

She was motionless and looked him directly in the eyes for full effect.

"Okay, we will eat as soon as you come down," he muttered.

He turned quickly and walked out of the room like a dog with his tail between his legs. It occurred to him that she might slip out the back door. However, ten minutes later, she came down and, without saying a word, finished setting the table. Dale rubbed her back, which she ignored.

He called for everyone to come in, and they had to wait several minutes for Michael to come down. Dale sat at the head of the table and directed his father-in-law to the seat directly across from him. Lizzie sat next to him, and the boys filled in the other seats. Dale liked to eat dinner as a family, and the boys knew to wait until he had said the blessing before eating.

Mr. Lawson got his first real look at life Johnson style. The boys were loud and abrasive. They liked to bait each other. Even Christopher acted like he was twelve years old and would stir things up for no apparent reason.

"Daddy, can you tell Michael to stop eating with his mouth open again," Christopher provoked.

Lizzie was quiet. She got up a couple of times to get something someone wanted, but she never really acknowledged her father.

"Did you know I'm named after you?" TJ asked his grandfather.

"Uh, yes, I did know that."

"So, people call you TJ too?" he followed up.

"No, most people call me Tom. When I was your age, everybody called me Tommy."

"Tommy?" TJ questioned with a look of disgust on his face.

His brothers laughed at that.

"Well, what do you want us to call you?" Michael asked.

"I don't know. You got anything in mind?"

"I know," TJ interjected. "How about 'Pop'? That's what uncle Daniel calls you."

"Yes, you can call me that. I would like that," Mr. Lawson acknowledged.

"Okay, Pop, tell us some stories about mom growing up. We never get to hear those," TJ said.

"Well, I don't know...your mother was always so perfect, you know."

"That's not what Aunt Wanda said," TJ challenged. "She said mom was the favorite and you let her get away with murder."

"Wanda said that, huh?" Mr. Lawson questioned.

"Yeah, she said that one time, mom put a plastic shower curtain in the dryer and ruined the whole thing, and you didn't even get mad," TJ asserted. "Daddy would have killed us if we did something like that."

"Gimme a break, you guys have done ten times worse than that, and you're all still alive and breathing," Dale refuted.

"I told you guys not to believe everything Wanda says," Lizzie spoke up finally.

"I don't think I had a favorite," Pop said. "But I will say that, Lizzie looks a lot like my mother. I was really close to my mom because I was the only boy. She died when I was in the Air Force, and sometimes I can see her when I look at my Lizzie."

Mr. Lawson was clearly caught off guard by the impact of his own words, and he had to fight to maintain his composure.

"Air Force, what was that like?" Christopher asked.

Turns out that the boys were very interested in knowing about their grandfather. All three had questions, which they freely asked. It was rare for them each to be focused on the same thing at the same time. Frankly, they interacted with Lizzie's dad in a manner that Dale had never done. Dale could see that Mr. Lawson was enjoying himself too. He laughed a lot and recounted events from his life that Dale had never heard before. It was fair to say that dinner was a success.

Later, they all relocated to the family room, except for Lizzie, who began cleaning up. At one point, Mr. Lawson announced that he had to go, and Dale called out to Lizzie to come in and say goodbye. They were all standing at the front door when she approached.

"Lizzie, I was wondering if I could speak to you privately for a moment," Mr. Lawson asked nervously.

Dale and the boys said their final goodbyes and scattered like leaves in the wind. Although he couldn't say for certain, it seemed to Dale that Lizzie spoke to her father there for almost an hour. He didn't hear any raised voices, so he assumed that it was going well. He was sitting alone in the family room dozing when he heard the front door shut. Dale got up and followed her into the kitchen.

"You okay?" he asked.

"Yes, I'm good," she responded with a sigh.

"Do you want to talk about it?"

"No, not really," she replied. She turned her back and started organizing food in the refrigerator.

"Are you still mad at me?" he inquired.

"Yes," she quipped.

"Is there anything I can do to make it up to you?"

"I don't know; ask me later," she responded with a twinkle in her eye.

Chapter 17

Sonja had a baby girl. They named her Brandy Lynette Murphy. Lizzie was very excited and made Sonja's mother promise to send photographs. However, Christopher had no reaction when they told him. Although he hoped he was wrong, Dale didn't foresee his son ever playing a significant role in his daughter's life.

Because Dale never knew his own father, he understood what an awful burden that was to carry. As a kid, he used to daydream that a big, strong man would miraculously appear out of nowhere and proclaim himself to be his dad and rescue him from the hellhole in which they were living. Obviously, the fantasy was ridiculous, but it reflected the aching need most kids in that situation have to feel the love of a father.

Christopher decided that he wanted to go into the Air Force. He was hesitant to tell Dale and had Lizzie do it. However, Dale thought it was a good idea. He'd been telling Christopher all along that he needed to learn a trade, or he would be destined for low-paying jobs all his life. Neither one of Dale's sons appeared to be mechanically inclined, so he was at a loss to provide Christopher with any further direction. He didn't know anything about the military.

According to the Air Force recruiter, after completing basic training in Texas, Christopher would be matched up with a career field based upon his aptitude. Basic training was eight weeks, and he would then be assigned to an air base in any number of places all over the world. Dale thought it was probably good for Christopher to get out of Schenectady and away from his friends, most of whom Dale considered bad influences. Lizzie's dad, who had now become a regular fixture in their lives, was thrilled about the idea.

Christopher left for basic training in August, and he graduated in October. After that, he was relocated to a different base in Texas and was assigned to the protective services program. While he was there, he tested positive in a random drug test and was kicked out of the Air Force. They literally put him on a bus and sent him home in a week's time. He officially received a general discharge, which is the type given when a service member's actions fail to meet military standards. Christopher was living at home again by Thanksgiving.

Dale and Lizzie were dejected. Christopher tried to tell them that the drug test wasn't administered properly, which resulted in a false positive. Obviously, they didn't believe him. The truth was that Christopher told himself so many lies that he couldn't keep them straight. He pretended to have everything under control, but deep down, he was still very insecure, and he hadn't developed a strength of character. Dale had hoped that the Air Force would have given him the additional confidence that he needed.

Over the next eighteen months, Christopher was fired from two jobs and totaled Lizzie's car by hitting a telephone pole. He generally slept until well into the afternoon, ate everything in sight, and hung out all night with his friends. Dale wanted to throw him out on the street, but Lizzie was dead set against it. He knew that she was giving Christopher money too, although he had told her not to do so. As it was, Christopher was asking her parents and Wanda for money all the time. The situation was making Dale insane and affected the entire household.

The first time that Christopher was arrested was for robbery—a felony. He spent a week in jail until he was released without having to post any bail. According to the victim's statement, Christopher had taken thirty dollars from him outside of a bar. In his defense, Christopher claimed it was a case of mistaken identity and that he was innocent.

However, Mr. Lawson found out that it was really a fake drug transaction, during which Christopher pretended to be selling crack cocaine to the guy and ended up just taking the money without providing the drugs. The charges were ultimately reduced to a violation, and Christopher was given credit for the time that he had already served in jail and was released from custody.

Dale hurt his back while fighting with Christopher. Michael was screaming early one morning, and Dale ran down the stairs to find Christopher pushing and shoving his brother against the wall. Dale immediately jumped between them and grabbed Christopher, who resisted, and they struggled against one another. Christopher never actually struck his father; the two were just wrestling. It ended when Lizzie ordered them to stop.

"I want you out!" Dale shouted. "Get your stuff and get out of my house! You have fifteen minutes before I call the police!"

Dale stormed up the stairs to his room and slammed the door. When he came out thirty minutes later, Christopher was gone. Dale left the house without speaking to anyone. He noticed then that he felt a little twinge in his back but didn't give it much thought. He was late for work. Two hours later, he could barely walk. He drove himself to the emergency room. The doctor prescribed muscle relaxers and bedrest. Lizzie had to come and get him because he couldn't drive home. He was out of work the rest of the week.

Christopher had gone to Lizzie's mom's house. Dale knew that wasn't a good development, but he stayed out of it. It was about a month before Mrs. Lawson made him leave. Dale wasn't sure what happened there, but Lizzie knew, and she never told him. It was the first time in their marriage that they were distant from each other.

Christopher was arrested five or six times over the course of the next several years. Most were for drug possession offenses. Dale refused to go to court or to the jail to visit him. Lizzie went to both places regularly.

The first time Christopher went to state prison stemmed from a violation of his probation. He was sent to a state drug treatment center, only to be released and returned to prison for yet another parole violation. It was just an endless cycle, and Dale felt oppressed by the public humiliation. Christopher would come to the house occasionally when he wasn't locked up, and they were cordial. But he never stayed overnight.

***

Dale couldn't help but wonder why all three of his sons had to struggle so much. If it wasn't one, it was the other. Unbeknown to his parents, TJ decided at one point during his senior year in high school that he no longer needed to take his medication. Soon thereafter, Lizzie called Dale at work one afternoon to tell him that TJ had been suspended from school for exposing himself to a group of kids.

By the time Dale got home, TJ was in a full-blown manic episode. He was very glad to see Dale walk in, and ran to him the way a two-year-old runs to his dad picking him up from daycare. He was elated, and his speech was incoherent. Lizzie said she had called the doctor, who instructed her to take TJ to the emergency room if she believed that he was a danger to himself. Dale slept on the floor outside TJ's room that night to make sure that he didn't do anything to hurt himself or try to leave the house.

The next couple of days were hell. At one point, TJ was crying and laughing at the same time. They finally had to take him to the ER, and he was admitted to the psychiatric unit for observation. Eventually, his mood stabilized, and he was released. However, the toll taken upon everyone was immense. Dale felt like he was dying a slow death. He just wasn't sure how much more he was able to take.

TJ had been seeing a therapist for years, ever since he was first diagnosed. As far as Dale could tell, she hadn't made a bit of a difference with TJ. Sue Ford's office was downtown in a small office building. Usually, Dale just dropped TJ off for his weekly visit and came back an hour later to pick him up. After the recent hospitalization, Lizzie had made an appointment for them to meet with her without TJ.

Dr. Ford's office was on the second floor, in the back. There was a young girl sitting in the waiting room when they arrived. They only had to wait a few minutes before the receptionist directed them to Dr. Ford's office. TJ's therapist was tall with auburn colored hair and she wore stylish glasses that suited her face well. She was young, in her early thirties. Dale thought she was very attractive.

"I was so disappointed to hear about this recent episode," Dr. Ford said. "When I last saw TJ in the hospital, he seemed to still be struggling a bit. How is he today?"

"He's a little better. He's home," Lizzie responded.

"Yes, I know. Well, I am glad you came in. I've meant to call you. I think we have come to a crossroads with TJ. He is at a point where I think he needs more supervision."

"What kind of supervision?" Lizzie asked.

Dr. Ford adjusted herself in her seat behind a modern-style mahogany desk and sat straight up.

"He needs to be in a place where he can learn on his own how to live with his condition. Bipolar disease is a chronic condition, as you know. It's not going away. TJ recognizes that most of the time. But the medication won't work if he doesn't take it. Psychiatric treatment is a waste of time if he isn't open to it. He's a smart guy. But he struggles with his own thoughts and insecurities."

"So, you think we should put him in some kind of mental hospital or something?" Dale asked.

"Not a hospital, but a supervised residential program that provides intensive and comprehensive treatment. He is eighteen years old now; he's technically an adult. Sending him back to school is a bad idea, in my opinion. It's just too much pressure. Hopefully, he will learn how to cope and go on to live a productive life in the community. I've spoken to him about it, and I think he wants to try something new. Frankly, he is concerned that you won't let him go."

"He said that?" Dale wondered.

"He doesn't want to disappoint you. Especially, you, Mr. Johnson. He is very sensitive. He knows that you love him."

"So, I'm the problem?" Dale blurted out.

"No, not at all," Dr. Ford said. "Please hear me, that's not what I am saying. TJ is sick; very sick. He has a disease where his brain doesn't function normally. It's not anybody's fault. You didn't do anything wrong."

There was a mail truck that Dale could see just outside of the window directly behind Dr. Ford. The driver was struggling to parallel park behind a pickup truck, and Dale was detracted momentarily by the action.

"We don't know what causes bipolar disorder," she explained, "About three percent of the people in this country have a diagnosis of bipolar disease, and 83 percent of those cases are classified as severe. So we have to accept it—see it for what it is. These things happen. You need to change your expectations about who he is and his limitations. That will help all of you."

"Well, that's the problem," Dale articulated. "No one can tell us what to expect from him. It's been very frustrating."

"I get that," Dr. Ford commiserated.

"Okay, so where are these places?" Lizzie asked.

"I have a packet I will give you," Dr. Ford responded. "It has several good options. There's one in Pennsylvania that I like. I believe it's thirty days inpatient. They help with local aftercare placement as well. But you look it over and tell me what you think."

It was over a month before they could get TJ into the program in Pennsylvania. It would have been longer, but they had a no-show. While Dale was critical of both Christopher and Michael in many respects, he did feel bad for TJ.

Deep down, he wondered if TJ had inherited this disease from him. Wanda's girls were normal and healthy. Daniel was doing well living in New Jersey and working in New York City.

Louis was convinced that their mother suffered from some undiagnosed mental condition; who knows what was hidden in their DNA? There clearly was enough evidence, however, for Dale to believe that he was the reason his son was being tormented by the devil.

TJ cried when they dropped him off. But it was impossible to read anything into his reactions. After all, he wanted to come to this place. Still, they tried to reassure him that everything would be okay. It was only twenty-eight days.

Dale understood TJ better than anyone, including his mother, who struggled greatly with her own feelings of helplessness when it came to her middle son. TJ felt trapped in a world that wasn't of his own creation. He just wanted what everyone else took for granted. He wanted to be in control of his life.

The drive home was a break for them. They were alone in the car for three hours without one of the boys sucking up all the air in the truck. It felt good. They barely spoke but enjoyed each other's company just the same. Their kids had become their whole lives, and they were starting to forget about the fairytale that brought them together in the first place—and the God who had orchestrated the whole thing.

Chapter 18

Lizzie's mother never got over the divorce, which was partly why Lizzie struggled with it the way she did. Dale wasn't surprised that Daniel didn't come back to Schenectady after college. Wanda and Lizzie were always coming up with ideas about how to get their mother to embrace life again fully, but none of them were successful. She suffered from depression and didn't want anyone to try to help her.

Truthfully, she probably would have taken her husband back despite his infidelities and her public humiliation, but he wanted the divorce. Everything worked together to wear on her greatly, and she soon looked and acted much older than her actual age. She had a stroke—but she died of a broken heart.

She passed away the same day TJ came home. The whole family took it hard, but Dale was most concerned about Lizzie and TJ. Lizzie was in shock and quickly retreated within herself. TJ, who ended up staying at the treatment center for forty-five days altogether because they had to change his medication completely, seemed confused about what was happening. Dale kept waiting for him to blow, but fortunately, it never happened.

Dale wondered whether he needed to get Lizzie to a therapist of her own. At first, she was busy making funeral arrangements, and then she got caught up with clearing out her mother's house and settling her affairs. She didn't want Dale to coddle her, and he knew enough to just let her deal with everything her own way.

At the same time, he was broken up himself. He loved Lizzie's mom too. He kept thinking about the time that she told him he was the man she had always prayed Lizzie would find. The feeling of loss was heavy upon his entire household, so Dale couldn't afford to lose himself in grief.

Christopher acted grief-stricken. He had been close to his grandmother. She had babysat him a lot when he was young, much more than she did with TJ and Michael. Dale didn't know much about how Christopher was living. They only knew he was on parole and that the state had found him a place to live and maybe even a job.

Before Christopher was released from prison six months ago, Dale and Lizzie were interviewed by some woman from the local parole office, and Dale had made it clear then that Christopher couldn't live with them. She said that she understood and thought they were taking the correct stand because Christopher was still in denial about his addiction. Her advice was that they should encourage him to fully commit to drug treatment and recovery.

Dale was driving home from work about a month after the funeral when he saw Christopher standing by the roadside. At first, he wasn't sure that it really was his son, so he made a quick turn and drove back around. As he slowly approached the intersection, he observed Christopher standing on the edge of the roadway holding a handwritten cardboard sign that read: "VETERAN, WILL WORK FOR FOOD."

Dale imploded. He told Lizzie as soon as he got home. She was speechless, which was a good thing because he was not.

He went into a rampage. Lizzie just listened. She didn't try to calm him down. So humiliated, Dale could hardly sleep that night. Only God knows how many people had seen Christopher begging in the streets of Schenectady in broad daylight. He was supposedly so overcome with grief over the death of his grandmother, yet he could so easily tarnish her memory and reputation in the community where she had lived most of her life.

But make no mistake about it, Dale took this as a personal affront. More than that, however, it was a public declaration before God and the entire world that his family was cursed and doomed—like sheep about to be slaughtered. The writing was on the wall, and it was foolish for him to deny what the whole world knew was true.

Surprisingly, TJ had enough credits to graduate from high school with a school diploma instead of a state regent's diploma. But he didn't want to go to the graduation ceremony. Instead, they had a family cookout in TJ's honor. Wanda came over with her family. Lizzie also invited her father, who was newly retired.

Christopher showed up later in the afternoon. Lizzie immediately ran to her husband and begged him not to say anything to Christopher. Dale promised reluctantly. However, she apparently didn't make the same promise to herself because she and Christopher had a heated exchange near the end of the festivities. It took place in the kitchen, away from everyone. Dale was cooking at the grill in the backyard, so he never saw or heard anything. He might not have ever known about it if Michael hadn't told him. By the time Dale made his way inside, Christopher was gone.

***

TJ wanted to live in the residential setting that Dr. Ford had found for him in Albany. They specialized in treating young people between the ages of eighteen to twenty-five who had emotional disorders. Purportedly, the staff worked to help individuals develop more life skills in terms of learning about themselves and living with their disease. It sounded good, and both Dale and Lizzie were excited that TJ was taking steps on his own to get better.

With TJ gone, Michael was the only one who was still at home. He was going into the tenth grade, which meant that it would be three years minimum before they were empty nesters. With the end possibly in sight, Dale figured all they had to do was tread water. Whatever his issues, Michael went to school on time, came home intact, and even occasionally managed to do his homework. He wasn't going to do anything that could get him suspended from school, nor was he going to get anybody pregnant. Things were looking up already.

However, Dale was very aware that he had no real connection with Michael. They were like oil and water. Dale was afraid to say anything to Michael for fear that Lizzie would get mad at him. Unlike the way he had handled Christopher and TJ, Dale never gave Michael any chores to do or made him pick up after himself. Michael was the little prince. He didn't even want a driver's license. Lizzie was always jumping up and getting him whatever he needed or taking him wherever he wanted to go.

TJ's parents didn't like his residential program, as it was a poorly run not-for-profit agency. It was hard to get ahold of him, and he still didn't have a job. They had gone there several times, and no one ever knew where TJ was or how long he had been gone. Granted, he wasn't in jail and should have some freedom, but they didn't like the idea of him running all over the city of Albany unsupervised. Dr. Ford said that the reports she had received indicated that TJ was adjusting well. He was taking his medication and participating in group sessions. He also had made friends and was growing in confidence.

Late one afternoon, someone from the Albany Police Department called Dale at work. The officer identified himself and said that he was calling because TJ had been arrested and was taken to the Albany Medical Center for a psychiatric evaluation. Evidently, TJ had become enraged about something and was observed chasing a city bus down Central Avenue with a stick in his hand while screaming and yelling obscenities. He was arrested when police officers couldn't get him to calm down and couldn't understand him.

Dale and Lizzie drove to the hospital in Albany, but they were not permitted to see TJ. The next morning, they received a call at home from the Capital District Psychiatric Center, asking them to come in. Dale immediately left work, and they drove back to the hospital. Following the directions provided, they went to the psychiatric floor and signed in. It was several minutes before a man appeared and introduced himself as Dr. Ramesh Syed. He appeared to be in his fifties, short and thin, and he wore a white overcoat that was much too big for him. He also spoke in a heavy Indian accent. He sat down hastily behind his desk.

"Thomas is your son, yes?"

"Yes, he is," Lizzie responded.

"How old is he?"

"Twenty," she replied.

"Is this his first time in treatment?"

"Yes," Dale replied.

"Really? No hospitalizations or in-patient treatment facilities?" asked the doctor.

"I'm sorry, I misunderstood," Dale apologized. "Our son has been treated for bipolar disease since he was a teenager in middle school. He completed one in-patient program for a month."

"Okay, that's what I thought...Well, he is doing good now. He is calm and knows where he is. He is very tired and sleeping. We are not sure what happened; if he is taking his medications or not. I think that maybe Thomas just got angry about something that happened to him that day, and it escalated in him."

"How long will he have to be here?" Lizzie asked.

"Fifteen days, I think. Maybe less. Two psychiatrists have examined him and determined that he is a substantial threat to harm himself at this point. Once we have him stabilized, then we will release him."

"Release him where?" Dale wondered.

"We can't tell him where to go. We need a court order to keep him involuntarily. The key is to get him stable again on the medications. Maybe we have to change them; I don't know. But this appears to be his first episode this year. So, yes, he is in pretty good shape."

"I'm sorry, but I don't understand. You're going to release my son without any kind of treatment?" Dale posed.

"We can only make recommendations. As soon as he is no longer a danger to himself, by law, we have to let him go. He should follow up with his regular doctor."

"But what is there to prevent this from happening again?" Dale inquired.

"We cannot guarantee that it won't happen again. Bipolar disorder is a chronic condition."

"Yes, we know that." Dale acknowledged. "Believe me; we know that. This nightmare has been going on for years now. But I am wondering what we can do to help our son. The answer can't be sitting around and waiting for the next episode and hoping that he doesn't hurt somebody or kill himself. We can't just keep doing this over and over again."

"Successful treatment of people with bipolar disorder is complicated," the doctor began. "And it is individualized, so it is not a one-size-fits-all approach. Even when there are no breaks in medication, mood changes can still occur. Extreme stress, alcohol, and drug use can trigger episodes. Or they happen for some unknown reason. A stable environment is a good start. Families have to learn to cope with mental illness. You're not alone."

"Honestly, we feel alone," Dale responded. "This is torture. To watch your child in pain year after year and know that there is absolutely nothing that you can do about it is the worst thing that has ever happened to us."

"Yes," Dr. Syed sympathized and shook his head up and down. "I understand. I really do. There is still so much that we do not know about this disease."

"But there's nothing else you can advise us to do? There must be something. We keep hearing the same thing. Might there be someplace where we can take him where they are treating people with good results? Anything like that?" Lizzie begged.

"No, not really. I wish that there was someplace like that. There are good therapies out there, no doubt. But there is no known cure."

"Huh," Dale let out a big sigh of despair.

"I am sorry," Dr. Syed spoke. "I wish that there was more that we could do."

"When can we see him?" Lizzie asked.

"Tomorrow. Just call the main number here and set up a time."

He handed her a business card.

They both left Dr. Syed's office feeling completely dejected. Dale felt like a condemned man who had just received a death sentence. The situation seemed hopeless. He had prayed so hard for TJ that he didn't have anything else to say to God about it. He kept thinking that there was something he was missing, that if he only asked the right question, they could find the cure. But that didn't appear to be the case. They drove home in complete silence.

They arrived back at the hospital right at one p.m. the next day to see TJ. Their moods remained somber. For some reason, Dale thought that they would see TJ in a hospital room. Instead, they were escorted to a large day room that looked like a reception area. The room was brightly lit with walls painted sky blue and several pine sofas upholstered with multi-colored fabric scattered throughout.

The room was empty. They sat there alone for about five minutes before a male attendant brought TJ in. He was wearing a hospital robe and his sneakers with no laces. He looked generally unkept and was in dire need of a haircut. TJ sat down at the table with them, and the attendant took a seat near the door facing them, just out of earshot.

"How are you?" Dale asked.

"I'm okay. Tired," TJ said without making eye contact.

"Why?" Dale wondered. "Are you having problems sleeping?"

"Yeah, a little. I think it's just...I don't know."

"Do you remember what happened?" Dale solicited. "Do you know how you got here?"

"Not really."

"Have you been taking your medication?" Dale questioned.

"Yes, I always take it. Has nothing to do with it," TJ snapped.

Dale was taken aback. He didn't expect TJ to be hostile to them.

"Honey, we are just worried and trying to understand what happened," Lizzie said.

"I told you that you don't have to worry about me," TJ blurted out. "Sometimes things happen for no reason. You can't just blame people."

"Nobody is blaming you," Dale contested. "Can we get you anything? Do you need something?"

"No!" TJ responded in a harsh tone.

The room was filled with awkward silence.

Finally, Lizzie spoke, "Honey, we are only trying to help. We don't understand—"

"I know. That's the whole problem," TJ interrupted. "Did they tell you how long they're making me stay here?"

"Not long. They are just trying to get you stable." Lizzie volunteered.

"How long will that take?" TJ demanded.

"I think they said about a week," Dale replied.

"A week? That's too long," TJ complained. He looked directly at his father for the first time.

"Why?" Dale inquired. "Do you have something you have to do?"

"No, I just want to get back to my friends," TJ offered.

"Well, your friends will have to wait," Dale asserted.

"What do you think about coming back home?" Lizzie interjected. "Just for a little while until you're better?"

Dale raised his eyebrows and looked in Lizzie's direction. He was shocked by the suggestion. They had not discussed the prospect of TJ coming home.

"I don't want to go home with you!" TJ objected. "I'm not a baby. I can take care of myself, thank you."

"TJ, we know you're not a baby," Lizzie defended. "But you need help right now. You could have hurt someone."

"Not true. I don't hurt people," he contested. "Sometimes, I get tired of fighting, and things happen."

"Fighting who?" Dale inquired.

"That's just a figure of speech," TJ protested. "I didn't mean it like that. That's why you don't understand. You can't understand because you don't know what it feels like. I don't even know why we're talking about this."

"Honey, we're just trying to help. We are your parents, and we love you," Lizzie said, her voice growing weak.

"Well, good for you guys," TJ replied dismissively.

"Please don't talk to my wife like that," Dale said in earnest. "Did we do something wrong? Why are you acting like this?"

"No, you didn't do anything," TJ shot back. "Not everything is about you, you know."

"I don't know what that means," Dale argued. "We came here because we're worried about you. We're not trying to hurt you, you know. Tell us what you want us to do!"

"Just leave me alone!" he said defiantly.

"You want us to go then?" Dale asked.

TJ just looked straight ahead. He didn't answer.

"Fine," Dale said and stood up. "You know where we are if you need us."

This time, Lizzie cried all the way home. Dale didn't know what to say to her. Whereas Christopher couldn't be trusted to tell the truth about anything, TJ lacked the ability to know what the truth was.

But there was no denying that TJ was determined to be independent of his parents, at least for the moment. Legally, he was of age, so they couldn't make him do anything anyway. Dale's truth, however, was that he didn't want TJ to come home. He was barely holding on to his sanity as it was. Still, the outright rejection hurt just the same.

Chapter 19

Lizzie's dad had a stroke approximately one year from the day that her mother died. Fortunately, he survived. But he couldn't use his right side and had to go to a rehabilitation center and then into a nursing home. For some reason, he had given his power of attorney to Daniel, who still lived out of state and never came home. Thus, Wanda and Lizzie had to do everything for him.

Dale helped clean out his father-in-law's apartment, which was a mess. Lizzie tried to visit him at the nursing home at least once a week. During one visit, she and Wanda met their twenty-five-year-old half-brother and his mother. Lizzie said that the woman appeared to be about their age. Although Lizzie and her dad had pretty much settled their differences, she was still working through her hurt and disappointment. She said that she wasn't ready to accept her father's love child.

Lizzie was always complaining about the level of care that her father was receiving. He could talk a little, but it wasn't easy to understand him. He developed bedsores at one point because the caretakers hadn't moved and turned him as often as they should have. Dale had never seen anything quite like that before. There were huge blue and red, blistered holes on his backside.

Lizzie was overwhelmed yet once again. Her dad was miserable and in a lot of pain. Dale hated going to the nursing home, but he would occasionally go to support her. It was so depressing. Mr. Lawson lasted two years before he mercifully died of pneumonia.

Dale couldn't find TJ to tell him about his grandfather's passing. He left a message for him at the residency. Dale would sometimes drop off supplies for him-mostly toiletries, clothes, and outerwear. He never knew for sure if TJ ever received any of the items. On average, TJ would get arrested and admitted to the psychiatric center every twelve to eighteen months. Although someone from the hospital always called his parents, TJ never reached out to them when he was admitted there, and they never visited him there again.

***

Michael enrolled in community college after he graduated from high school. Of course, he didn't want to go, but Dale insisted. Despite the protection of his mother, Michael knew that he could only push his father so far. Lizzie drove him to his classes and picked him up most days. Occasionally, he took the bus.

Michael was the first one in the family to get a cell phone and a personal computer, and after that, his life was complete. However, Dale also made him get a job, and he ended up working at that same Burger King downtown where Louis used to work. The smell on his clothing brought back memories.

***

They were awakened one night by the phone ringing. Dale hated unexpected phone calls in the middle of the night.

From experience, it was never good news. This time it was something about Christopher. As they ventured out into the night to Albany Medical Center once again, they were only slightly panicked. Sadly, they had grown accustomed now to the dark storm clouds that regularly hovered over them.

Christopher was found unconscious in Washington Park, not far from the capital buildings in Albany. He had been beaten very badly and had a severe head injury that required surgery to relieve the pressure on his brain. His condition was critical. They were taken to a waiting room on the surgical floor and told that the surgeon would come out and speak to them after the procedure.

Six hours later, an exhausted-looking doctor appeared in scrubs and said that Christopher had done well and that his chances for recovery were good. He would be in the intensive care unit tomorrow. They were only permitted to see him for a few minutes. He looked like he was hit by a truck, and they barely recognized him. Almost his entire head and face were bandaged, and the parts of his face that they could see were bruised and swollen. There were tubes and machines everywhere, and his parents were horrified.

Fortunately, Christopher made a slow and steady recovery over the course of the next several days. Either one or both of his parents, along with Wanda, were at the hospital every day until he was discharged two weeks later. Lizzie insisted that Christopher complete his recovery at home, and, unlike TJ, Christopher couldn't wait to come home. Dale felt like he really didn't have a choice.

Christopher claimed not to know who beat him up or what happened that night, but Dale didn't believe him. Dale was experiencing what it feels like when you love your adult children, but you don't like them very much. Christopher was a chip off the old block, his grandmother's block, that is. As soon as he was able, he was staying out all night again and sleeping all day. Dale was livid. He felt like a hostage in his own home.

After nearly three months, Christopher called one morning and informed his mother that he was in jail again. He was arrested for selling drugs to a police informant. He said that it was entrapment. Dale didn't know what he meant by that, but Christopher wanted them to get him a paid lawyer so he could fight it. Dale laughed aloud at that. It was several months before Christopher finally entered a guilty plea to a drug felony and was sent back to state prison.

Joe remained Dale's only friend. They managed to get together every few weeks or so. They found that they could easily pick right up where they had left off. The good thing about Joe was that he had no filter when he was with Dale, and listening to him was often like being at a comedy show. When Joe got on a roll, Dale would laugh so hard that he felt like he would pee his pants. The bad thing was that Joe's directness often cut deep.

"So you finally got rid of Christopher, huh?" Joe asked over a game of pool.

"Yeah, this is his second felony," Dale responded with a heavy sigh. "I don't think he'll be out again anytime soon."

"You should have never let him back into your house in the first place."

"What was I supposed to do? He almost died," Dale contended.

"I don't know," Joe admitted. "Maybe you should have driven him back to the park where they found him. That's what my dad would have done to me."

"No way, man." Dale balked. "I don't believe that."

"Are you kidding me?" Joe contested. "One time, I came home from the playground crying because some kid punched me in the face. My dad walked me back there and made me find that kid and fight him again."

"What happened?" Dale asked.

Joe took a moment to try to make a difficult shot and missed badly.

"I got beat up again," he revealed with a wide grin.

"We're talking about my son's life here, not a black eye," Dale protested. "I just couldn't leave him out there to get attacked again."

"Why not? They shoot horses, don't they?" Joe countered.

"Man, get out of here. You don't even know what that means." Dale contended while shaking his head. "Just take the shot."

"Maybe not, but I know dead weight when I see it."

Dale knew better than to take anything that Joe said to heart. But he did have a point. Having Christopher home was too much of a risk on so many different fronts. It's not like Dale didn't know how things with him would turn out. Christopher never hid the fact that he wasn't even trying to do right. He was completely void of sound judgment and would have sold drugs right out of their house if the opportunity presented itself. It would have been Dale's fault if something worse had happened.

Lizzie would travel to whatever state prison where Christopher was being confined to visit with him whenever possible. Dale went with her only once when he drove her to Auburn Correctional Center, located near Syracuse, because he didn't want her to drive alone in bad weather. But he waited for her in the car during her visit.

At first, he wasn't even sure what the problem was. He knew that he wasn't trying to punish Christopher further, even if that was how it might have appeared to others. However, a large part of it was that he simply refused to see his son locked up like an animal in the zoo. Ultimately, he concluded that he needed to protect what little was left of his sanity.

When he thought about Christopher, and he often did, Dale saw him running through defenders on the football field for touchdowns. When he scored in high school, Christopher always looked for his dad in the crowd as he ran triumphantly off the field with his teammates. Sometimes their eyes connected. It was a special moment that the two of them shared. Christopher was on top of the world and proud. They both were.

***

It was Father's Day, and Lizzie thought it would be nice to go to church as a family—Michael too. Dale resisted. He hadn't been to church in months, and Father's Day was one of those made-up holidays, as far as he was concerned. It had been years since their boys acknowledged Father's Day, or Mother's Day, for that matter. He never celebrated those holidays as a kid either, so it was no big deal. He preferred to stay home and rest. Unfortunately, Lizzie preferred that he didn't.

When they arrived five minutes late, they barely found seats in the back of the sanctuary. Pastor Harris was sick at home, and there was a guest speaker. His name was Reverend Harry Jones. He was an older man who appeared to be in his sixties. He had a commanding presence, and Dale was immediately caught up as he ministered from the Word of God.

The topic of the message that morning was "The Prodigal Son and a Loving Father" from Luke 15:11-32. Dale opened his Bible and listened intently. Of course, he had read the passage many times and even had several notes highlighted in the margins. Dale had always sympathized with the older son, who had stayed home and tended to the father's affairs while his younger brother went out into the world and squandered his inheritance. Reverend Jones used as his key passage verses 20 and 32:

> So he returned home to his father. And while he was still a long way off, his father saw him coming. Filled with love and compassion, he ran to his son, embraced him, and kissed him. (Luke 15:20 NLT)

> We had to celebrate this happy day. For your brother was dead and has come back to life! He was lost, but now he is found! (Luke 15:32 NLT)

Reverend Jones summarized his main point by saying, "Good fathers don't run away. Only children run away from home. God, the ideal father, is loving, kind, and forgiving, and he will never rest while his son is in the midst of the ashes."

The sermon was well-received, and Dale was visibly moved. After service, he and Lizzie stood in a reception line to meet Reverend Jones. They told him how much they enjoyed the message. Dale was quiet for the rest of the day.

He went straight to his room and only came out to get dinner, which he ate in his room. Lizzie asked him several times if something was wrong, but he just said that he was tired. However, the truth was that he was convicted by the message. He felt like a fake. He knew better than most about the need for a father's love, yet he had fallen woefully short in his role as a good father figure.

The tension was rising in him like a sickness. At one point, just as he was getting ready for bed, he started to feel a little light-headed. Without saying anything to his wife, he walked down the stairs, out the front door, and stood on the porch to get some fresh air.

There was a light breeze. It was still a little muggy, but the night air felt good. He was lost somewhere deep in his thoughts and didn't hear Lizzie open the door. He was startled when she walked up from behind and put her arms around him. She pressed the side of her face hard between his shoulder blades and squeezed him tightly.

"Are you ready to go see about your boy now?" she prodded.

Chapter 20

Dale had no idea how to find Louis. He had only received the one postcard from him—and that was over thirty years ago. If Louis was still on the African continent, that didn't mean he was still in Kenya. He had such little information to go on. He didn't know the name of the organization that Louis and Desiree worked for or if Louis was still an American citizen. Dale knew that Louis had not paid back his student loans because the default notices still came to his mother's residence.

Finding Louis turned out to be easier than he thought. Lizzie suggested that he call Bruce Goodman, a Schenectady police investigator who knew her father. Bruce referred Dale to another investigator, Josh Charles, a young guy who was more than happy to help. It took a few days, but Josh appeared at the police garage one afternoon, and they spoke privately in the breakroom.

"It was hard because Louis Johnson is such a common name and the social security number you gave me is incorrect," Josh began. "I called the office of alumni affairs at UB, but they had nothing."

"Oh, really?"

"So I changed lanes and started looking for Desiree Johnson or Desiree Sally. That led me to a John Sally, who resides in Akron, Ohio. I called him, and it turns out that he's Desiree's younger brother. It took some convincing, but he finally told me that he hadn't spoken to her in months, but she was in Uganda. He had a telephone number, which I called. It was some kind of a hospital or medical clinic. The person who answered the phone said that Desiree worked there, but not Louis Johnson. Bottom line, I didn't find your brother, but I found his wife. Here is the number," Josh declared proudly.

"Thank you," Dale said while looking at the phone number written on the piece of paper.

"If I were you, I would keep calling the number until you speak to her," Josh advised. "Don't leave a message, just in case she doesn't want to talk to you."

"Right. Okay," Dale agreed.

"Also, when you call, remember that Uganda is six hours ahead of us," Josh explained.

"Thank you very much. This means so much."

"Not a problem," Josh said. "Let me know if I can help any further. Good luck."

Dale was excited and nervous at the same time. This was all happening so fast. He wasn't sure what he would do if Louis didn't want to talk to him, but he knew that he had to try. Lizzie encouraged him all through dinner.

"I can't image Louis not wanting to talk to you," Lizzie stated.

"Really? Well, he hasn't called me in all of these years."

"But you never called him either," she shot back.

"He never gave me his number," Dale resisted. "I'm just saying that if he really was interested in having some kind of relationship with me, don't you think he would have reached out to me by now? He's the one who moved to a country on the other side of the world."

"Maybe there's a reason why he couldn't," she persisted.

"Like what?" Dale probed.

"I don't know," she responded. "But let me put it to you this way. If he was in some kind of trouble over there, you're the one person he would expect to come looking for him."

"I'm just worried that—"

"You have to call," she interrupted. "You know you do. And you want to. So just swallow your pride and make the first move."

"That's what you think this is?" he challenged. "Me being proud? I want to see him."

"I know, but you're making it too hard on yourself by overthinking it."

"I know you're probably right," he conceded.

He barely slept that night. Although he never mentioned it, Louis had been on his mind a lot lately, even before Father's Day. But he felt helpless to do anything about it. His mother would occasionally ask about him too. The truth is that he did feel guilty for his part in how they had left things. He had been arrogant; he could see that now. His own sons didn't even have the kind of relationship with him or each other like he had with Louis. Sometimes Dale missed him straight to his soul.

He was so anxious that he had a hard time sleeping. He planned to get up at 6:00 a.m., an hour earlier than normal.

That way, it would be the middle of the day in Uganda. He found himself wide awake at 4:30 a.m. Rather than just lying there and torturing himself further, he decided to try to reach Desiree now. The connection didn't go through the first time he dialed it so he tried again.

"Hello?" a voice said.

"Hello, may I speak to Desiree Johnson?" Dale nervously spoke into the receiver.

"Speaking," Desiree said.

"Uh...hello, Desiree, this is Dale Johnson in New York. I am trying to reach my brother Louis," Dale said anxiously.

"Oh, oh...hello, Mr. Johnson...um...I'm really sorry to have to inform you that my husband...he recently passed away suddenly—"

"Excuse me, what did you say?" Dale spoke in a panic.

"Uh yes, Louis died last year actually; I'm very sorry."

Her tone was professional but distant.

"Oh, my god! What? How?" Dale cried out.

Dale was ambushed by his grief. He could feel the blood coursing through his veins at warp speed. He broke out in a sweat and was struggling to catch his breath. He dropped to one knee and bent over slightly to take in more air.

"Um, he was bitten by something on the back of his leg, and it got infected," she explained calmly. "It became sepsis, and he went into septic shock. There was nothing anyone could do."

"Okay, but...wait...no, wait a second...why wasn't I told?" Dale pressed.

"Well, I didn't know how to reach you, for one thing," Desiree defended.

"What do you mean? I've been here the whole time. You never had any intention of ever telling me anything?" he snapped.

"That may be true, but it wasn't my responsibility to try to contact you," she said smugly.

No longer able to restrain himself, Dale shouted into the receiver, "What do you mean, 'not your responsibility'? He was my brother! He was...my brother!"

"Mr. Johnson, I know you're upset, but please don't speak to me that way. You need to lower your voice," she deflected.

"I don't understand. All you had to do is send a telegram, a note...something. Oh, my god! This isn't happening!" Dale shouted.

He was enraged and foaming at the mouth.

"Like I said, it wasn't my responsibility," Desiree rationalized. "We had a beautiful life, with beautiful...you turned your back on him, and now you're trying to play the victim. Well, he was my husband whether you like it or not; I lost my husband! Show some respect!"

"Before he was your husband, he was my brother!" Dale roared. "I was there taking care of him when you still needed someone to wipe your butt. This is one of the most evil, mean-spirited things I've heard of anyone ever doing! What kind of Christian woman are you?"

Completely out of breath, Dale was panting, and his entire body was shaking.

"Again, Mr. Johnson, you need to calm down," Desiree instructed. "I refuse to take any more of your abuse—"

"What did I ever do to you? Tell me! I want to know!" he demanded.

"You already know this, and all of your bullying won't bring Louis back," she debated. "I hope that you—"

"I hope no one ever does anything to you like what you've done to me," Dale argued.

"I'm sorry, but this conversation is over!" she said.

She hung up the phone.

He continued to rant and vent into the air until Lizzie pulled him into her arms in an attempt to console him.

"I'm so sorry. Baby, I'm so sorry," she cried.

He could feel himself free-falling into the depth of despair. His instinct was to fight, but he felt defenseless. He began crying out from the bottommost parts of his heart, and he was surprised himself to hear an odd groaning sound coming out of his gut. He had never experienced that before. Lizzie was kissing his face and head over and over. He was drowning in pain and remorse that was more than he could bear. This was it for him. He knew it at that moment. His agony was all-consuming, and there was no way he was ever going to be able to come back from this.

Both Lizzie and Michael helped him sit down on the sofa. Michael began rubbing his father's back, and Lizzie made him drink some water. He was no longer crying, just dazed. Eventually, they led him up the stairs and back to bed. As soon as he laid down, he curled up into a fetal position. He stayed that way the entire day as he faded in and out of consciousness.

He forced himself to call his mother the next day. He considered driving over to her place to tell her in person, but that required more effort than he was willing or able to put forth. He wasn't concerned in the least that she would be overcome. She was in remarkably good shape for a sixty-nine-year-old woman who never bothered to take care of herself. It was hard to predict exactly how she would react.

"Hello," she answered.

"Hey, it's me, Dale."

"How are you?"

"I have some bad news to tell you," he began. "Uh, I'm sorry... I just spoke to Louis' wife. She said he died last year."

He was fighting back his tears and didn't want her to hear the pain in his voice.

"Died...last year?" she asked.

She sounded bewildered.

"Yes," he whispered.

"What happened to him?" she questioned.

"Uh, she said he got an infection in his leg, and the doctors couldn't get rid of it."

"Do you think that they could have caught it if he was here instead of in another country like that where the doctors are probably not as good?"

"I don't know, maybe," Dale hedged.

"Are they gonna send his body home?" she asked. "I mean, so he can be buried here?"

"No, I don't think so. It's way too late for that," he replied.

"Why didn't his wife call you as soon as he got sick?" she wondered. "Why did she wait a whole year after he died to call?"

"I don't know," Dale stated.

"There is something behind that. Trust me, she ain't tell'n it all," she reasoned.

"I don't think we will ever know," Dale conceded.

"You're probably right...I told you when he first went way over there that it was a bad idea," she recalled incorrectly. "I never understood why they wanted to go there in the first place. Now look at what happened. Most of the people who live over there want to live here in the United States."

"He wanted to help people," Dale spoke. "That's a good thing."

"Yes, sir, he always did have a good heart," she remarked.

Chapter 21

In the three months since he learned of Louis' death, Dale barely left the house other than to go to work and run necessary errands. He was still wrestling with the guilt and grief that had taken residence in his soul. He just couldn't believe that Louis was only a phone call away all these years. Lizzie was right; he had let his pride come between him and his brother. Desiree was never the issue. He had made Louis feel as though he could never come home.

Lizzie had a surprise for him, but he didn't want it. She was taking him on a trip and wouldn't say where they were going. She promised to take care of everything. He didn't even have to pack. He reluctantly agreed to go.

They hadn't traveled much over the years because money was always tight, and it was hard with the boys. She deserved a nice vacation. He knew what she was trying to do, and he really did appreciate it, but a change of scenery wasn't going to resurrect his brother or his broken spirit. Nothing could.

It wasn't until they were at JFK airport in New York that she told him that they were going to Jamaica, to their honeymoon resort. He was very surprised, but he wasn't sure what to think about it. Not all his memories of their honeymoon were good, and his energy level was at an all-time low. Suddenly, there was the added pressure of not wanting to ruin everything for her. He needed to figure out a way to push himself through this, which probably was the point in the first place. At least Lizzie wasn't pregnant this time.

He agreed to do whatever she wanted to do. They sat by the pool, went for walks by the ocean, and even sat in the hot tub. The food was good too, much better than he remembered. His body and mind relaxed, if not his soul. The wounds were just too deep. He knew that he still loved Lizzie as much as he ever did. However, for the first time since they met, that wasn't enough.

Midway through the week, Lizzie decided that she wanted to let the locals braid her hair. She said she would be gone all morning. Dale was sitting on a recliner by the pool alone, reading the frayed Bible that Louis had given him when a handsome Jamaican waiter approached him. He appeared to be in his twenties.

"Good morning, sir. Can I get you a drink?

"No, thank you, I'm good," Dale replied.

"May I ask where you're from?"

"Upstate New York"

"New York," the young man repeated. "How do you like the island? Very nice, huh?"

"Yes, it is. We're having a good time."

"I see you're a believer," he said and pointed to Dale's Bible.

"Yes."

"I have been born again for many years too. Me and my wife, we work at our church, doing what we can, you know."

"That's great," Dale said.

"Can I ask you a question?" he asked.

"Sure."

"Why are you so sad?"

He had a look of great concern on his face. He took a few steps forward and was standing over Dale.

"Uh, what do you mean?" Dale questioned.

"Your eyes, your eyes, mon. They reveal your pain. I can see it very clearly."

"Um…I just lost my brother. He got sick and died. It's a long story."

"Was your brother a believer like you?" he asked.

"Yes, yes he was."

"Then you know that he is not gone forever," he said with a smile. "You will see him again. We don't mourn like the people who do not know God."

"Yes, I know," Dale agreed.

"You will be okay. God will provide, yes?"

There was a presence about this stranger that caught Dale completely off guard and unarmed him.

"Yes, he will. Thank you," Dale forced himself to say.

"You're very welcome. Have a good day, sir."

"You too."

Dale was more than a little intrigued as he watched the man turn and walk away. He had traveled only a few feet when he suddenly stopped and turned around.

"Oh, I am supposed to tell you that God loves you more than you know," he shouted. "More than angels."

The waiter kind of shrugged his shoulders and looked Dale squarely in the eyes before turning and walking away. Dale watched him until he disappeared down a walkway.

His eyes slowly filled with tears. He was motionless, and there was a stirring within him. He lowered his head and cried for several minutes. He tried hard to regain control but was helpless. However, by the time he met up with Lizzie for lunch, his mood had changed completely.

"I love it! Your hair looks great!" he exclaimed.

"Really? She added some hair to it. You don't think it's too long?" she questioned.

"No, I don't. You're still the finest girl I've ever seen."

"Hmm…what's gotten into you?" she asked cautiously.

"Nothing. I just know a stone-cold fox when I see one."

"Is that right?" she solicited.

"Damn straight."

The last three days of their second honeymoon were the best. His sadness was still present—it would be there forever—but it lifted just enough so he could think clearly and see that he had a whole lot of living left to do. While he needed to own his mistakes, he also could accept the undeniable truth that God was active in his life, which meant that he was not defeated because that wasn't possible with God. Louis had taught him that.

Although there were lapses from time to time, Dale continued to fight his way through. If nothing else, he understood TJ's battle with depression and mental illness a little better. He loved his wife and his boys, even if things weren't perfect at home. He needed to be there for them. Sometimes he was going to be sad—he could live with that fact. But he still trusted that God hadn't left him alone.

***

His mother called. She needed to pick some things up at the supermarket. Dale usually drove her to the store and waited in the truck while she did her shopping. Sometimes he went in with her and picked up something they needed at home.

They rarely talked about anything of substance, mostly just small talk about the weather and such. She was beginning to complain more about minor ailments, which included nagging dental issues. She was still fond of Lizzie and she always asked about her. But she never inquired about her grandchildren.

Once back at her apartment, he carried her groceries inside for her. The beer she had bought wasn't bagged. He put everything on the kitchen counters and was starting to leave.

"Thank you. I'll put it all away later," she said and sat down at the kitchen table.

"Okay. But you need to put the milk and the eggs away now," he directed.

"Yeah, I will."

"Alright, I'll see ya," he remarked.

He turned and was walking toward the door.

"Okay. Thanks," she replied. "Oh, and Dale…I'm sorry about Louis. I know how much he meant to you."

"Didn't he mean something to you too? I mean, he was your son," he said with an edge.

It just came out of his mouth before he knew it. He turned around and faced her directly. There was a storm brewing inside of him.

"Yes, I know, but I know how close you were to him," she explained. "That's all I meant."

"Right. But how come you never loved him? I'm sorry, but I really need to know. This is one of the things that always bothered me about you," he said.

"I know you hate me for it, but I did the best I could," she rebutted.

"The best you could? Are you kidding? You've got to be kidding!" He couldn't believe what he was hearing. He could feel the veins on both sides of his neck throbbing.

"Yeah, the best I could!" she contested. "You don't know anything about me or what I went through or anything that happened," she yelled.

"And whose fault is that?" he countered. "You never told us anything—"

"Because none of it is any of your damn business!" she yelled back.

"Why our mother is so screwed up is none of our business? What a joke! Well, you can choke on your little secrets, for all I care."

"You can go to hell!" she shouted.

"Too late. Living with you was hell!" he attacked.

"Okay, you wanna know so bad...okay, here it is...I was fourteen years old when I got pregnant. I was just a baby myself. Your father was the boy who lived next door. I lived with my grandmother, who got me out of foster care. He was in high school, and I thought that he was a nice boy. But he was evil. He didn't want anything to do with me after I got pregnant. He laughed at me, called me a ho, and spit in my face. He did all that stuff because he knew I didn't have no daddy to fight for me. That's the way that men are. Low-down, dirty swine! Every single one."

Dale was silent.

"He hurt me bad because he said he loved me," she ranted. "But he was only using me, just like everybody else! So after you were born, I said, 'what the hell.' I didn't much care about anything anymore. I did a lot of stuff I am not proud of. I didn't care. I got pregnant again. I never even knew who Louis' father was. I wanted to get an abortion, but I didn't have any money."

"Big deal!" Dale fumed. "You're not the first teenager who got pregnant. Boys say nice things to girls all the time that they don't mean. You didn't have to lay down and die. All Louis ever wanted you to do is to love him. He was just a boy, a little boy. But you wouldn't do it."

"I tried! I did!" she contradicted. "But I couldn't! I did love him. He was a part of me, whether I liked it or not. But he reminded me that I was nothing but a piece of meat. My mother was a prostitute. I guess I was pretty much one too. At least I had a say with you. With Louis, someone just took advantage of me."

"Sounds to me like you don't know what happened there. Maybe you took advantage," Dale asserted. "But that doesn't explain why you just left us by ourselves all the time so people could do the same thing to us."

"Not true! That's not true!" she refuted. "I know what you're talking about, and that is not how it was. When I found out what Barbara Jean was doing to you, I made her stop. I knew that you were trying to blame me for all that!"

"I was ten years old!" Dale bellowed. "That was your friend who you brought home. You knew that she would come into our room every night. You knew she was sleeping in the same bed with me. What did you think she was doing?"

"I don't know! I don't know! I wasn't thinking right," she cried. "You were a boy; I thought it was different for boys."

"Well, it wasn't!" he yelled. "She was awful...and I hated it. She smelled like beer and cigarettes and...funk all the time. Just disgusting. My God! She made my stomach turn. Just the thought of it made me want to—"

"Stop!" she demanded. "I'm sorry, but I didn't know. You never said anything. You know I made her stop. We got into a big fight, and I made her leave you alone."

"Toya, you never did anything for us, and we both know it!" Dale protested. "You were supposed to protect us, but you were too busy trying to get your groove on that you left your kids to the wolves!"

"I made a mistake," she confessed. "I was just so mad and so ashamed that I couldn't see straight. Especially after my grandmother died. She was the only one who ever cared even a little about me. I had nobody to help me!"

"You never even tried to be better than you are," he alleged. "You were only looking out for you. But I made sure nobody ever did anything to Louis. I made sure!"

"I know you did, and that's why—"

"And he loved you too," Dale interrupted. "That's the thing. I don't know why. But he really did love you. And what did he get in return? You rejected him and dumped on the one person who loved you the most. Just hateful for absolutely no reason."

"I'm sorry!" she shrieked. "I don't know what you want me to say! Don't you think I know I didn't do right? Everything was so messed up, right from the start. It wasn't as easy as you're trying to say, and don't you dare look down your nose at me like everybody else. I was his mother! I'm the one who gave birth to him! Not you!"

"Just so you know. I don't hate you," he claimed. "Maybe I used to. Now, I mostly feel sorry for you. You could have had a better life if you really wanted it."

He stood still and glared at her. She waved him off with one hand and immediately turned away. She started frantically looking around for her cigarettes.

He left her that way. His anger, no longer simmering, had come to a bubbling boil, and he punched the wall as he walked down the stairs. He probably should have waited until he had calmed down before driving home, but he only paused momentarily before starting his truck and driving away. He just wanted to get as far away from her as possible.

He told Lizzie everything as soon as he got home. She listened quietly as he unloaded. He was spewing out years and years of suppressed anger that refused to be quenched any longer. It had taken ahold of his senses completely.

"So you were molested, and you never told anybody," she said softly.

"No," he said.

"Not even me?" she asked.

"I couldn't, don't you see?"

"No, not really," she admitted. "I always knew that your mother had hurt you. But I never imagined anything like this. How awful! You know, you just can't walk away from something like that and think it was just going to go away."

"Honestly, I believed that God would take the memory away. And he did—mostly. I still have the scars, for sure, but it doesn't hurt the way it used to. Louis never knew. I never wanted anyone to know."

"But maybe if you talk to somebody," she suggested.

"Not everybody heals the same way," he asserted. "I never wanted or needed to talk it out with anyone, other than maybe my mother. It's not the sex. I always knew it wasn't my fault. But I felt betrayed by her because it was like she did it on purpose to punish me or something. I hated her for it. I don't know if I will ever be able to forgive her, especially now that Louis is gone."

"But you really don't have a choice; you have to forgive her. It is the best thing for both of you," she said. "You know I've been there too."

"I honestly don't know if I can; part of me wants her to pay for what she did," Dale confessed. "There's no way she did her best with us. No way!"

"So what are you going to do?" she pushed.

"I'm pretty sure Louis would want me to forgive her," he pointed out.

"What happened to your hand? It looks swollen."

He hadn't noticed his hand. It looked a little puffy around the thumb area.

"It'll be alright," he replied while examining it from both sides.

"Is there anything I can do to help you?" she asked lovingly.

"Um, yes, can you call her and make sure she's okay?"

Nothing his mother told him had come as a surprise to him. He always knew that she was a teen mother and that he and Louis had different fathers. The real revelation was the impact of everything on how she saw herself and how she lived her life. She had a victim's mentality and viewed everything through the lens of someone who had embraced her pain. He and Louis were just casualties of her feeble attempt to self-medicate. Because he had spent his whole life resenting her, it was all that he knew.

Chapter 22

Lizzie bought Dale a cell phone for his birthday, and he hated it. He couldn't understand why anyone would want to carry a phone with them wherever they went. He kept losing it and forgetting to charge it. He was getting old. He and Lizzie were great grandparents; Christopher's daughter had a baby. Lizzie had kept in touch with Sonja's mother even after Sonja graduated from high school and moved with the baby to Chicago. They hoped to have a chance to meet their great-grandson one day.

And as if he wasn't already feeling his age, Dale woke up one morning and couldn't move because his back had completely seized up. The doctor said that it was muscular and not a disc impingement. Regardless, he couldn't believe how bad it hurt. The pain radiated over his entire backside. Lizzie had to dress him to get him to his doctor's appointment. The medication that they gave him for the pain gave him no relief, and he was out of commission for a week.

Dale's mood these days could best be described as guarded. He continued to make every effort to put his best foot forward. He was never a whiner, nor was he ever one for deep introspection. His incessant brooding aside, he figured he could continue to fight as long as he was still standing.

However, now it was abundantly clear that much of his thinking in the past had been harmful. The failure to confront his mother all these years was a mistake—the elephant in the room. Clearly, both he and Louis could have benefited greatly from clearing the air, even if she never changed her behavior or attitude.

Now when his moping was brought to his attention, he would just hit the reboot button in his head. But he knew that that was only a temporary fix. He was dealing with more than his fair share of disillusion and disappointment. As a result, he was frustrated and sad. He allowed himself to bask in his discontentment when it was convenient, meaning when no one else was around. He had to do it. Somehow it gave him the strength he needed to go on.

***

Joe called him and wanted to meet. Dale got there first, and he knew something was wrong as soon as Joe walked through the door and headed directly toward the bar. He looked like he was carrying a heavy weight. Not wanting to pry, Dale waited for Joe to tell him. It didn't take long.

"So, they tell me that I might have cancer," Joe said slowly.

"What kind of cancer?" Dale inquired.

"I have a tumor on my brain."

Dale felt like someone just kicked him in the chest. But he refused to react.

"So, what is the treatment?" he asked.

"We went to the Sloan Kettering Cancer Center in New York last week," Joe disclosed. "They're going to do surgery."

"What kind of surgery?"

"To remove it," Joe explained.

"When?" Dale asked

"We don't know yet. Probably schedule it within the week."

Dale was silent while he processed what he just heard. Joe was thinking too.

"How are you feeling now?" Dale questioned.

"I feel pretty good," Joe replied. "I've had these headaches, but it hasn't been that bad. Sometimes my eyes do this weird thing, and I can't see or hear clear for a few seconds. It's like a little seizure."

"How bad is it? What do they say?" Dale probed.

"They don't know," Joe explained. "Hopefully, it's not cancerous. They're going to take out as much as they can and get a biopsy. My neurosurgeon says we're going to have to just wait and see."

"How's Tracy?" Dale wondered.

"Good as can be expected," Joe replied. The woman is a rock. But I can see that she is tore up inside."

Joe lost his composure for a couple of seconds and began to cry. Dale's foundation shook, but he bore down.

"You're the first person I've told, other than my kids," Joe said once he was steady enough.

"What? Why? I don't understand," Dale questioned. "What about your other family? I'm sure they would want to know. You have to tell your sister."

Joe took a big gulp from his glass. He leaned forward in his chair. His face was flush.

"You know why…please don't make me say it, man," he begged.

The two men stared into each other's eyes for a couple of seconds before looking away quickly at the same time.

"Okay, I feel you. I feel you, bro," Dale acknowledged.

Overcome by the moment, both men needed another minute to regroup. It was Dale who finally broke the silence.

"Is there anything I can do?" he asked.

"Matter of fact, there is," Joe declared. "If anything happens…I know it won't…but just in case…I want you to know that all of my important papers are in the safe in the basement at my house. There's a letter in there with your name on it. It's the things that I want done. I want to make it easier for my family. Just tell Tracy to open it for you."

"Okay," Dale obliged.

"And that's it. That's all I got," Joe said.

"Do you want me to come with you to New York?"

"No, buddy, I appreciate it. We don't know how long the whole thing will take. Tracy knows to call you."

They sat there together for another half hour, making small talk. It was uncomfortable, like they were lovers breaking up and saying one last goodbye. At one point, when Joe wasn't looking, Dale stole a look at his friend's profile and stared hard. He needed a picture in his head to remember, just in case.

They walked out of the bar together and said their goodbyes at the front entrance. Joe extended his hand, and Dale pushed it aside and embraced his friend. The two men held on to each other unashamedly. It was as much a spiritual connection as it was physical. They wept quietly together; neither one able to hold back.

Dale always knew that Joe was important to him, but he'd also taken their friendship for granted. Neither one of them had ever tried to define it or figure out why it was that they worked together. As long as he had known Joe, it was still hard to take him seriously because he made everything a joke. He liked to have fun, and there was hardly an outward expression of genuine affection between them. One more missed opportunity. He was beginning to see the pattern.

Dale managed to make it to his truck before he broke down. He was spiraling downward. He cried over Joe. He cried over Louis and his boys. And he cried over his mother and a world full of disappointment and needless suffering. He felt tired, like he had been running against the wind since the day he was born. All hope was fading.

Lizzie was already in bed and asleep when he arrived home at 10:30 p.m. She had left the light on for him in their room. He stared lovingly at her for a minute. This was something he still liked to do, but it was another thing he had to hide because she thought it was weird. He pulled the blanket up over her, turned the light off, and headed back down the stairs. There was light coming out from underneath Michael's door. Since he graduated with an associate degree in nothing, in particular, Michael rarely left his room and stayed up late most nights.

Dale went into the living room and sat down slowly on the recliner that they bought for him to sleep in when his back pain prevented him from lying flat in the bed. The only light in the room was coming from the clock underneath the television. He watched the numbers on it change in succession and grew uneasy with each passing minute because they seemed to signify that he was running out of time.

He found it difficult to settle down. Something was seriously wrong with him. He felt oppressed. Everything that came to mind brought anguish with it. He didn't know what to do with any of it—and that, in a nutshell, was his private hell. He prayed all night before drifting off to sleep just before Lizzie woke him up at 6:30 a.m. to get ready to go to work.

Joe called the next day and told him that the surgery would be on Friday, which was just two days away. He sounded optimistic, almost happy. Dale wasn't sure what to say back to him.

"Promise me you're going to fight," Dale implored.

"I promise," Joe pledged.

"No matter what," he begged while trying not to sound fearful.

"No matter what," Joe repeated.

Dale was a wreck all day Friday. He was having a hard time concentrating and had no appetite. For some reason, he was under the impression that the surgery would be first thing in the morning and he would hear something right away. He kept checking his phone.

When he hadn't heard anything from Tracy by dinner time, he was convinced that something bad must have happened. Lizzie kept telling him that he should call Tracy, but he didn't feel comfortable doing that. His phone finally rang at 8:15 p.m.

"Hello."

"Hi Dale, it's Tracy."

"Hi," he said with hesitation.

"Joe is in recovery. They said it went good," Tracy reported. "They think that they got all of the tumor. The biopsy showed that it was cancerous grade II, but there's a good chance it was just in the one spot and hasn't spread."

"Why did it take so long?" Dale wondered.

"They took him into surgery at 6:00 a.m. this morning. But the actual start time kept getting delayed. So they didn't start until around 2 p.m. And then they had to wait for the lab report to come back on the biopsy. I wanted to wait before I started calling people until I had something to say."

"Oh, I understand," Dale conceded. "How are you?"

"I have definitely had better days, you know," she confessed. "I haven't seen him yet. All the kids are here with me and Joe's father and sister, so we have each other."

"Is there anything I can do? Anything at all?" Dale asked.

"Ah, I don't think so," she replied. "I think we're good for now. But thank you. I will call you if there's any change in anything. Joe insisted I call you first."

"Thank you so much. It means more than I could ever say…" he trailed off.

Choking up, she said, "Dale, I know that my Joe doesn't always say what he feels all of the time. Actually, he never wants to talk about anything serious. But I wanted you to know that you really mean a lot to him. You're like the brother he never had, and he thinks the world of you."

"Thanks…I feel the same way. I've been worried," Dale said while holding back his tears.

"I know how you guys are," she acknowledged. "Look, I will call you tomorrow."

"Okay. Thank you again."

Dale was elated. He knew Joe wasn't necessarily out of the woods yet, but this was definitely good news. He had started to prepare himself for the worse. As crazy as it sounds, he had been blaming himself. For a while now, something inside had been telling him that he was the reason bad things kept happening to the people he cared about. It was a crippling feeling because not only did it make him feel guilty, but it also made him want to isolate himself to not put others in jeopardy.

Tracy called the next morning to report that Joe was awake and conscious. She said he looked good. However, he was experiencing some pain. His treatment plan included both radiation and chemotherapy. She anticipated that they would be in New York City for about a week, and then the rest of his treatment would be at Albany Medical Center.

Although Dale was relieved, he was worried about his friend. Some of the guys at work told horror stories about people they knew who had brutal bouts with cancer, all of which only added to his anxiety. Tracy continued to call Dale regularly with updates and even put the phone to Joe's ear once so Dale could say hello.

He decided that he wanted to go to the hospital. New York City was a little over two hours away, and he knew that he would feel better if he saw Joe. Lizzie decided to come too. They went on the Tuesday morning following the surgery. The traffic into the City was a nightmare, and there was nowhere to park when they got to the medical center. Dale had to drive around for about thirty minutes before he found a metered parking spot on the street several blocks away.

Tracy was alone in Joe's room with him when they arrived there. She was delighted to see them and jumped up from her seat to greet them. Joe was asleep at first but opened his eyes when he heard them talking. They had shaved his head, which was partially covered by a large bandage.

"Joe, honey, look who's here," Tracy said.

Joe opened his eyes but otherwise made no gesture of any kind.

"How are you doing, buddy?" Dale asked.

"Good," Joe managed to say.

"I had to come to make sure you were behaving yourself," Dale spoke.

Joe smiled. Dale took his hand.

"Hi Joe," Lizzie said.

"Hi," Joe responded.

"What happened to your hair?" Dale asked. You didn't tell me they were going to shave your head. You look like a white Michael Jordan."

"I don't want to look like him. I want his money," he managed to say with a raspy voice.

"Yeah, me too," Dale responded and smiled.

He wasn't surprised that Joe still had his sense of humor and wit. That had to mean something, he hoped.

"Since you guys are here, I'm going to go get some coffee. Can I get you something?" Tracy asked.

"No, thank you," Dale answered,

"I need to go to the ladies' room, so I will walk with you," Lizzie said.

"Yes, I can show you." Tracy offered.

The two women walked out together. Dale remained standing next to the head of the bed.

"How bad does it hurt?" Dale whispered.

"Like hell."

"Does the medication help?" Dale asked.

"No...maybe a little."

"Well, they got it all, so that's good news."

"Uh-huh," Joe muttered and closed his eyes for a second. He looked tired.

"Go to sleep if you're tired," Dale said. "It's okay. Rest."

"Okay," Joe said and immediately closed his eyes again.

Dale stood there watching him. He prayed silently for several minutes and asked God to take the pain away.

Joe opened his eyes again when Lizzie walked back into the room. But he immediately closed them.

Dale and Lizzie both sat down, but they didn't speak until Tracy came back. The three of them quietly discussed Joe's status. The radiation was the source of the pain. However, they still expected Joe to be discharged within a week.

Dale and Lizzie were there about an hour altogether. Joe was in a deep sleep when they left, and they didn't want to wake him. Tracy walked them to the elevator, hugged them both, and thanked them for coming. Dale felt a little better that he got to see his best friend and to pray for him.

There was a parking ticket on Lizzie's car when they walked up. Dale was annoyed. He couldn't have been more than a few minutes over if that. He hated the city. They were thinking about maybe trying to get dinner or something before heading back, but he wasn't in the mood to drive around. They made it to Albany in just over two hours, stopped at one of their favorite restaurants there, and had dinner.

They arrived home at 8:30 p.m. They were both very tired. When they opened the door, they could hear the muffled sound of the television and movement. To their utter surprise, Michael was sitting in the living room on the sofa with a young girl. She was plain, slightly overweight, and wore a sweatshirt and jeans. She had shoulder-length blonde hair and blue eyes.

Michael jumped up when he saw them and was acting coy and nervous. She introduced herself as Amber Greene, and she said that she worked at the convenience mart with Michael. She seemed nice enough, and after some small talk, Dale and Lizzie said goodnight and headed up the stairs.

Just as they made it into their room, they looked at each other, and without saying a word, they erupted in hysterical laughter. For Dale, it was the kind of laughter that came from his belly, and he had to bend over to keep from falling over. He had tears in his eyes. It felt good.

"All I know is that you better stop laughing at my baby," Lizzie managed to say before gushing in laughter again.

The phone rang at 2:15 a.m. Dale was awake. He had been waiting. Joe had a seizure. He died an hour ago.

Dale went into automatic pilot mode again, refusing to allow himself to feel anything. He showed no emotion after hanging up the phone. He was all cried out. He told Lizzie what Joe's son Joey had just reported to him on the phone and then rolled over as if to go back to sleep. She spooned him from behind and held him close while crying softly.

He felt like he was slowly dying inside himself—and there was absolutely nothing that he could do about it. Praying didn't seem to change anything. His life from the outside didn't look any different than people who didn't know God—and probably looked worse. Nothing made sense; there was no point in trying to figure anything out. Dale resolved that if God chose not to rescue him, then he was probably meant to suffer.

Tracy had the envelope that Joe had left in his safe delivered to him at home unopened. It was one of those big manila envelopes. Dale examined it suspiciously. He had imagined something much smaller. He sat down at his kitchen table and opened it slowly. Inside was a handwritten two-page letter and four business-sized envelopes. The letter read:

> Dear Dale,
> If you're reading this, then it means that I didn't make out too good. I figured as much. Anyway, I only want a Mass. I do not want calling hours. This is very important to me. I also want to be cremated and my ashes buried in the Catholic cemetery where my Mom and grandparents are buried. In this packet is my life insurance policy. Please give this to Tracy. Tell her to call my supervisor, Kevin McQuiston, and find out about my death benefits through work. Also, there are four envelopes in here. One is for Tracy, and one for each of my kids. I want you to give these letters to them exactly one year from my death. Please don't let them know you have them. I appreciate you taking care of this for me. You're the only one I can trust to do it the way I want. This is very hard. It is even hard for me to write this. I will miss everybody. Thank you for being my good friend for all of these years.
> Joe

Dale took the entire week off from work. He was as helpful to Tracy and her kids as he could possibly be. The funeral Mass was in the same church where the one for Mr. Carbone was held. It brought back memories. He clearly remembered the smell inside and the lingering sadness.

Surprisingly, he heard from Mrs. Carbone, who called him to offer her condolences and see how he was doing. He appreciated that because he still felt close to her and her family. She said she was doing well but didn't ask about Christopher like she used to.

By the end of the week, he was running on empty. It felt like every muscle in his body was screaming, which was a good thing because, even if he couldn't settle his mind, at least he could rest his body. However, his sleep was anything but peaceful. He figured that he should probably get used to the feeling.

Chapter 23

At first, Michael denied that Amber was his girlfriend. When Dale asked him about her, he was evasive and aloof. He said that they were just friends and turned to walk away.

"Wait, come back," Dale commanded. "Don't walk away from me when I'm talking to you."

He turned back around to face his father. "Oh, sorry," Michael said. "I didn't mean to."

"Have you had sex with this girl? Are you sleeping with her?"

"No, not really," Michael reported.

"What does that mean?" Dale asked.

Michael just shrugged his shoulders and lowered his eyes.

Dale continued, "Listen, if you want to act like a man, then be a man. If you like this girl, then treat her like a lady. She is a person God loves, just like you. We don't use people. Sex is a big thing. You know the difference between right and wrong."

"Yes, I know," Michael muttered.

"Then act like you know," Dale reloaded. "Don't make the same mistake Christopher made. He has a daughter out there who he doesn't even know."

"Daddy, I know. So, can we please—"

"Listen, if you get this girl pregnant, or any other girl for that matter, you're gonna have to deal with me. I'm gonna be on you like white on rice. Do you understand me?"

"Yes," Michael whispered.

"I mean it! Don't do anything stupid!" Dale yelled.

"I heard you!" Michael stressed.

Dale knew that Michael was afraid of him in a way that Christopher and TJ never were. He also knew that it was probably much too late for the sex talk with a thirty-one-year-old man. But Michael was hardly the typical guy, and there was at least a chance that he would think twice about whatever it was he was doing with this Amber. Dale was only trying to save his son from himself.

A part of Dale's new candor was the acceptance that he wasn't responsible for how his sons turned out. He was only their father. Their choices were their own. He had spent too much time blaming himself for things that were completely out of his control. His boys might be broken, but he didn't break them. Maybe he could have been a better father, who knows? But he was always there; he never left home.

Briana, Wanda's youngest daughter, was salutatorian of her high school class. She was planning to attend Cornell University. She was a wonderful girl, sweet and respectful. There was a big graduation party, and Dale was truly proud of his niece and her accomplishments. But deep down, he was also jealous. The comparison to his boys was stark. It seemed to him that black girls were advancing at a much greater rate than the boys.

Indeed, most of the minority kids he watched graduate that afternoon were girls. He knew that there were many successful black men in the world, but he didn't know many of them. Daniel had done very well for himself, but something wasn't right there. Dale couldn't help but wonder if he would have made out better if he had daughters instead of sons. He was ashamed of himself for thinking that way.

TJ's birthday was the day after the graduation party. Lizzie wanted to see him. Dale had developed a bit of a knack for finding him. For one thing, they were still notified whenever TJ was involuntarily confined to the psychiatric center due to an episode, and the social workers who called always gave him an update on TJ, including where he was supposedly living. He also knew that TJ liked to hang out downtown near the arbor hill area with the same guys. He always started looking there in the morning. Generally, it was impossible to find TJ in the late afternoon or evening.

They found him sitting in a group outside a church in arbor hill that provided services to the homeless. It was 9:45 a.m. There was an empty lot directly across the street from the church, and Dale parked there. They sat there for a couple of minutes and watched TJ before Dale got out and called to him. TJ waived and started walking toward them. Lizzie got out of the truck and embraced her son immediately.

"Happy birthday, honey. How are you?" she asked.

"I'm good," he said.

"How are you feeling these days?" Dale wondered.

"I'm taking my medications, if that's what you mean," TJ replied.

Dale had to fight to ignore TJ's edge. He seemed abrupt and defensive and didn't show any excitement at seeing his parents for the first time in several months.

"No, that's not what I was asking," Dale defended. "You look thin. Are you eating?"

"Yeah, I eat. I walk a lot."

"Do you need anything?" Lizzie questioned.

"No, I don't," TJ answered sharply.

"Do you need any money?" Dale asked.

"No, I don't shop much. Plus, you know I get disability now."

"Hey, guess what? Brianna graduated from high school yesterday," Lizzie interjected. "I can't believe that she's all grown up. She had a graduation party. It was really nice. She asked about you."

"Really?" TJ remarked. "Tell her I said congratulations."

"I will," Lizzie replied. "I am just having a hard time with everyone growing up and leaving home. It makes me feel old."

"Uh-huh."

TJ seemed preoccupied. It was clear that he didn't want to be there talking with them. Perhaps they embarrassed him. Going there was probably not a good idea.

Dale punted, "Hey, man, listen; we just wanted to see you on your birthday and wish you a happy birthday. You know where we are if you need anything."

"Yes, I know," TJ said.

"Honey, take care of yourself. I love you." Lizzie expressed.

"I will," TJ agreed. "But I'm doing really good."

"Happy birthday again," Dale stated.

Lizzie hugged TJ again. Dale shook his hand, and TJ immediately turned and ran away. They stood there and watched as he partially disappeared into the small crowd.

There simply are no words to describe how Dale felt after the encounter. Not only did TJ look unkempt, but he smelled bad too. Dale's eyes watered a little when TJ first approached them, and he had no idea how Lizzie could have hugged him without passing out. His son wasn't one of those people who learned to live and function effectively with bipolar disease.

The drive home was quiet. There wasn't much for either one of them to say, so they kind of entertained their own thoughts. As a parent, it's hard to accept the fact that nothing can be done to help your sick child. As a Christian, it's even more difficult because the cry of your heart for every second is for your children, who are God's gift. There are so many scriptures that say that God is a healer and a present help.

***

Dale's relationship with his mother mainly remained unchanged. They never again discussed anything about her past. Once was enough for them both. He couldn't think of anything else to say to her.

However, she was beginning to need him more as she was getting older. She was admitted to the hospital the week after Joe died. She called him because she noticed that her right foot was swollen, and he had to take her to the emergency room and sit there with her for hours. Initially, they were concerned that she might be diabetic. It turns out that her kidneys were not functioning properly. She was only in the hospital for two days, but now he had the added responsibility of checking in on her more often.

Similarly, Dale was starting to see a decline in his own health. In addition to his chronic lower back pain, he developed high blood pressure and carpal tunnel in his right hand. Sometimes he completely lost feeling in his dominant hand, and he had a hard time gripping his tools at work. There was quite a bit of pain, too, especially at night. His doctor advised against surgery for now. While he was somehow able to manage everything that was coming at him, his overall sense was that things would only worsen over time.

He was beginning to think about retirement. Next year would be his thirty-fifth year with the city. No one had been at the garage as long as him. He needed to be sixty-two years old to collect his retirement, and he was still a few years off. But he and Lizzie were beginning to talk about it. Their mortgage would soon be paid off, and they could sell the house and move wherever they wanted to go. A complete change of scenery is what he needed. Somewhere out west sounded good to him.

There was really nothing to keep them in Schenectady other than Michael and his mother. But Michael was a grown man now, and it was time for him to act like one. There was no chance that Dale was carrying him forever. He firmly believed that the whole point of parenthood was to raise children to be able to go out and pursue their dreams. Although he wasn't exactly sure where Lizzie was concerning Michael long-term, he knew enough to anticipate a tough conversation coming in the future.

But his mother was going to be a much bigger problem. He was all she had. He couldn't just leave her in Schenectady and go off on his merry way without looking back. He recognized that she was his responsibility. It was important to him that she be cared for, but he had no idea exactly what that meant for him.

Chapter 24

Dale had always been a bit obsessive about his lawn, which he always mowed twice a week in the summer, whether it needed it or not. After Christopher ruined the front yard once by cutting it too low and leaving several bare patches, the most that he would allow the boys to do was put down mulch and pick weeds out of the flower beds. He had a system, and the front lawn looked especially like a putting green. He liked the idea that this was the same lawn that Mr. Carbone used to care for.

It was early one Saturday morning in August, and he was cutting the grass in the backyard when Lizzie called to him from the back window. He couldn't hear her over the sound of the mower, but she was waiving her hand and gesturing to him to come inside. Reluctantly, he turned off the engine and headed for the door. He didn't want to take his boots off just to turn around and have to put them back on again, so he stood at the back door and shouted out to her.

"Lizzie, what is it?"

She poked her head around the corner and waved again for him to come inside. She had a pressing look on her face. He took his boots off and walked through the kitchen into the living room. He was surprised to see a young woman sitting on the sofa next to Lizzie.

Hello," Dale said, and he extended his hand.

Hello," she replied and smiled.

She was brown-skinned, slender built with short-cropped hair. She was also stunning and looked like a runway model. Her almond-shaped eyes seemed to jump right out, and she wore the perfect amount of make-up. Dale couldn't help staring at her as they shook hands.

"Please have a seat," he urged. "How can I help you?"

"Dale, this is Johanna," Lizzie said. "She is Louis' daughter."

"Who?" he asked instinctively. "I'm sorry, who are you?"

"Mr. Johnson, I am Johanna Johnson. My father is Louis Johnson, your brother, I believe."

He was confused and having difficulty connecting the dots. He looked at Lizzie for help. His words had escaped him momentarily.

"Johanna is Louis' daughter," Lizzie repeated. "She is here in the United States to go to college. She is starting at NYU."

Dale was suddenly completely transfixed by the young woman. She didn't look anything like Louis or Desiree.

"Dale, did you hear me?" Lizzie asked.

"Uh…uh…yeah, uh, I'm sorry. I don't mean to be rude, but I didn't know my brother had a daughter," he muttered.

"I understand," she stated. "I'm sorry for intruding at your home without calling first. I didn't have your phone number."

"No, that's okay," Dale said. "How old are you?"

"I'm nineteen."

"Desiree is your mother?" he inquired.

"Yes, Desiree Johnson," she responded.

"Does she know you came to see me?"

"No, she doesn't," the young woman replied. "I will tell her when I can. Please allow me to explain. My mother is a very good woman, and I love her very much. But she is also very demanding of the people she loves. She would be angry if she knew I came here. You see, she doesn't think very highly of you. She says you disrespected her, and you didn't want my father to marry her. She said they had to move away to get away from you."

"None of that is the truth," Dale protested.

"I know. My father told me," she acknowledged. "He always said that you were very loving and kind. But my mother didn't want you to know where they were living. She made him promise not to tell you."

"But I don't understand. Why would Louis ever agree to that?" Dale questioned.

"My mother...she is very strong."

"But why did she even have to know?" Dale wondered. "He could have called me on his own."

"He promised her," she said pointedly. "He had to keep his promise."

Dale nodded his head. But he still didn't understand. That sounded crazy to him.

"Can you tell me how my brother died?" he shifted.

"He was bitten by something, a rat, we think," she explained. "It put poison in his bloodstream. He had a very high fever, and his leg got very big from the infection. He only lived a short time after."

He noticed her accent for the first time. It was only slight.

"Was he happy before he got sick?" Dale asked. "Did he have a good life?"

"Yes, my father was a very respected man," she reported. "He helped to bring much change to the area where we live. He worked with the government officials and was able to get them to focus more on helping the people. The government has many bad people in it, and there is much corruption and distrust of Americans. But the people loved my father. There was great mourning in the district when he died."

"I thought they went to Kenya, "Dale quizzed. "How did they get to Uganda?"

"They were only in Kenya a very short time," Johanna noted. "A few months, I think. They met some people who wanted to do ministry in Uganda, so my parents went with them. I was born in Uganda. My brother was born in Uganda too."

Dale's held his breath and his eyes got big.

"You have a brother? Louis has a son?"

She closed her eyes and hesitated.

"Yes, my brother is fifteen years old," she affirmed. "He is in boarding school."

"This is unbelievable!" Dale gushed. "Your mother, she said nothing."

"I'm very sorry," Johanna said. "She is very wounded. Her life as a young girl here in America was very difficult, and she feels that she cannot trust much. Sometimes she makes people angry with her. She had a hard time getting pregnant at first, and that made her sad. But she was a good wife to my father."

"So my brother was happy?" Dale probed.

"Yes, sir, he was loved, and he was happy."

Dale burst into tears. "Excuse me," he managed to say before he jumped up and walked out.

He went into the bathroom, shut the door, and sobbed. He felt like a blubbering idiot. He thought he was through crying for Louis, but this revelation picked the scab off his deep wound and resurrected much of his pain. He had convinced himself that he would never know what happened to his brother. The guilt was suffocating.

"Dale?" Lizzie interrupted from the other side of the door.

"Yes."

"You okay?"

He opened the door.

"I've asked Johanna to stay for dinner. She took the train and the bus to get here. Can you believe it?" she asked in a hushed tone.

Dale went out back to finish mowing the lawn while Lizzie and Johanna got acquainted and prepared dinner. It gave him time to think. The visit from this young woman was truly a gift from God. It was a much-needed reprieve from the devil's gloating.

He had a lot more questions, but he didn't know how much he should ask or how much he really wanted to know about Louis' life without him. If Desiree was that vindictive, then he questioned how happy Louis could have really been with her. Most people would consider the act of isolating one's spouse from his or her family to be abuse. He made a mental note to be very careful about anything he said about Desiree.

Johanna was a delight. Even Michael was smitten with her. It was usually like pulling teeth to get him to sit through an entire meal with them. But there he was. He clearly was enjoying spending time with his cousin. She was thoughtful and well-spoken. She was also caring and sensitive, unlike her mother. Dale was convinced that she was her father's daughter.

"How did you find us?" Lizzie wondered.

"The U.S. Embassy. I needed your address to enroll at the university."

"Can you tell me about your brother? What is his name?" Dale asked.

"His name is Louis too. He is a very strong boy. And a good student. He wants to come to the U.S. to study to be an engineer. He is tall like you. My father called him Dee."

"Why Dee?"

"Because he said that my brother is you," she explained.

Dale was touched, and he held his breath a little. This was the proof that he needed that his bond with Louis was never really broken.

"Your mother let him call your brother that?" Dale delved further.

240

"He told her to never tell him what to call his son. He was adamant."

"She accepted that?" Lizzie questioned.

"Everybody, they call my brother by the name of Dee."

She smiled to herself.

"Johanna, I must say that you have the most beautiful skin I have ever seen," Lizzie remarked.

"Thank you," Johanna replied.

"I like her eyes too," Michael said.

'Did you ever think about modeling?" Lizzie wondered.

"My major is chemistry. I think I might want to be a pharmacist. But I am not sure."

"You mean like a drug store?" Michael asked with a bewildered look on his face.

"Back in Uganda, counterfeit medicine is a very big problem."

"You're a remarkable young woman," Dale declared.

"Thank you, Uncle."

They decided that it made more sense for Johanna to stay the night with them and for Dale to drive her back to school in the morning. She resisted at first, but they insisted. They put her in Christopher's old room. The four of them sat in the living room talking until just after 9:00 p.m., when Lizzie decided that they should let Johanna get some rest.

"Oh my! I almost forgot, "Johanna exclaimed before excusing herself and running up the stairs.

She returned momentarily and handed something to Dale.

"I brought these for you," she announced.

There were several photographs. The first one was of Louis sitting behind a desk. He looked older than Dale remembered, and his face was fuller—but it was definitely Louis. The lump in Dale's throat felt like it was the size of a softball.

As he looked through the rest of them, he would quickly wipe away the tears from his eyes before they ran down his face in a futile attempt to hide the fact that he was crying. He then handed each one individually to Lizzie, who then passed it along to Michael. In one photo, Louis was holding baby Johanna, and in another he was standing with a boy outside of a church. She said that the boy was Dee, who looked to be about nine or ten years old.

Dale examined each photograph as closely as he could. He was looking for evidence of anything that might reveal Louis' state of mind-anything at all. He was desperate. Most men he knew didn't like women who were overbearing.

"I have more. These are the only ones that I brought with me."

"I couldn't possibly keep these," he contended. "They must mean a lot to you now."

"I want you to have them," she maintained. "It would make me very happy."

"Thank you."

Lizzie had considered riding with them to New York City, but she had a doctor's appointment in the morning. She said it was too late to cancel. It was clear that she really liked Johanna, and the two women had an emotional goodbye after breakfast as they headed out the door.

On a whim, Dale asked Johanna if she had time to meet his mother before they left. She indicated that she did. When he called Latoya, he just told her that he was on his way over with someone he wanted her to meet. She didn't ask any questions. He was only slightly concerned about what she might say to her granddaughter.

Dale knocked on the door and waited a few seconds before using his key to unlock the door. As soon as they walked inside, Latoya walked out of her room. Her hair was wrapped in a scarf, and she had on a floral-print robe and slippers.

"Hello," she said.

She was staring at Johanna.

"Hi, "Dale replied.

"Hello," Johanna echoed.

"I have someone here who I would like for you to meet," Dale stated. "This is Johanna. She is Louis' daughter from Uganda."

"Who?" LaToya asked with a puzzled look on her face.

"I know. That was my reaction too," Dale said. "This is Louis' daughter. She is here in the U.S. to go to college."

"It's very nice to meet you," Johanna said with a smile.

"Uh, I didn't know that Louis had a daughter," LaToya said while adjusting her scarf.

"He has a son too," Dale interjected with a smile.

"Really? A son?" she repeated. She looked confused.

"My brother is fifteen years old. He is in boarding school in Uganda," Johanna recited.

"Have a seat. Have a seat...you're a very pretty girl, you know," LaToya complimented after closer examination.

"Thank you very much," Johanna said mildly.

It finally registered to Dale that she wasn't vain in the least and that she didn't much like the attention that her looks garnered.

"Were you with Louis when he died?" LaToya asked and leaned in closer to her granddaughter.

"Yes, I was there."

"Um...did he suffer much?" LaToya asked.

Her question caught Dale off guard. He never thought to ask that.

"He was heavily sedated. He wasn't in pain," Johanna responded.

"How come no one called us to let us know?" she investigated further.

"I didn't know who to notify here in the U.S."

"Oh yeah, that's right," LaToya said.

"My father didn't have any addresses or phone numbers," Johanna explained.

"That's funny; I've lived in this apartment longer than you have been alive...um, I'm sorry, please forgive me. I'm getting old. I just say things sometimes."

"Of course," Johanna replied politely.

"Are you going to be here in Schenectady long?" LaToya wondered.

"I start my classes tomorrow at the university in New York City."

"So, you're pretty and smart," LaToya concluded. "You know, Louis was smart too. He got a scholarship to college."

"I didn't know that," Johanna admitted.

"Yes, he did. That's probably where you got it from."

"That is kind of you to say," Johanna stated.

"I wish you grew up here. I would have loved knowing that I had a granddaughter."

"Me too," Johanna admitted. "We only had our parents. No other family." Johanna sucked on her lower lip and lowered her eyes a bit.

"I think that's a shame, "LaToya complained. "I never had much family myself. I wish somebody would have told us."

She looked sad. Dale wasn't expecting that. Usually, her go-to reaction to anything unpleasant was anger. But considering he had put her on the spot with this surprise morning visit, she was handling herself remarkably well.

There was an awkward silence.

"Look, we really have to go," Dale announced as he stood to his feet. "I promised Lizzie I would get Johanna back to school at a decent time."

"It was so nice to finally meet you," Johanna said as she extended her right hand.

"Would it be alright if I hugged you?" Latoya asked and stretched out both of her arms and leaned back slightly.

"Yes, of course," Johanna replied.

Their embrace was surprisingly loving. Johanna let go first.

"Thank you," she said. "I hope you can come back and see us soon."

"I will. I promise," Johanna committed.

"Johanna brought some pictures of Louis. I will bring them over tomorrow for you to see," Dale offered.

"Okay, I would love to see them," LaToya said.

"Goodbye, Mrs. Johnson."

"Goodbye," LaToya replied. "Um, I just want to say that...um...Louis was my son, and he loved me. I know he did. That means the world to me now that he's gone...and that makes you and your brother special to me."

"Thank you for saying that," Johanna said with tears in her eyes.

Dale had never been more surprised by his mother. He really wasn't sure what to make of what she just did. Noticeably, she didn't say that she loved Louis. However, to be fair, she had never claimed to be better than she was. She just never tried to improve herself. Truth be told, he always knew she wasn't completely dead inside.

It was a beautiful day for a drive. The sun was bright in the sky, and the weather was pleasant. Dale was looking forward to this time alone with Johanna, and they talked steadily during most of the drive to NYU.

She was direct and had a lot of questions of her own about what Louis was like when he was growing up. Apparently, Louis had shared more with her than Dale had ever discussed with his boys. She knew all about their issues with their mother.

"My father told me that she was dependent on alcohol. Did she ever get help for it?" she asked.

"No, not really," he answered. "She still loves her beer. But she is older now, so she can't do a lot of the things she used to do. I think she has a lot of regrets."

"Maybe, you could help her," Johanna suggested.

"Help her how?" he inquired.

"Perhaps if she knew you loved her, then maybe she could get to the point where she believes she has value. Women need men in a way that men do not need women."

"I'm not sure many women in this country would agree with that," he contended. "It's different here."

"Yes, I have heard this. But the Bible teaches that husbands should love their wives. It doesn't say for wives to love their husbands. Women need love; men need respect."

"I'm her son," he argued. "I'm not her husband."

"You're the only husband she will ever have. Can you imagine what it must be like never to feel loved?"

"I don't know if I can give her that," he admitted. "It's much too late for us, I think."

"No, it is not," she disputed. "You're both still alive. I miss my father every day. I will miss him on my wedding day, and even after I have a husband and children of my own. But I know he is still with me. He told me that he loved me so often that I feel like I can do anything...even come all this way to the U.S. by myself."

"I think you're very brave," Dale stated.

"My father's love made me brave."

"What about your mother's love?"

"She is different from my father. She has not settled herself. She doesn't have many friends, just her work at the medical clinic. She works very hard and misses my brother when he is in school."

"It is important to me that you know I never disrespected her," he appealed. "I only met her the one time. I never said anything dishonoring to her or about her. I just didn't think that Louis was ready to marry anybody, and I told him so. Maybe, I was wrong. I don't really know. But it was nothing against Desiree personally. I didn't even know her."

"She likes to take things personally," Johanna divulged. "I think I know what happened. I am sorry for you."

"I just need to know how angry Louis was with me," Dale probed. "All these years, I couldn't understand it. I still don't understand, and it's killing me. It was like the punishment didn't fit the crime. You know what I mean? I thought I knew him."

Johanna took some time to herself before speaking.

"The last few days before he died, he was very bad with the fever," she began slowly. "He was sweating and shaking all over as his body tried to fight the infection. His eyes were rolling back in his head, and I was very afraid. He was talking in his sleep, and it was very difficult to understand what he was saying. But I listened closely, and I heard him say your name, 'Dale,' many times. My mother, she heard it too. There was a moment just before he died that he became calm and opened his eyes. He said your name again. He was looking at me, but he said your name."

She was obviously revisiting the scene in her head. Her voice was shaky.

Dale took his eyes off the road for a second and looked her in the eye. Together now, they were staring at the mountain called grief and despair.

Johanna gathered herself first.

"My dear uncle, I do not believe that my father was angry with you…not at the end… He loved you very much. So much that he called out to you—to you—with his dying breath."

Dale was shaken to the core. He could feel his soul groaning down deep. There was also a sharp pain in his heart, screaming out like a toothache. It took everything that he had to stay composed and not lose control of his truck in rush-hour traffic.

He couldn't think of anything else to say or ask. It was as if his brain had short-circuited entirely. It seemed like it was the same for her, too, in that she didn't speak much for the last forty-five minutes while he drove uneasily into the city toward NYU.

It wasn't anything like the rural campuses to which he had grown accustomed. He parked as close to her dorm as he could get, and they got out of the truck.

"Thank you so much," she said. "I enjoyed meeting you and your family very much."

"We enjoyed meeting you too," he replied. "My family is your family too now, and, as my mother said, we want you to feel free to come to Schenectady anytime that you want to. You're welcome anytime you have a break. You can stay as long or as short as you want. You don't have to take the bus, just call me, and I will be more than willing to come and get you."

"Thank you, I will," she promised.

"And call me if you need anything," Dale offered. "I hate the idea of you being here all alone."

He hugged her tight and struggled to let her go. He handed her the small bag she had brought with her.

"Thank you for telling me what happened to my brother," he whispered. "You saved my life."

She kissed him gently on the cheek and pulled away.

"I always knew in my heart what I had to do," she said. "I needed to bring my father's memory home to you so he can rest now." She smiled through her heartbreak and walked away.

As he watched her disappear into the crowd, Dale was reminded of the first time he dropped Louis off at college.

Chapter 25

Life is a great mystery that one day we will clearly understand. The Bible teaches that death is a part of life. That is, there is an appointed time for each of us to die, and the death of someone who believes in the Lord Jesus is precious to God and celebrated in heaven by the saints. Death is the last enemy to be defeated; after experiencing it, we will all rise in victory to live again the way Jesus did.

However, the transition from the here and now is often traumatic, especially with an unexpected or violent death. The prospect of coming to terms with one's own mortality—or worse yet, the death of a loved one—is easily the cruelest part of living in this world.

Moreover, we each have various thresholds for agony and different relationships with the creator. It is possible to love God with all your heart and still have a hard time withstanding the pain of living in a seriously broken world. Although words are powerful and God's Word is supreme, the cries of the flesh can resound at such intensity that everything else is drowned out, so those words have little or no effect against the profound hurt that has burrowed a hole in the soul.

To be clear, few men have ever loved a woman the way that Dale loved his Lizzy. He was devastated. By the time she was diagnosed, Lizzie's breast cancer was stage four. There was a large tumor in the right breast. Worse yet, the cancer had spread to her stomach. The chosen treatment was a double mastectomy and chemotherapy delivered in a solution through a heated tube and administered directly into the chest cavity. There was a five-year survival rate.

At first, Lizzie didn't want anyone to know except Wanda. They had to tell Michael what was going on, but they didn't inform Christopher or TJ. Dale let Lizzie dictate their course of action. She was scared and confounded like anyone would be, but she was also calm and focused—determined to live and not die.

Her faith level was so much higher than her husband's, and her attitude was amazing. She and Wanda were a great team. Neither one ever said a negative word. Wanda organized a prayer group that met regularly at the house and often accompanied them to the hospital. Cancer was the enemy. So they believed God and fought hard against it.

In contrast, Dale initially tried to distance himself from his emotions again, but it was much more difficult to do this time around. Suppressing his anger and fear was like trying to hold back a tidal wave. He quickly realized that even attempting to fight that way was a complete waste of time, something that frankly he simply couldn't afford to do. He needed to be present, which meant he felt everything.

Although intense at times, his own torment was secondary. He decided that the best approach wasn't to deny it or hide it; rather, he taught himself to manage it. If Lizzie could be strong, then he could too. If she needed to lean on him, he was determined to be there, standing straight and tall. In the end, that was what she needed most from him.

He read all the materials that Lizzie's oncologist gave him about how to care for a loved one with cancer. He really wanted to know what to expect. Serious psychological consequences could result if the caregivers do not give themselves the right to grieve. Admittedly, he didn't know how to express his fear and concern in a healthy manner. Complicating matters, he was having a hard time being confident that she would beat this thing, which meant he was guilt-ridden too.

Most of the time, Lizzie didn't look sick. Fortunately, the chemotherapy didn't cause her to lose her hair or to be too nauseous. The real issue was the pain. The thing that makes this disease so demonic in nature is that she had absolutely no symptoms before she was diagnosed. Once the disease had progressed to the point where it was difficult to treat was when the pain became intense. It was obvious that this attack on his wife was premeditated and calculated—the enemy had specifically singled her out. Dale believed that with all his heart.

Suddenly Lizzie was obsessed with Reverend Harris, who had been their pastor for about two years. He was a young man in his forties of average height with a slim build. Dale had only spoken to him a few times casually before all this happened. Reverend Harris had an attractive wife and a few cute little girls who wore their hair in long braids and looked alike. Prior to getting sick, Lizzie had never said anything much about him one way or the other.

Reverend Harris came to pray with her weekly. He brought with him the lifeline she badly needed, and she was always in a better place after they prayed together. He usually came with a couple of women from the church. Dale avoided praying with them if he could because it was hard for him to keep it together when he prayed.

One Saturday morning, Reverend Harris approached Dale, who was sitting alone in the kitchen while Lizzie met with the prayer team in the living room. The pastor was dressed in casual slacks and a long sleeve dress shirt with an open collar.

"So, brother, I meant to check in with you. How are you doing?" the pastor asked.

"Oh, I'm as good as I can be, you know," Dale mechanically replied.

"Mind if I have a seat?"

"No, of course not. Can I get you anything?" Dale inquired.

"No, no, I'm good, thank you," Reverend Harris said.

He sat down in one of the chairs across from Dale and was fidgeting in his seat.

Reverend Harris began, "Uh, I know how hard all of this must be on you and your family."

"We just want Lizzie to get better. Taking it one day at a time," Dale responded.

"Yes, I get it," the pastor sympathized. "It is really hard to watch someone you love suffer in any way. And in this case, it must be really hard. But she is a strong woman of faith. She knows God is on her side."

"But is he really?" Dale asked with almost no expression on his face. He shrugged his shoulders and raised his eyebrows in a manner that came across as much more disrespectful than he intended.

"What do you mean?" Reverend Harris questioned.

He sat straight up in his chair.

"Well, what do you mean when you say that God is on her side?" Dale baited.

"I mean just that he is our helper when we need him," the pastor pronounced.

"Is he planning to heal her?" Dale challenged. "Take the cancer away? Is that what you're telling me?"

"God is God. He moves as he sees fit," the minister explained. "Nobody can promise you a particular outcome because we cannot possibly know the plans and purposes of God." His tone was more forceful. He was clearly irritated.

"I'm not sure that's enough," Dale responded dryly.

Reverend Harris fired back, "What other choice do you have? We're supposed to worship God for who he is, not because of what he can do for us. God is not our genie in a bottle. He never promised that Christians wouldn't suffer here on earth. In fact, it's just the opposite. The Bible teaches that we will have many trials in this life."

"So, what's the point? Heaven?" Dale repositioned.

"Well, there is that, but no. I don't think that's it either," Reverend Harris defended. "I'll tell you how I've always chosen to look at it. To me, it's worth serving God even if there is no heaven simply because he is just that awesome! As a comparison, would you say it was worth loving your wife all this time even if she dies and leaves this earth prematurely?"

Dale didn't answer. He just looked at the pastor.

Reverend Harris continued, "Obviously, we believe that that won't happen and that she will be fully healed and delivered from this attack. But even if that doesn't happen, wasn't it still worth it? Loving her and having her in your life all these years, I mean. You tell me, is Lizzie worth it?"

Dale felt cornered. He wasn't sure exactly how to respond to what seemed to be a trick, like fool's gold. His silence revealed his shaky position.

Pastor Harris resumed, "I think that the same thing goes for God. He alone is supposed to be enough. He's the one who sent Jesus into the world to save us. He alone gave us life, and he is the reason we persist and keep on fighting—even against all odds."

"I'm sorry, but I want more from him. I want him to do something to help my wife. Is that so wrong?" Dale asked.

"No, that's not wrong," Reverend Harris conceded.

"That's the reason that I accepted Jesus in the first place, to make my life better," Dale articulated.

"I'm not sure that that's the best reason. How would you feel if your children only loved you because of the things that you could do for them? Tell me this, who would you rather serve, if not God?" the pastor asked theoretically.

"I don't know, maybe no one," Dale suggested.

"How is 'no one' better than God almighty?" the pastor inquired and paused for effect. "How is anyone or anything greater than our God?"

"I'm not saying that," Dale retreated.

"Brother, it's a mistake to let hurt and disappointment cloud our perception of who God is," Reverend Harris expounded.

"How can it not?" Dale asked defiantly. "I'm not sure anybody truly knows who God is."

"Maybe, but most people don't even know who they are either," the pastor asserted. "We were created to worship God, not to be fat and happy on this earth; it's not our actual home.

God's people must continue to love and trust him, even when we don't understand."

"With all due respect, that's easy for you to say," Dale argued.

"Actually, it isn't," Reverend Harris said solemnly. "I have had my fair share of pain and loss too. I've been through a lot that nobody knows about. No one is immune from getting hit below the belt, not even the men and women who preach the gospel. I'm just trying to encourage you to give God a little bit of credit. Maybe he knows what we can survive."

Dale had enough and quickly stood to his feet. He looked at the clock on the wall.

"Pastor, I'm sorry, but I have an appointment, and I have to run."

"Oh, I understand. I'm always available anytime you would like to talk," Reverend Harris offered.

"Thank you. I appreciate it."

Pastor Harris sprung to his feet, and the two men shook hands.

Dale hurried out the front door, leaving Reverend Harris alone in the house with Lizzie and her friends. He wasn't angry. He understood that the good reverend was just trying to help him, and he also suspected that Lizzie had orchestrated their impromptu meeting. He appreciated the fact that people were worried about him too. However, he didn't want to talk to anyone about what was going on inside his head. His preference was that all the focus be on Lizzie and easing her pain.

Ultimately, the exchange with Reverend Harris did very little to change his perspective or his disposition. It just made him feel more lost. He had no idea what to think and was working hard just to keep his head above water. The fact is that his doubts were real, and his faith was under attack. But he no longer cared about himself. Lizzie was the only one who mattered. At this point, she was his reason for breathing, not God.

Dale didn't lie, exactly. Although he didn't have a set appointment, he needed to pick up his mother's medication from the pharmacy. She always waited until she had taken the last pill before she called him. He hated that she expected him to drop everything and run her errands. But it was easier just to do it than to complain to her about it.

Regardless, the trip to the pharmacy today was a much-needed excuse to get away. He felt that he was losing the debate with the pastor. She was asleep on the couch when he arrived. It was 1:30 p.m. She woke up when he knocked on the door and was in the process of sitting up when walked in.

"Sorry, I didn't mean to wake you."

"It's okay. Are those my pills?" she inquired.

"Yes, this is your last refill, so you need to make an appointment with the doctor before you run out again."

"Okay."

"Do you need anything else?" he asked.

"No, I don't think so. How are you?"

"I'm good. Tired."

"You look tired. Is something wrong?"

"Everything is wrong," he said with a slight chuckle.

He felt like he was a teenager complaining to his mother about how much he hated his life.

"Did something happen? LaToya pressed. "How is Lizzie?"

"She's sick," Dale uttered.

"Sorry to hear. What's wrong?"

"She has cancer," Dale stated flatly.

"What kind of cancer?"

"Breast cancer. It's in her stomach too."

"Bad?" she wondered.

"Yes." He was downcast.

"Is she in the hospital?" LaToya explored.

"No, she is doing chemotherapy," he responded.

"How come you didn't tell me before?"

"She didn't want anyone to know," he explained.

"Well, I'm sure she will beat it. She's still young," LaToya encouraged.

"I'm scared," Dale blurted out before he knew it. Tears were pooling in his eyes.

"I know, but you're the strongest person I know," she stated emphatically.

"No, I'm not!" he shot back.

"Yes, you are!" she insisted. "If anybody can get through this, it's you." She sounded so confident that he was caught completely off guard.

"I don't think that's true," he committed. " I don't think that you understand how serious this is. Her doctor told me that the chances are against us."

"I don't care what no doctor says. I know you," she defended. .

"You're not hearing me. I'm not strong. I'm nobody," Dale stated calmly.

"A nobody? Is that what you think?" She looked baffled. "You can't mean that. Okay, just listen. I meant to tell you something, but I just never did before..."

Dale just looked at her and waited for her to speak.

"I saw what happened to you...at your wedding, I mean. I saw it."

"I'm sorry, but I don't know what you're talking about," he contended.

"I think you do...while you were standing up in front of everyone with Lizzie and the preacher. I saw what happened to you," she maintained.

"What exactly did you see?"

"Something I had never seen before," she recounted. "It was some kind of vision or something, I think. But it was real, you know. There was a strange light, and it shined down on you...only you, no one else... I saw it as clear as day...it was like, I don't know, like God was somehow there with you too... standing there. I saw it! And I saw you take to him too. You had a choice, and you said yes to him. That's how I know."

She was clearly choosing her words carefully as she reflected. But there was also an intensity in her expression and a meeting of the minds when their eyes met.

"You never said anything about it before," he positioned.

"But you know it's the truth, don't you? Tell me I'm lying. You know I'm not making it up."

"I don't know anything. How come you never said anything before?" he insisted.

She began scratching her scalp through the scarf on her head and hesitated for a moment. She was struggling with something.

"Um, honestly, I think I was a little jealous... I know that's a terrible thing to say, but I would have given anything for that to have been me standing there. I wasn't always like this, you know. My grandmother taught me to love God. But I turned my back on him because I got mad because of what happened to me and everything. I ended up cursing him."

"I still don't get what you're trying to say," he reacted.

"Don't make the same mistake I made," she implored. "You're one of the ones God really loves. Those of us who live in the dark can always see the light. Even if we don't want to, and we try to hide from it."

"Then tell me this, why would God let this happen to me? Without Lizzie, I will die too."

"None of the bad stuff that happens to us is God's fault," she argued. "Don't forget that there's evil in the world too. Believe me, I should know."

"But if he could have prevented it," Dale persisted. "I never would have imagined in a million years that this would be my life. I'm nothing but a broken mess. After...after this is over, I'm through—I mean it. I really do. I will have absolutely no reason for living, and I don't care what happens to me."

"You don't mean that. That's just the pain talking," she deflected. "You're a good man."

"I just feel like it would have been better if I was never born at all."

"Then I wouldn't have survived either. I would've died a long time ago," she stated.

Her words stunned him like a tackle to the midsection that he never saw coming. It nearly knocked the wind out of him.

There were tears in her eyes. He realized just then that he had never seen her cry—not even once. She took a few slow steps in his direction and stood directly in front of her son. With her right hand, she reached up and gently cupped his face just under his chin, which startled him at first, and he jumped back a little. But he caught himself and relaxed enough to let her lovingly caress him. Her touch was soothing, and he began to melt inside. His mouth was suddenly dry, and his upper body shook inside as he fought against the whirlwind of emotion taking hold of him.

"I know that you don't like me much, but you're the best thing that ever happened to me," she whispered.

"No, please don't say that. I can't handle any more. I'm sorry, but I just can't do this."

Like a punch-drunk prize fighter, he was dazed. The last thing he expected was a pep talk from his mother.

He had never mentioned to anyone what he experienced during his wedding—not even to Lizzie. And no one had ever told him that they saw anything peculiar. But he couldn't deny that his mother was on point. However, in his mind, he never had any reason to believe that God especially favored him. As far as he was concerned, God loves everyone the same. And other than Lizzie, there was no clear evidence in his life of added blessings.

He had to beg her off. She wanted to see Lizzie right away, but he needed to prepare his wife beforehand. She was genuinely worried about Lizzie, which was nice. She had always acted like the two of them were closer than they really were.

Dale was convinced, however, that she would not have shown the same level of concern if it had been one of his boys who were sick. She was never very interested in her grandchildren before Johanna, to whom she had spoken to once on the phone since their first meeting. She clearly struggled in her relationships with all males.

Dale had trouble sleeping that night. He kept tossing and turning. He hadn't thought about his wedding in years. After Lizzie was resting soundly, he got up and took their wedding album out of the closet. Although they hadn't done it in a while, they used to love to look through it from time to time and laugh and reminisce.

However, what stuck out now was that most of the closest people to him in the world were gone. There were several photos of Louis, one with him walking their mother down the aisle. Joe was in many photos, too, and there were even a few of Mr. Carbone laughing and sitting with his wife. And then there was Lizzie's mom looking beautiful.

When Dale looked at the photos of himself, all he saw now was a naïve boy who had no idea that there is such a thin line between happiness and heartache. Of course, Lizzie looked stunning in every photograph. He was being torn open bare with every image of her smiling back at him. It exposed a nerve, and the pain was deep. He felt like he was under attack.

Contrary to what his mother had said, however, there was no discernible aura about him that he could see in the photographs. God must have grown tired of him or forgotten about him. Perhaps his lot in life was to suffer the loss of everyone he ever held dear. If that was even partly true, then there was nothing he could ever do to change his destiny. Perhaps this late-night stroll down memory lane wasn't such a good idea after all.

Notwithstanding, by all accounts, an ongoing marriage of thirty-five years was something to be proud of. It seems that so many people today see marriage as anything but what it really is—a covenant with God. Promises made on earth have eternal consequences in heaven. Any strain on their marriage came from the everyday pressures of life, not from their commitment to each other lessening.

It was tough with their boys. There is no denying that. When children—especially adult children—struggle and disappoint, their parents must grieve the loss of their hopes and dreams for the future. He wasn't blaming his kids exactly, just reflecting honestly upon the impact of their failures and shortcomings.

But he and Lizzie always had each other to lean and depend upon, which was enough for him. They never fell out of love—like that was even a possibility. If anything, he loved her more now, maybe even too much. He would gladly take her place in this battle if he could. But his worst nightmare was coming true. Their fairytale was about to crash and burn. Now the one tangible proof he ever really had of God's love for him was being mercilessly ripped from his grip.

Chapter 26

Johanna kept her promise and visited them twice during her freshman year. The first time was at Thanksgiving, right after Lizzie was first diagnosed and before she had her surgery. They told her of Lizzie's illness when she came back up four months later during spring break. After the initial shock, she was terrific. She rolled up her sleeves and tended to Lizzie's every need like a pro. She had such a caring spirit and her being there gave Wanda a break from having to be there when Dale was at work. Needless to say, Michael was no help at all.

Dale was sitting in the living room one night after dinner alone, and Johanna brought him a cup of coffee.

"Oh, thank you. You didn't have to do that," Dale exclaimed.

"How are you doing, Uncle?"

"Um…I'm hanging in there. Is my wife asleep?"

"Yes, she is. Is there anything else I can do to help?"

"No, I don't think so, Dale responded. "But thanks for asking. I really appreciate it."

"What does the doctor say?" Johanna asked.

"She said that Lizzie is not responding to the treatment," Dale divulged. "The cancer is aggressive. We could participate in some clinical trials, but we aren't too keen on that idea."

"How long then?" Johanna asked.

"Six months," he recited calmly. "Maybe longer."

"I am so sorry," she whispered. "My heart is broken."

"I know..." he trailed off. "Hey, did you ever tell your mother that you met us?"

"Yes, I told her at Christmas."

"How did it go?" Dale wondered. "Was she angry?"

"Yes, she was hurt at first, I think," Johanna spoke and paused thoughtfully. "But I explained to her why I had to find you. I told her that you were a good and honorable man."

"Thank you," he said.

"She knows that she was wrong about you," Johanna stated. "She wanted me to tell you that she was sorry for the way she treated you on the phone and for not letting you know when my father died."

Dale didn't react initially. But he had no interest in holding a prolonged grudge against his brother's widow. He had learned his lesson.

"You tell your mother that I forgive her, and I'm glad that my brother had people in his life who loved him. Please tell her that for me," he requested.

Johanna was clearly moved by the gesture. She reached out and kissed him on the forehead.

"I will tell her. Thank you," she said.

"By the way, I think you would make a great doctor. You really would. You should definitely think about it," he urged.

"I will. Thank you."

When it came time for her to go back to school, she insisted on taking the train. He was saddened to see her go, but Lizzie was getting worse, and he didn't want Johanna to have to witness that kind of suffering so soon after her experience with her father's death. She was still so young. She wanted to come back every weekend and help, but he refused. He wanted her to focus on her studies.

Dale thought watching Lizzie give birth three times was hard, but nothing compared to watching her fight stomach cancer. She said it was a constant burning pain that varied in intensity. When it was bad, she often employed the Lamaze panting techniques that women in labor are trained to use. She always had a low tolerance for pain, which only exacerbated her present condition. He felt helpless because he fully accepted that he should be able to help her somehow as a man.

She was prescribed a pain management regimen that included opioids, but they didn't always work. Sometimes all he could do was rub her back as she lay balled up in a fetal position, and cry with her. There was no way to anticipate when it was going to be one of the bad days. They were on an emotional rollercoaster and were very much aware that the next rise and fall might be the last one before their ride ended.

Lizzie was admitted to the hospital several times for different reasons. Most recently, she had become anemic. She was also experiencing growing fatigue along with some nausea and bloating. She was never in the hospital more than two or three days at a time, but they both preferred outpatient treatment. For one thing, she rested better at home. Also, he didn't like to leave her if she was in the hospital, so he ended up sitting in her room all day. It was easier to do other things, like go to work part-time, when she was home.

He knew there would come a time when he would have to take a leave of absence from work, and he wasn't looking forward to that because work had become his only refuge. For at least a few hours, he could forget about his private hell and focus on something menial that was entirely within his control.

Dale hated that people felt sorry for him. He could see it in their eyes. There was always someone from the community dropping off a meal or a cake or something. Surprisingly, it helped him. It really did. But he dreaded the small talk. He never knew what to say, and neither did most people who came over. He learned that the trick was to keep it light and disguise his hurt as much as possible. His go-to was to ask visitors about their lives, their kids or jobs, or just talk about the weather. He got pretty good at it, too, as there were only a handful of instances when his tears betrayed him.

On one such visit, a little old lady from the church appeared at the front door who brought food. He didn't recognize her, although he pretended that he did. She appeared to be much older than his mother, although there was no way of knowing for certain. She wore a short, dark wig that looked more like a hat than natural hair. She said her name was Vernice Tyson, but everybody called her "Mama."

"I can't stay," she began. "My grandson is waiting for me out in the car, but I wanted to bring you this food I made for you. I got some fried chicken, some greens, macaroni salad, and banana pudding."

"Thank you, that's very kind," he said. "It smells wonderful."

She handed him two big brown bags. They were heavy, and he immediately placed them on a coffee table.

"I love banana pudding!" he said. "You didn't have to go to all that trouble."

"Yes, I did! I have been meaning to get over here but seems like something always kept getting in the way. How's your wife doing?"

"She's okay. She's fighting hard," he recited for probably the tenth time that week.

"Praise God! Such a beautiful woman. I used to think that every time I saw her at the church."

"Thank you," he stated. "Please keep us in your prayers. We really need it."

"I most surely will, sir!" she replied. "I lost my husband, Jimmie Lee, about ten years ago, and there's hardly a day that goes by when I don't think about him. I'm tellin' you the truth, not even a day. When he first had his heart attack, it nearly killed me too. We were so close that people used to say we looked like twins. I knew something was wrong the very second when it happened, and he wasn't even at home. I look back at it now, and I can see how God prepared me and how I got over."

"How did he do that...if you don't mind me asking?" Dale inquired timidly.

"No, I don't mind at all," she answered. "You know how the Bible says that our faith is tested by fire?"

"Yes, I do," he affirmed.

"Well, I know that I have almost been burnt up by the fire myself. I got scars on top of scars." She chuckled to herself, more than a little amused at her choice of expression.

269

"I'm not gonna lie," she continued. "When Trina, my oldest daughter, passed less than a year after my husband died, I was broken up bad. I could hardly breathe. I didn't want to live, and I prayed to God to take me too. I couldn't see at the time how he was perfecting me through the fire."

"Really?" he questioned. "Perfecting?"

"Even though our lives are tied to other people, we walk alone with God. I must say that I am both stronger and wiser now, and I know, as sure as I know my own name, that I couldn't have made it on my own. See, I know for myself now just how good God really is, and that is why I continue to speak his praises."

"Well, I can see you're a woman of strong faith like my wife," he said politely.

"What about your faith?" she asked directly. "You know that her faith can't save you."

"Yeah, I know," he acknowledged. "I am trying to walk it out day by day as best I can."

"That's a good thing you're doing there, brother," she exhorted. "I know it gets hard because our bodies get tired. I surely do. But God will never leave you to fend for yourself. I can promise you that."

"Thank you for saying that. It helps. And thank you for the food."

"You're very welcome. Let me know how you like the banana pudding. I think I put my foot in it if I say so myself."

Chapter 27

Time loses all meaning in periods of desperation. Dale noticed that for sure. He was having a hard time even remembering what day of the week it was. Once he was in his truck on his way to work when he realized that it was Saturday and the shop was closed. When he got there, he just sat there in the parking lot, looking out the window for about an hour.

Wanda had to keep reminding him about Lizzie's doctor appointments. They had missed a couple of them because he had simply forgotten about them. There were so many. He had taken over all of Lizzie's household duties and chores, and there was the added pressure of keeping the house clean because he never knew when someone was going to stop by. The takeaway was that he no longer trusted himself to remember where he was supposed to be at any given time.

However, there was one exception that was indelibly etched in his subconscious. Tomorrow was the one-year anniversary of Joe's death. He had called Tracy and asked if he could stop by. He told her that he had something he needed to give to her. She didn't ask any questions, but he was nervous about going there. He had kept all four letters in the original yellow envelope that Joe had given to him, and he had only removed the note that was addressed to him personally along with the life insurance policy.

His primary concern was that he didn't want to upset Tracy or her kids any more than they already have been. A voice from the grave is, without a doubt, unsettling to most people. As he was pulling into her driveway, he was praying that Joe knew what he was doing.

She looked different. She had lost a lot of weight, and it made her look older somehow. Her hair was much shorter than it was the last time that he saw her, which was the day of the funeral Mass. He didn't know whether to comment on it or not. He decided to play it safe and keep his observations about her appearance to himself.

"How is Lizzie?" she asked as she handed him the glass of water he requested. Then she sat down next to him on the living room sofa.

"She's okay," Dale recited. "She's a fighter. It's hard, you know."

"Yes, I do," she agreed and sighed heavily. "I'm so sorry; I wanted to stop by, but…I can't."

"No, I understand," he replied. "Oh, thank you for the fruit basket."

"You're welcome," Tracy said.

He took a big gulp of water.

"Well, I don't really know how to do this," he began slowly. "But I have something here for you from Joe."

"Joe?"

"Yes, he wanted me to wait a year and then give this to you."

He handed her the envelope.

"What is it?"

"They're letters for you and the kids."

"You're kidding!" she exclaimed.

"No, I'm not kidding," he responded softly.

"But I don't understand...why?"

She looked dismayed.

"I don't know," Dale spoke. "But he made me promise. It was very important to him."

She looked bewildered and stared at the envelope like it was a bomb set to explode any second.

"Well, I can't open this right now," she stated. "Only one of the kids is even in town and—"

"No, I know," Dale interrupted. "I wasn't expecting you to. I'm just the messenger. I'm sorry if this upsets you. I know Joe thought that these letters would help somehow. He loved you."

She appeared troubled, just as he had feared.

"Thank you," she whispered and exhaled loudly.

He stood up. He was uncomfortable and anxious to leave.

"You're welcome. It was nice seeing you again," he remarked.

She stood too, and he started to turn toward the door. She abruptly put her hand on his shoulder to stop him.

"Uh...Dale...excuse me...I know you're dealing with a lot now, and I certainly don't want to make things harder for you or say the wrong thing..."

"Not at all. What is it?" he asked.

"I just want to say that this has been the worst year of my life. I still wake up most mornings thinking that it is all just a terrible mistake and that my Joe is still here. I listen for the sound of him breathing next to me or singing in the shower. But I never hear it. It's not a dream, more like a nightmare. I miss him so much, and the thing that bothers me the most is… everything happened so fast that we didn't have time to even think, you know. I tell people that he just had a bad week and died. He was here one second and gone the next…just gone forever! I feel robbed! I got cheated out of the chance to say goodbye the way I wanted to, the way I needed to. I am glad Joe got the chance to write whatever he put in these letters… but what I'm trying to say is that my best advice is for you to make sure that you and Lizzie say everything to each other that you need to say face-to-face. Don't hold anything back. Time has value, and this time you have now is a gift, a special gift… especially for you…because you still have to live in this world without her. Please don't waste it feeling sorry for yourself. Trust me; there will be plenty of time for that later. If you do, you will regret it for the rest of your life!"

Dale could feel his heart pounding like it was about to come through his chest. He also could feel the Spirit of God moving within him. Most people don't get that God is a spirit and he doesn't live on the earth. He uses ordinary people to accomplish his purposes, and Dale heard the clear voice of God in every word she spoke. Moved with compassion for her and deep gratitude, he instinctively reached out and pulled her into his strong arms. She immediately went limp and began to sob.

"I'm so sorry," she said. "I didn't mean to do that. I really didn't. I'm still so emotional."

She was wiping her eyes and face with a tissue.

"Oh, please don't be sorry," he implored. "I want you to know that I heard everything you said, and I can't tell you how much this means to me."

"I'm glad," she breathed. "People like us need to stick together. This is a club that no one wants to be in."

"I've been so lost lately," he divulged. "And so mad at everything. Joe once told me that he thought I had an anger problem, but I wasn't listening."

"Oh, he's one to talk," she chimed in. "One time, he actually flipped the dinner table over because he got mad at some football player who dropped the ball or something. Food flew everywhere, including all over the baby, who screamed bloody murder. My parents were mortified. Don't imagine that he ever told you about that."

"No, I'm sure it just slipped his mind," Dale said.

"Yeah, right, what a goof!" Tracy kidded.

They laughed.

"Hey, Dale, you know you can call me any time, right?" she probed. "I just feel so bad."

"Yes, I know. Thank you for everything."

"Oh, no problem, and thank you too…You know what he used to say about you, don't you?" she asked.

"No, what?"

He would say that he liked talking to you about things because you're holy," she revealed.

"Holy? Really?" Dale reacted. "I can't imagine why he said that."

"Because you go to church even when it isn't Christmas or Easter," she explained.

"Oh, that's crazy," Dale said while shaking his head.

He left her house with renewed purpose. In the end, it was just a minor shift in perspective, but, nevertheless, it made all the difference. The things everyone else had been saying to him, although all true, simply didn't resonate with him; it was too much too soon. He just kept thinking that no one really understood him. He felt that he was different from them, that his hurt was deeper and superior to their hurts.

However, when Tracy spoke, it was like the blindfold had been removed from his eyes, and he could suddenly see what had always been there. He knew all along that he was missing something but just couldn't figure it out. Now it was abundantly clear that he had been short-sighted—and that closedmindedness was hurting them both. The bottom line was that it wasn't just about what was good for Lizzie because he mattered too, and while she was about to be set free, his life sentence was to live on with only the memory of her.

Even recognizing that this unexpected epiphany had great value for him, it still didn't mean he suddenly accepted everything that was happening to his wife or the ravaging of his heart. He just needed to appreciate whatever time they had left. He wasn't perfect—not even close. He never said he was. In the end, he was just a man in love with a woman.

Chapter 28

Dale used to tell Lizzie almost everything. He liked to save up things in his head that happened during the day to share with her later when he got home. But he didn't do that anymore. He couldn't. Now they mostly talked about her daily routine and how she felt.

She knew he was struggling, and he never tried to hide that fact from her. She was always very sensitive to his pain, and she witnessed him get emotional several times. But the cancer also changed the way that they related to one another, both physically and emotionally. He started to grasp that this was just the beginning of a whole new world for him, one he never imagined that he would ever experience.

To add insult to injury, his back started bothering him again. It was getting harder to sleep at night. While it was better when he slept sitting up in the recliner in the living room, he didn't like leaving Lizzie alone in the bedroom all night. He didn't trust that she could or would call out if she needed something. He eventually made an appointment with a chiropractor and started seeing him weekly. He discovered that he was carrying a lot of stress in his back. The treatments seemed to help some, but now his back was always a little stiff and sore.

The strain was getting to Wanda too. She developed a painful rash on her neck and back, covering her right shoulderblade. She was diagnosed with shingles, which meant she was contagious and couldn't be around Lizzie, whose immune system was already severely compromised. Dale felt bad for her because she was completely devoted to her sister's care, and this development was very hard on her. He tried to reassure her that he was on top of things, but deep inside, he didn't believe it. He felt like he was living in a house that was falling down with a leaky roof, and it was pouring rain.

However, all things considered, the next few months weren't that bad. He changed his hours at the garage so he could keep working. He also insisted that Michael, who was working the three to eleven p.m. shift at the convenience store, assist his mother in the mornings. Michael didn't really have to do anything but be there. Some of the women from the church assisted with Lizzie's personal care, and she seemed to be feeling a little better. She could do a lot more for herself and spoke to Wanda every day on the phone.

Right on cue, TJ had another involuntary admission at the psychiatric center. Dale explained the situation involving Lizzie to the counselor, who called him from the hospital, and he asked whether it made sense to let TJ know what was going on at home. The counselor advised against it, suggesting that he wait until TJ was stabilized. But she did agree that he needed to be told, and kindly offered to help with that at the right time.

***

Daniel appeared at the front door early one afternoon without any notice beforehand. He was wearing a business suit and was perfectly groomed. He had a light beard that appeared to have been professionally trimmed. Even with the beard, he looked a lot like Lizzie. Dale was surprised to see him since they hadn't heard from him in months. Lizzie had called him before she had her surgery, so he knew all about it.

"I hope it's okay, me just dropping by like this," Daniel apologized.

"Yeah, of course," Dale replied. "C'mon in. Lizzie is going to be excited to see you."

"Well, I had to come up for a conference in Albany, and I just thought that I would swing by this way," Daniel explained.

"I'm glad you did," Dale replied.

"How is she doing?" Daniel asked in a hushed tone.

"I'm not gonna lie, it's been rough," Dale acknowledged. "But you know your sister; she's a fighter."

"Yeah, I know," Daniel agreed.

"So, how are you?" Dale asked. "How's everything going with the job?"

"Good. Really good. I work a lot of hours, but I can't complain, you know. Advertising is a pressure-driven business."

"Well, I'm glad it's working out for you," Dale replied. "Do you know about Wanda getting shingles?"

"Yes, yes I do," Daniel answered.

"Are you planning to stop by and see her too, since you happen to be in town?"

"I don't know. Maybe. I'm supposed to be at the conference right now, but I slipped away," Daniel explained.

Dale hesitated only slightly. He was considering whether to speak up and say what was on his mind. True to form, he opted to go for it.

"Look, I am not trying to start anything, but I have been meaning to ask you something," Dale began. "Did we do something to offend you?"

Daniel was clearly caught off guard by the question. He had a puzzled look on his face.

"I don't know what you mean," he said.

Undeterred, Dale continued, "It's just that Lizzie has been sick with terminal cancer for over a year now, and you don't come to see her even once. This is the first time, and you live less than three hours away. And your only other sister is flat on her back with shingles, and you can't be bothered to go see about her when you happen to be in town."

"Dale, I don't think that's fair," Daniel protested. "There is more to it than that."

"Right, that's what I thought," Dale prodded. "That is why I am bringing it up. Would it be possible for you to explain it to me so I can understand? Because I really want to."

"It has nothing to do with you," Daniel deflected.

"Oh, see there, I disagree!" Dale refuted. "It has everything to do with me. In case you've forgotten, that's my wife up there fighting for her life. She loves you with all of her heart, and you should have been here helping to make things easier for her. But for some reason, you intentionally decided that you don't want to do that. I am asking you, man to man, to tell me why."

"It's complicated! Besides, I'm not a damn nurse!" Daniel resisted.

Dale was incensed, and he had to fight to keep his voice down. The last thing that he wanted was for Lizzie to hear him.

"That's really your answer?" Dale mocked. "You're not a nurse? That's all you got? Thanks so much for clearing that up. I stand corrected."

"Please, I don't want to do this," Daniel pleaded. "Look, I'm sorry. I know how it looks, but can we just please not do this now?"

"Sure thing," Dale derided. "Just let me know when you do want to do it. I wouldn't want to trouble you too much. I know how busy you are. For the life of me, I have no idea how you sleep at night. Honest to God!... Excuse me; I will tell Lizzie that you're here."

Dale headed up the stairs. What he really wanted to do was to grab Daniel by his ears and shake some sense into him. Lizzie was in the master bathroom. He told her through the door that Daniel was downstairs. He tried to sound normal. In response, she sounded surprised and thrilled. It didn't appear that she had heard them arguing.

Dale sat down on the bed and waited for her to come out. He had no desire to go back down and talk to Daniel. Besides, he knew Lizzie would sense the tension in the air and be upset at him for saying anything. Both Lizzie and Wanda treated Daniel like he was still twelve years old. Dale couldn't bear to watch it, not today.

He heard Michael's voice downstairs and assumed that he was talking to his uncle. Lizzie looked good when she opened the bathroom door. She had put on a little bit of makeup and combed her hair. She made her way downstairs. Dale stayed put.

281

The visit lasted about an hour, which was probably fifty minutes longer than Daniel had intended. Dale went down only after Lizzie called out to him, presumably to say goodbye.

"Daniel needs to run," she said. "He wants to go by and check on Wanda."

"That's good," Dale said.

He glanced quickly at Daniel, who averted his eyes.

"Dale, do you want to send any of that food that is in the kitchen over to Wanda?" Lizzie wondered. "We're not going to eat all of it. It doesn't make sense to let it go to waste."

"No, I'll call over there later and see if they need anything," Dale responded.

"Well, it's so good to see you, Danny," she said enthusiastically. "You gotta come back soon. I really miss you."

She leaned into him, and they had a long embrace.

"I will, I promise," Daniel said. "Please let me know if there is anything I can do to help out."

"Okay, you know I love you," she proclaimed.

"I love you too, sissy," Daniel replied. "Goodbye, Dale."

He never looked directly at his brother-in-law.

"Take care of yourself," Dale managed to say.

They stood at the door and watched Daniel get into a late model BMW. Lizzie waved goodbye as he pulled away. There were tears in her eyes. Dale was still angry. He loved Daniel too, but there was something wrong with him. Whatever rapport that they once had was gone now. The guy was a stranger.

"And so?" Dale asked as he closed the door.

"Pretty sure he's gay."

"Did you ask him?"

"No"

"Why not."

"What difference does it make?"

"It doesn't excuse his behavior."

"I know it doesn't."

"Then what did you talk about?"

"Mostly his job in New York…minus everything personal, especially his love life."

"I don't understand why you would let him get away with that," Dale resisted.

"That's because you never really understood Daniel," she maintained.

"You're right about that," Dale defended. "You don't understand him either."

"Yes, I do! He is very tenderhearted," she explained. "He doesn't know how to fight for his place in this world."

"Tenderhearted?" Dale questioned. "You're kidding?"

"Look, I promised myself that the next time I saw him I would make sure I told him how much I love him. And I did that. So, now I'm good."

She had a satisfied look on her face that, although good to see, he couldn't comprehend the source of her contentment.

"I'm sorry, but I don't understand a black man who doesn't know how to fight," Dale countered. "Maybe, if you cleared the air, he can stop hiding and find some peace. Did you ever think about that?"

"He is at peace when he is hiding," she argued. "Please don't ever tell him that I suspected."

She looked him squarely in the eye. He knew her well enough to know by her tone that she meant it.

"I won't," he promised and shrugged his shoulders.

Chapter 29

Dale had mixed feelings, but he knew he was doing the right thing. This winter had been particularly harsh with heavy snowfalls and record cold temperatures. He would have put this trip off indefinitely if possible. The roads were snow-covered and slippery, and visibility was poor.

However, Lizzie's condition worsened considerably just before Christmas. She was now in excruciating pain most of the time, and the medication that she was taking mainly made her drowsy. She was confined to bed now and slept most of the time. She was also having problems swallowing, which meant that she had no appetite. She looked thin and frail.

Mid-State Correctional Facility is a medium-security level prison in Marcy, New York. It should have taken Dale less than two hours to drive there from home. This Saturday, it took him four hours from door to door. Christopher had just recently been transferred there.

The state preferred to move inmates frequently. Dale had called Christopher's counselor to be put on his approved visitor's list because he was a first-time visitor. It took a while to get inside because he had to be "processed," which required him to complete paperwork, stand in a slow-moving line, and submit to a body search.

Eventually, he was led into a huge room that looked like a school cafeteria. There were tables arranged throughout, and inmates dressed in identical dark-green uniforms were sitting at individual tables. It only took a couple of seconds before he spied Christopher sitting in the middle of the room. Dale put his head down and walked intently in his son's direction. When he reached his destination, he sat down.

"Hi, Daddy," Christopher said.

He looked better than Dale thought that he would. He clearly had been working out, and his biceps protruded from his short-sleeve shirt and were well defined. Dale was seated in the chair directly across from his son.

"Hi, how are you?"

"I'm good. Did something happen to mom?"

"Yes, she's sick," Dale said.

"What's wrong with her," Christopher asked.

"She has cancer," Dale stated.

Christopher's eyes got big.

"What kind of cancer? Is she in the hospital?" he inquired.

"No, she was diagnosed with breast cancer, and now it has spread to her stomach."

"Oh, how she's doing?"

"Not good."

"But she's gonna be okay, right?" Christopher asked in earnest.

He appealed with his eyes how he used to when he was five years old, asking his dad if they could go to the park and throw the football.

Dale could only shake his head.

"I don't think so," he whispered finally.

Christopher erupted, "What do you mean? Don't say that… please don't say that! Can't they do a transplant or something? There must be something that they can do."

"I'm sorry, Christopher."

"Daddy, please…," Christopher begged. "You gotta do something." He covered his face with both of his hands and began to sob with all his might. The people at the other tables were staring. A corrections officer immediately walked up to their table and asked if everything was alright. Dale just nodded, and the officer turned and slowly walked away.

Dale didn't know what to do. There were signs on the wall that prohibited physical contact, among other things. He knew that their firstborn would be upset, but he was hoping that Christopher didn't completely fall apart.

"Christopher! Christopher!" Dale eventually called out under his breath.

When Christopher didn't look up, Dale decided just to sit and wait for him to regain his composure. It took several minutes.

"Christopher, I need you to listen to me," Dale directed. "I know it's hard, but your mother knows I'm here. We wanted you to hear about this from us. Is there anything that you want me to tell her from you?"

"I don't know what to say…" Christopher trailed off and started rubbing the top of his head. He wept without restraint.

"Yes, you do, "Dale spoke firmly. "Think about how she must feel. She is too sick to come here and see you herself.

This is much harder for her than it is for us, and it could be your last chance to say anything to her. What do you want me to tell her?"

Christopher lifted his head. His face was covered in tears, and his nose was running. Dale reached in his pocket, took out a tissue, and handed it to him.

"Um...tell her that I'm sorry I wasn't a better son," Christopher cried. "Tell her I'm gonna change. I promise. Tell her thank you from me for loving me."

"I will. I'll tell her, man."

"I can't believe this is happening," Christopher cried. "Why is this happening?"

"I don't know," Dale voiced.

"How are you, Daddy?"

"Me? Honestly, I just force myself to keep moving."

"You're a great husband to her, you know. I tell everybody about you guys."

"Thank you for saying that."

"You were a great father too."

"I don't know," Dale admitted. He wasn't expecting the compliment.

"It's true," Christopher contended. "It's not your fault the way I turned out."

"What happened to you? How did we get here, Christopher?" Dale solicited.

"I was stupid and didn't listen to anybody," Christopher vented. "I'm an addict. I know that now. That didn't just happen to me. It was the choices I made."

Dale wasn't impressed by his son's revelation. There was way too much water under the bridge for him to be easily taken in by this show of honesty. Christopher's words couldn't be trusted.

"That sounds like something people say when they are in prison and then forget as soon as they get out," Dale responded dryly.

"Maybe, but, Daddy, everybody can't be like you."

"Why not? There's nothing special about me," Dale argued.

"That sounds like something people say when they don't know how good they are at something," Christopher responded using the same tone that his father had just used.

"I don't know anything about that, but I will never apologize for wanting you and your brothers to be better than you are," Dale countered. "All your mother and I ever wanted was for you to stand up and be a man."

"You act like it's easy being your son. What if this is all you ever get from us? What if we can't do better because we don't have the right stuff like everybody else?" Christopher unloaded.

"If you really believe that, then that is where I failed you," Dale spoke. "That's probably one of the worst things any son can say to a parent."

"Why? Maybe you just expect too much from us. Why can't you just accept us the way we are? I admit that I have made a lot of mistakes, but nobody's perfect," Christopher argued.

Dale grimaced. Christopher's words cut through him like a dull knife. They hurt more than the pain that was now shooting down his lower back, buttocks, and legs. The chair that he was sitting in was garbage. He didn't respond to Christopher immediately. Rather, he searched his heart for the right words to say. He didn't come all this way to tear down his son. He forced himself to sit up straight, reached across the table, and placed his right hand on Christopher's lower arm.

"I sit by your mother's bed sometimes and watch her sleep," he reflected. "She's in so much pain. Even in her sleep, I can hear her bearing down against it. It breaks my heart in a way I didn't even know was possible. And there's absolutely nothing that I can do to help her...but she's fighting with everything she has for just one more day, for just one more breath. I couldn't be prouder of her. You would be, too, if you saw her. But the truth is that I've never seen you show anything near the toughness she has shown. I'm talking about fighting with all that is within you. Christopher, I know that addiction is a disease, just like cancer is a disease. But God loves best the men who resist the enemy. The ones who simply refuse to stay down. So, it doesn't matter what happens as long as you fight like hell to the end. I feel like I didn't teach you boys that, and I blame myself more than I blame you."

"I'm sorry, Daddy," Christopher cried. "I want to do better. I really do. I want you to be proud of me."

When Dale looked at his son, he could see himself in Christopher's features. It was like looking into a mirror thirty years ago. Tears rolled down Christopher's face again, and Dale could feel his massive aching need. In truth, their overriding inner struggle was the same. Neither man ever felt like he measured up. His hope was always that his sons would be better than him in that area. Unfortunately, all hope was failing.

"I know. Me too. I'm sorry too." Dale declared and rubbed his son's forearm.

He couldn't wait to get out of there. Being in a prison is much worse than being in a hospital. It was more like being on a modern-day plantation, minus the cotton. Most of the men who were dressed in green sitting in this capacity-filled room were black and brown men. Undoubtedly, the natural by-product of being in a place like this was having the life sucked out of you, along with your identity and self-esteem. All men were created in God's image to have the freedom of choice and movement. If Christopher really meant all the things that he said about wanting to change, then his journey back home would be a difficult one.

Dale almost didn't survive the drive home. By the time he had completed his two-hour visit with Christopher, his back was throbbing and screaming like a banshee. As soon as he got to his truck, he took two of his muscle relaxers. He had to sit perfectly straight, or else he was hit with a painful spasm like a lightning bolt. At least the weather had cleared up a bit, and the roads were freshly plowed. He managed to make it home in less than three hours, but he was in agony.

Lizzie was awake when he walked in. She was sitting up in bed, and the aide they just hired was sitting with her. Her name was Lisa, and she seemed very nice. She was a middle-aged woman with rough hands but a kind heart. She arranged to have a hospital bed delivered, and they had set Lizzie up in the living room to limit the trips up and down the stairs.

Lizzie smiled when she saw him, and he leaned over and kissed her on the lips. She didn't appear to be in any pain. He took a sigh of relief.

"How are you feeling?" Dale asked.

"I'm okay," she said. "You okay?"

"I'm good," he replied. "Did you eat something today?"

Lizzie nodded her head.

"Yes, she did," Lisa spoke up. "She ate most of her oatmeal for breakfast, and for lunch, we had a little soup and a fruit cup."

"There you go," Dale encouraged. "I need to eat something myself, but first, I'm going to go up and take a shower. I will be back down to sit with you after. Okay?"

"Yes," Lizzie said.

Dale hobbled up the stairs, stripped down, turned on the water in the shower, and stepped inside. The full force of the hot water pounding against his back felt like heaven. He closed his eyes and let out a deep groan that the neighbors across the street probably heard. His mind immediately began to replay the events from the day. He was troubled in his spirit and allowed himself a brief cry. He figured that he must have needed the release of tension because he didn't shed a single tear during his visit with Christopher or the painful drive home. He was hungry and tired, and he felt internally drained.

Lizzie was sleeping soundly when he came down, which meant that he would eat his dinner now. He could hear Lisa from the kitchen if Lizzie woke up and they needed something. The hospital bed was a good idea because everything was easier when she was sitting up. He typically slept the same way she did, sitting up in his recliner, which he had placed in the corner of the room facing her. But his sleep was anything but restful because he had pretty much trained himself to wake up every time she moved.

"Dale, is there anything else I can do for you before I leave?" Lisa asked from the doorway.

"When was the last time she took something for pain?" he wondered.

"Not since this morning, "Lisa reported. "She hasn't complained about any pain, but she's probably due. I left everything on the coffee table for you."

"Okay, thanks," he replied.

"I'll be back in the morning. Make sure you get some rest too. It's important for you to keep your strength up, too, you know," Lisa lectured.

"Yes, ma'am. I'm going to warm up a little something to eat now and then settle in for the night. Drive carefully; the roads are very slick in spots," he warned.

"Okay, thanks. See you in the morning. Oh, by the way… it helps if you rub her throat a little when she eats. It helps her to swallow better."

"Okay, I'll try that. Thanks."

"Good night."

"Thank you. Have a good evening," Dale said.

The refrigerator needed to be cleaned out. It was stuffed with old food that should have been thrown out days ago. He'd been meaning to get to it but never found the time. Wanda used to help him with that kind of stuff, but she didn't come over as much as before. She preferred to just talk to Lizzie on the phone when she was up to it. Dale understood. Wanda owed it to both herself and her family to make her own wellbeing a priority.

He decided to make himself a sandwich. There was plenty of lunch meat and cheese, and he didn't have to dig through stuff to get them. He was just sitting down to eat it when he heard the front door open. It was Michael. He peeked his head into the kitchen.

"Hi, Daddy."

"Hi, how is the weather?" Dale asked.

"Not bad," Michael replied. "It's just cold."

"Can you shovel off the front steps before you go upstairs? My back is bothering me pretty good right now."

Michael made a face, but he thought better of saying what he was thinking.

"I'll do it in a minute, okay?" he asked.

"Just don't forget and don't wake your mother," Dale directed.

Michael took off up the stairs. Dale could hear him walking around. The house was old, and the wooden floors creaked. It turned out to be the perfect place to raise his family. The neighborhood was quiet, and they never had any problems there. It had felt like home from the very first day they had moved in, and he knew Lizzie always loved it there. But he wasn't sure if he wanted to keep it. It was full of memories— and not all of them were good. Maybe if he sold it, he could use that as the stepping-stone to getting Michael into his own place.

Despite his instruction, there was a loud scraping sound coming from the front porch as Michael pushed the snow off it. Dale got up and checked on Lizzie, who apparently wasn't bothered by the noise and was still asleep. Dale was making himself another sandwich when Michael came back in.

"I thought I told you to keep in down," Dale said.

"I tried to," Michael contended.

"Well, try harder next time!" Dale commanded. "What are you doing now?"

"Nothing."

"Come in here; I want to talk to you," Dale ordered.

"About what?" Michael questioned.

"You want a sandwich?" Dale asked.

"No, I already ate," Michael responded.

"Please sit down," Dale said.

Michael threw his body in one of the chairs at the kitchen table. It was clear that he didn't want to be there. Dale chose to ignore the small protest coming from Lizzie's baby boy and finished making his sandwich.

"What did I do now?" Michael wondered.

"Nothing, I just want to talk to you," Dale indicated. "Is that too much to ask?"

"I just don't want to get yelled at," Michael explained.

"Boy, please. When do I ever yell at you?"

"All the time," Michael offered. "You yell at everybody."

"That's not true," Dale contested.

"I heard you yelling at Uncle Daniel. He probably thinks you hate him."

"I don't hate Daniel, and I also don't care what he thinks," Dale explained calmly. "This is my house. I can say whatever I want in my house."

Michael rolled his eyes and moped. Dale poured himself a cup of coffee and sat down across from him.

"I saw Christopher today," Dale said.

Michael just shrugged his shoulders.

"You don't care. He said hello," Dale exaggerated.

Still no acknowledgment came from Michael as his expression didn't change.

"Alright, I was just wondering how you're doing with all that's going on with your mother," Dale remarked. "You haven't said anything."

"I don't know what you mean," Michael said. "What do you want me to say?"

"I mean, we're losing her. You know that. You must have some thoughts." Dale questioned.

"I feel bad, of course," Michael said defensively.

"Well, have you told her that?" Dale asked.

"No."

"Why not?" Dale interrogated.

Michael diverted his eyes and squirmed in his seat.

Dale was getting frustrated. This was a conversation one would expect to have with a teenager. Michael had a way of making his father feel like everything he said or suggested was outright ridiculous.

"Look, I'm not telling you want to do or think," Dale unloaded. "But you're not a child; you know what all of this means. I thought that maybe there was something that you might want to say to your mother now. I know that you love her. Just tell her that. I am sure that she would love to hear that from you."

"Did she say something?" Michael wondered.

"No, but she shouldn't have to, should she?" Dale presented. "She ran around this house taking care of you and your brothers for all these years. It's time for you to stand up. She gave you kids everything she had. Christopher and TJ aren't here. But you are, and you need to take advantage of this opportunity before it's too late."

"Do you mean now?" Michael asked. "I don't know what to say."

"No, not this very minute. You don't have to say it perfect. Just tell your mother what she means to you."

"Okay," Michael agreed.

"But if I were you, I wouldn't wait too long," Dale warned. "Just talk to her from your heart. You can do it. I know you can. I promise you won't regret it."

"Okay...can I go now?" Michael asked.

"Yes," Dale uttered and put his head down to eat.

He figured that it was worth a shot with Michael. The truth is that he wasn't at all sure Michael could do it. Other than recognizing Michael's shortcomings, they had no clue why Michael was stuck emotionally at puberty. He clearly struggled to feel empathy for others, so what his mother was going through must be difficult for him to process. She was always his anchor.

They should have pushed for a proper evaluation through the school district long before he graduated from high school. To her credit, Lizzie once stated at a parent-teacher conference that there was something developmentally wrong with Michael. In response, they pointed to his test scores as being indicative of the fact that he was in the average range. Dale was convinced they had all missed something there.

Lizzie was awake. She needed to go to the bathroom and didn't want to use the bedpan. She probably could have walked, but he didn't want her to fall, so he carried her to the bathroom. Afterward, he gave her a sponge bath and gently rubbed baby oil over her body, including into the folds of skin on her chest area that had become darkened in places. He then changed her gown and her bedding. She was alert and more like herself than she had been in a couple of days. There were fewer of these moments lately. She barely ate anything, but he got her to drink enough to get her pain medication down. This was a good day.

"Did you see Christopher?" she asked.

"Yes, I saw him."

"How was he?"

"He looked good," Dale volunteered.

"How did he react when you told him?" she investigated further.

"You know Christopher," Dale said. "He was pretty emotional."

"Hmm," she sounded. She closed her eyes tight and put her head back on the pillow.

"He wanted me to tell you that he loves you, and he wishes he was a better son." Dale recited.

Her eyes shot open. "He really said that?" she asked.

She stared at her husband. He could still see remnants of the magic that used to dance in her eyes.

"Yes, he did," Dale responded measuredly.

"Poor thing," she commiserated. She looked apprehensive.

"He also wanted you to know that he has changed and that he will be different when he gets out," Dale continued. "He wants you to be proud of him."

"That's nice. He always did know what to say," she told herself.

298

Ed Thompson

"No, he doesn't," Dale resisted.

"Maybe not, but what he said was nice."

"Yes, it was good, and I know he meant it," he conceded. "I think that maybe he is finally starting to grow up a little."

"I am so happy to hear that. Thank you for going to see him. I know it was hard for you," she noted.

"It wasn't as bad as I thought," Dale related. "I think that... we probably needed to talk."

"See, I told you," she contended. "You liked seeing him."

"Yes, and I also really enjoyed getting felt up by a fat corrections officer, although I must say that his touch was surprisingly tender."

She giggled, making his heart dance.

"Don't make me laugh; it hurts," she insisted.

He reached out and gave her a peck on the side of her face.

"Oh, and Christopher also told me to tell you thank you for loving him," he whispered.

She gasped and put both hands over her heart. Her eyes filled with tears.

And his heart stopped.

Chapter 30

Dale took a seat in an orange plastic chair in the small lobby area as he had been directed. He realized it was broken upon sitting, so he stood and waited for TJ to come down. This was the address the counselor had given him, and he was hoping that TJ still resided here. It was on Lark Street in downtown Albany, and there was no parking, so he had to find a spot on the street.

At least the roads had been plowed, and this was a much shorter drive than the one he took yesterday to the prison to visit Christopher. He was very concerned about his back, too, because it bothered him all night. His appointment with the chiropractor wasn't until the day after tomorrow.

He had been standing there for almost ten minutes when TJ appeared. Dale was immediately relieved because he wasn't looking forward to driving around Albany trying to find him.

"Hi," TJ said.

He looked like he had been sleeping. It was readily apparent that his personal hygiene hadn't improved much.

"Hi, TJ; how are you?"

"I'm good. What's going on?"

"I need to talk to you," Dale said.

"Okay, we can talk over here."

TJ led his father around the corner to an open space that Dale would never have guessed was there. No one else was present, and there were several wooden folding chairs scattered around the room. However, they remained standing.

"What's going on? Is something wrong?" TJ questioned.

"Yes, your mother is very sick," Dale stated. "She has cancer."

"Oh. Is she going to be okay?" TJ asked.

"Probably not," Dale articulated. "I'm sorry."

"So, she's gonna die?" TJ asked in disbelief. "Is that what you're telling me?"

"Yes, that is what I am saying."

TJ's eyes filled with tears.

"When?" he demanded. "How long does she have?"

"The doctor says not long," Dale reported.

"Not long? Like any day now?" TJ grilled.

"I'm sorry," Dale replied.

"I can't believe this! Are you kidding me? This is crazy," TJ emoted.

He dropped his head and started taking deep breaths, fighting his emotions. Dale felt for his son, but he was at a complete loss of how to console him. He had considered bringing the counselor with him today, but he wasn't sure what she could do. There was a chance that this news could trigger an episode of some kind; however, it was doubtful that having somebody there would make a difference. Dale knew from experience that it was impossible to predict how TJ would react or to reason with him after he did. Dale had said a quick prayer in the truck on the ride over.

"Are you interested in seeing her?" Dale offered. "I could bring you to see her and bring you right back here. You wouldn't have to stay long. But it's up to you. No pressure."

"She's in the hospital?" TJ asked.

"No, she's home," Dale responded. "There isn't anything more they can do for her in the hospital."

TJ looked lost. He was thinking and suddenly appeared desperate. Dale was now completely on edge.

"Daddy, if I give you something, do you think you could give it to Mom for me?" he asked.

"Yes, I can give it to her," Dale committed.

"Okay, can you wait here? It's in my room. I have to go get it."

"No problem. I'll wait here," Dale replied.

"Okay, I'll be right back."

TJ turned and scurried away. Dale sat down in one of the folding chairs. It was very uncomfortable. There was a chill in the air. He could tell that this old building didn't have good insulation. There was also a stale smell, like an old warehouse or something. The only sounds were of the traffic outside and the wind hitting against the windows. Hopefully, this was the last time he had to be the bearer of this news. He was beginning to think of himself as some kind of messenger for the angel of death.

He was especially tired of having to endure the look of shock and devastation that appeared on people's faces when they first heard about Lizzie's condition. He always felt responsible, like he was reporting his own failure as her husband. Each recitation took a little more out of him. Now he was literally scraping the bottom of the barrel to even get the words out.

TJ suddenly reappeared and rudely interrupted Dale's dip in the pool of self-pity. He was carrying a large, white cardboard box that originally contained a coffee maker. It was opened at the top, and something was sticking out.

"Can you give her this?" he asked.

"Yeah, sure. What is it?" Dale wondered.

"It a silk flower arrangement I made," TJ explained. "I'll help you carry it to the truck. The vase is glass."

"Okay, that'll work." Dale stammered.

They walked the few blocks to Dale's truck in silence. It was cold, and TJ wasn't wearing a coat. Dale opened the back door, and TJ put the box on the floor behind the passenger's seat.

"You got another new truck?" TJ asked.

"I got it last year."

"It's nice."

"You need to get back inside before you get sick," Dale spoke. "This wind goes right through you."

"Okay."

"TJ, your mom wanted me to tell you that she loves you," Dale conveyed.

"Tell her I love her too," TJ professed.

"Okay," Dale promised. "Take care of yourself."

"Daddy, um…thank you for coming to tell me…and for taking care of my mom…You know I would help you if I could, right?" he declared.

He looked completely disheartened.

Dale reached out and grabbed TJ by the back of the head and squeezed his neck the way he used to do when the boys were young. But this time, there was no squeal of delight from his son. He quickly turned and got in the truck. He waved goodbye as he pulled away.

After leaving TJ, Dale drove directly to his mother's place. She had called him just before he left home that morning. She wanted him to come get her. She had been coming over about twice a week for the last few months. Surprisingly, she was a big help when she was there. She didn't want to just sit around, and she insisted upon being put to work. There was no task beneath her, and she was devoted to Lizzie. She also seemed to get along nicely with Lisa. Dale was very appreciative of everything that she did for them.

He had put the word out that Lizzie was no longer receiving visitors at home. It was just too hard for her to get through visits now. Most people were uncomfortable being there anyway. Of course, that pronouncement didn't apply to the pastor or the prayer team, who usually came in the early afternoon. But they never stayed for more than twenty or thirty minutes.

Lizzie was asleep when Dale arrived home with his mother at 1:15 p.m. Only Lisa was there. Michael was already gone. Dale announced that he had a headache and that he was going to take a nap. His back was bothering him again.

He fell into a deep sleep as soon as his head hit the pillow and had a dream that he was being chased by a man dressed in black clothing whose face he couldn't see. In the dream, he was terrified and running with all his might. He could feel that the enemy was gaining ground, and he tripped and fell into a ditch. He was struggling hard to get up off the ground when he woke up suddenly. His heart was racing, and he was sweating profusely and panting.

He looked at the clock. It was 5:30 p.m. Startled, he jumped up. He couldn't believe he had slept so long. Standing at the bathroom sink and looking at his reflection in the mirror, he hardly recognized himself. There was heartache and disappointment written all over his face, and they had aged him like a harsh desert sun. No wonder people were worried about him. There was a broken old man looking back at him.

His mother was sitting with Lizzie in the dark when he walked into the living room. Lizzie was asleep, and the television was on with the volume so low that he could barely hear it.

"I'm so sorry. I never intended to sleep that long," Dale said.

"It's okay," LaToya answered. "You needed the rest. You're running yourself ragged."

"How long has she been sleeping?"

"Not long. She already had dinner. She didn't eat much, so she might be hungry later. She was having a little pain, poor thing. Lisa said to tell you to give her the medication at 7:00 and 11:00."

"Okay, what about you? Did you eat? I can make you something," Dale offered.

"No, thank you. I had lunch with Lisa," she explained. "It's too early for me to eat again. But why don't you go fix yourself a little something?"

"I'm not hungry either," Dale contended.

"Doesn't matter. You're going to make yourself sick. Go eat anyway!" LaToya ordered. She sat up erect and pointed in the direction of the kitchen.

"You're probably right," Dale said. "Are you sure I can't make something for you too?"

"Yeah, I'm sure. But if you make coffee, I'll take a cup," she remarked.

"Alright, coming right up," he replied.

He went into the kitchen and started the coffee. There was leftover spaghetti in the refrigerator in a plastic container, and he pulled that out and put it in the microwave. He started thinking about his dream. It wasn't the first time he had awakened in fear of being overtaken by an adversary. He already believed that he was being persecuted, and now the oppression had extended to his sleeping hours. He was a man without a haven.

His mother always loved his coffee. She used to say that he should open a coffee shop. He just thought she was buttering him up because she was too lazy to make it herself. She drank two cups while he sat at the kitchen table and ate his dinner while his truck warmed up in preparation to drive her home. He was wrong; he was hungry. He gobbled down the spaghetti in no time.

"Are you ready to go?" he asked after he finished and was rinsing his plate.

"Yeah, I'm ready," she replied.

"Michael is here. He can listen for Lizzie," he stated.

They didn't talk at all during the short ride to her apartment. Under the cover of darkness, they were free to entertain their thoughts. Dale wasn't really thinking about anything. His brain jumped around from thought to thought without rhyme or reason. If there was a pill to help settle his mind, he would have gladly taken it. He drove up to her apartment and parked on the sidewalk where no parking was permitted.

"You don't have to get out," she said. "I can take it from here."

"Okay, but watch your step," Dale directed. "You don't want to fall on the ice."

"I will. Call me if you need me," she reiterated. "I'm not doing anything but sitting here."

"I will. Thank you, Mom," he said.

"You take care of my girl and—"

She froze in place and turned to look directly at his darkened form. "What did you call me?" she asked.

"Uh, Mom," he said again.

"You never called me that... Louis did sometimes, but never you."

"I know. I'm sorry," Dale spoke. "I was wrong."

"No, I understand," she said softly.

"Yeah, but I need to tell you that I was wrong...and I want to apologize for hurting you," Dale expressed.

"I forgive you, sweet boy," she said with audible anguish.

"I forgive you, too, with all of my heart," Dale declared.

***

This time he remembered to take TJ's gift out of the car. Lizzie was still asleep. He needed to wake her up to take her medication.

"Babe...babe," he spoke softly.

She opened her eyes.

He smiled warmly.

"Hi," she said under her breath.

"I'm sorry to have to wake you, but you have to take your medication. Do you need to go to the bathroom?"

She nodded her head.

This had become their nightly ritual. He carried her to the bathroom and then cleaned her up. Just as he was putting her back to bed, she asked, "What's that?"

"Oh, it's a gift for you," Dale stated.

"It's beautiful. From your mother?" she guessed.

"No, it's from TJ," he replied.

"TJ?" she questioned.

"Yes, he made it," Dale relayed.

"Made it?" she repeated in astonishment.

"Yeah, he made it and wanted you to have it," Dale said. "He wanted me to tell you that he loves you."

"Aww, how precious is that?"

"He really felt bad that he couldn't come to see you," Dale reported.

"Make sure you tell him that I love it."

"I will," Dale asserted.

Chapter 31

Dale was sitting with Lizzie watching television. It was in the middle of the afternoon, and she was alert. Michael walked in and announced that he had something he wanted to show them. He had his laptop in his hand and started connecting it to the television. Dale had no idea that he knew how to do any of that. He seemed nervous. Dale wasn't quite sure exactly what to expect.

"Um…you ready?" Michael asked.

"Yeah, we're ready," Dale responded.

It took a couple of minutes. At first, there continued to be no picture, but Michael made some adjustments, and suddenly his laptop screen was projected onto the television. The first screenshot read, "The Johnsons: Look at what God has done!" There was music too. Then began a succession of family photos, like a slideshow.

Dale and Lizzie were suddenly captivated as they viewed photographs of their family through the years. One showed Lizzie, big and pregnant, displaying a huge smile. There were baby pictures of all three boys and their high school photos. The display included photos of their extended family, too, including a nice one of Lizzie's mom and dad in the beginning.

They laughed at the two of Dale and Lizzie posing before both proms they attended.

There were several photos from their wedding and close-ups of their wedding party. Another was of the whole family standing in front of their house on the day they moved in. There were also two clips from the newspaper of Christopher scoring touchdowns and being heralded by the community.

Interspersed throughout were funny shots. For instance, there was one of Dale sleeping on the sofa with his buttcrack prominently on display. Another was a picture of Michael as a toddler, wearing only a diaper and a pair of his mother's high heels.

The last photograph was probably taken twenty-five years ago. It was a black-and-white picture of their family dressed in their Sunday's best standing on the church steps. Dale could remember that day like it was yesterday. It was Easter Sunday, and neither boy wanted to go to church that morning. They kept fighting with each other in the car on the way, and Dale had to threaten physical harm to get them to settle down. The photograph was taken after the service. They were all smiling, and Lizzie was beaming with pride. Dale was too.

Michael ended with a final slide that he read aloud:

> This production is dedicated to our parents, Dale and Elizabeth Johnson. To our father, we honor you as a man after God's own heart. You taught us to be strong and set the right example. To our mother, we call you blessed and love you more than words can say. Thank you both for not giving up on us!
> Christopher Johnson, TJ Johnson, and Michael Johnson
> Written and Produced by Michael Johnson

Special thanks to Wanda Spears for her creative
assistance.
No portion of this production can be used without
the prior permission of the producer.

Caught completely off guard, Dale and Lizzie were both
left speechless for several seconds after the screen went dark.
They had watched the whole thing without hardly taking a
breath. Then they erupted in applause and cheers, and they
were both laughing and crying at the same time.

Michael looked confused.

"Come here, baby!" Lizzie exclaimed.

He leaned into her, and she reached out and began kissing
and pecking his face.

"I can't believe you did this! How wonderful!" she
exclaimed.

"Really?" Michael asked.

"That was truly amazing! It really just blessed my heart so
much," Lizzie gushed. "I am so proud of you!"

Dale rose up, touched Michael on the shoulder, and left the
room. He figured that they needed this time alone. Besides, he
wanted a few moments to gather himself. Interestingly, viewing
old family photographs wasn't as much of a strain on him the
way looking at wedding pictures had been. Although it was
bittersweet, he still rather enjoyed reminiscing with Lizzie, and
he felt a little uplifted at the end.

Of course, he had seen the photographs before, many of
which Dale had taken himself. But somehow, Michael had
managed to present them in such a fashion that his attention
was momentarily redirected away from his present suffering

to a simpler time of bygone days. He was suddenly painfully aware of just how dull his senses had grown over time such that he presently lacked the ability to see the faithfulness of God and the blessing of family. Their life together was a mixed bag of joy and sorrow.

However, nothing against Michael, but Dale was pretty sure that the printed words he had read to them at the end of the presentation were Wanda's words and not his own. They were perfect, just the things that Christian parents would most want to hear their children say. Unfortunately, it was also true that neither one of their boys had any idea who God really is or any desire to know him. They were lost—that fact alone would always be his biggest failure as their father.

Minutes later, Dale was in the kitchen when Michael walked in. He looked like he was carrying the weight of the world on his shoulders. Although Dale felt for Michael, he really didn't have to resist any impulse to reach out and physically comfort his son.

"Mom wants you," Michael reported.

"Okay, I'll be right there," Dale said. "You okay?"

Michael nodded. But the pained expression on his face spoke volumes, as did his teary eyes.

"You sure?" Dale asked. "You want to talk about it?"

Michael just stood there. His shoulders were lowered, and he was looking down at the floor. He was clearly struggling.

"I feel sick," Michael expressed.

"Here, drink this," Dale said and handed Michael a bottle of water.

Michael grabbed the bottle, took a big swallow, and handed it back to his father. He was carrying his laptop in one of his hands.

"You know, I have never been prouder of you than I am now," Dale voiced. "What you did tonight for your mother was good. It was perfect."

"But I don't understand why this has to happen at all. Did I do something?" Michael asked.

"No, you didn't do anything," Dale rebuked. "Why would you think that?"

"Because mom doesn't deserve this. She has always been so good."

"I know," Dale responded. "But all of us will eventually die. Death is just the beginning of a new journey in a better place, a perfect place."

"That would make sense except for the pain," Michael articulated. "I feel bad that she has pain all the time. It's horrible. It's like the worst thing I have ever seen happen to anyone!"

"There's pain when a baby is being born into this life, and unfortunately, there's pain when we are being set free into a new life," Dale explained.

"Well, I didn't know it was going to be this bad," Michael asserted.

"Neither did I," Dale admitted.

"You better go check on her," Michael reminded.

"Right," Dale said and hurried out of the room.

Lizzie was sitting up with tears in her eyes.

"What's wrong?" he inquired. "You need your pain meds?"

"No," she whispered.

He sat down on the bed next to her and began stroking her face.

"Wasn't that something what Michael did?" she asked. "I am so proud of him."

"Me too. I just told him that."

"See, the boys aren't all bad," she urged.

"Of course, they're not all bad," he agreed. "They were each conceived in love, and they have a wonderful mother who they love very much."

"Thank you," she said. "But I can't help but worry about them."

She grimaced as she adjusted herself in bed.

"We've done the best we know how. We can't live their lives for them. The rest is up to them," Dale stated.

"Michael is worried that you're going to make him move out of the house," Lizzie reported.

"What does he think I'm going to do?" Dale questioned. "Just throw him out on the street?"

"Yes," she replied. "That's exactly what he thinks."

"Well, I never told him that," Dale defended. "Is that what you think?"

"No, but please don't... for me, please."

"I love him, too, you know. He's my son too," Dale protested.

"I know you do. But you and Michael still have to come to an understanding. Promise me that you won't force him to do something he might not be ready for."

"I don't know what that means," he maintained.

"Yes, you do. Promise me," she insisted.

Dale was offended and suddenly became sullen.

"I promise," he said.

"I know I can trust you, Dale Johnson, because you always keep your promises to me," Lizzie articulated. "I trust you with my life, and my family is my life."

He was salty but couldn't show it. He felt like he was being manipulated and accused of planning something nefarious. In his mind, nothing had changed concerning Michael. While it was true that he didn't want Michael living at home into his forties, he would never jeopardize his son's safety to achieve that goal.

He knew Michael was fragile, but he believed that was a problem. Boys must be taught how to be real men—something that doesn't just automatically happen because they inherited an X chromosome or can grow hair on their chests. Women, in general—and black women, in particular—are oftentimes willing to accept excuses when their sons are slack or trifling.

Indeed, Dale still stood by what he did years ago with Christopher, who was both disrespectful and morally deficient. But Michael wasn't Christopher. He wasn't TJ either. He was going to be a project, and projects take time. Rome wasn't built in a day. But it bothered him that Michael would say something about his concerns to his mother in her condition and not a word to his father. That, in a nutshell, was a big part of the problem.

Dale knew, however, that he wasn't exactly in any position to plead his case to Lizzie. At this moment, her peace of mind was the most important thing to him. He desperately wanted to protect her as much as he could. Ever since the day that she was first diagnosed, he hadn't given any thought to how he would live without her. That was a place his mind refused to let him go.

Recently, Dale overheard Wanda talking to someone on the phone about "how hard he was taking it." While he understood where she was coming from, he was so tired of people, however well-intended, giving their opinions of how he should feel or should be reacting. He wanted to be left alone. And he wanted to wake up tomorrow and discover that the last year and a half had just been a bad dream, that the one that God had created for him to love was as vibrant as ever. Short of that, he had no plans about the days after tomorrow.

Regardless, this was another good day. Lizzie's spirits were up, and her pain seemed to be intact. She even ate a little. Michael's presentation had a positive impact on her, and Dale was very grateful for that.

She was sound asleep by 7:00 p.m. He sat as close as he could and held her hand, content for the moment because all he wanted was to be by her side, loving her. While this was far from the idea, at least they were together.

"Dale?'

"Huh?" he sounded as he jumped up from his dozing. "What's wrong?" he asked

"What's this?" she wondered.

"What?"

"All these flowers on the bed," she said. "What's going on?"

"Oh, you noticed," he proclaimed. "I didn't think that you would?"

"Who could miss all these roses?" she contended. "What's happening?'

"Happy anniversary, baby!" he said with a big smile."

"What? Really?" she asked.

She perked up.

"Don't tell me that you forgot Valentine's day is our day?"

"Today?" she marveled.

"Yes, today is the day that the whole world celebrates us," he decreed.

"No, it's not," she disputed.

"I told you that the brothers invented the romance game," he teased lovingly.

"Yes, you told me," she whispered.

"Happy anniversary. I love you," he said.

"I love you too," she replied.

Chapter 32

Dale stopped going to work altogether. He couldn't focus on anything for long now, knowing that Lizzie was home in great pain. Some woman from the hospital came and spoke to him about end-of-life care and signs that the body was shutting down. He listened carefully. He needed to know what to look for if he would mount a successful attack against it. He didn't ask any questions. His secret game plan was to pray over her every morning and rebuke the death angels. It seemed to be working so far.

As bad as it was watching his wife fight for her life, the alternative was still unimaginable. The nights were the worse. However, there were still moments when she was lucid and was right there with him. He was committed to doing whatever he could to help her fight.

Wanda had basically moved in with them now. She was using TJ's old room. If she went home, it was never for long—just a few hours or so. The overall mood in the house was gloomy. There was rarely a word spoken that wasn't necessary or said louder than in a hushed tone. Dale didn't much like that the house seemed like a morgue, but he couldn't think of anything to talk about himself.

Lizzie was noticeably weaker with each passing day, and he was no longer able to hide his anguish. It hurt to swallow, and it hurt him to breathe. He was an emotional wreck, and he was in no mood to commiserate with anyone.

Dale made a casserole for dinner that even Michael liked. Wanda liked it, too, although she understandably didn't eat much of it. She had spent most of the day alone with Lizzie, and Dale sensed that he needed to stay in the background. He knew that she and Lizzie had a double-secret meeting a couple of nights before, and, although he didn't know the specifics, it was clear that they were now in a different place. Sisterhood is one of the most powerful forces on earth.

"Do you want any help cleaning up in here?" Wanda asked.

"No, I got it."

"I want to change Lizzie before too long," she said. "Is there anything else I can do?"

"No, I can't think of anything. Thanks."

"You don't have to thank me," she countered.

"I know, but—"

"You know Dale, I always thought you were a great guy," she volunteered. "But I have to say that this past year you have been truly amazing."

"Amazing? I don't feel amazing," he replied.

"It's not a feeling." Wanda admonished. "Maybe it's better if we focus on the things we know rather than on the things we don't. You are the son of Lord God Almighty. No matter what happens, that's who you'll always be."

She walked up to him, put her arms around him, and hugged him as tightly as she could, the way that only Lizzie held him.

It caught him completely off guard. She only drew him closer when he instinctively tried to pull away. Finally overcome, he gave in fully to the ocean rising within him and held on to her for dear life. Although he would have preferred otherwise, he wept there in front of her for a moment.

"I'm sorry," he cried. "It feels like I'm being tortured."

"I know, I know it does," she whispered and rubbed his back with her right hand in a circular motion. "It's okay... it's alright," she reassured. "You're going to make it through this...Please don't ever tell my husband that I said this, but I've always envied the way you love my sister. I've never seen a real-life love story before. It's not only beautiful to behold, but it was divine."

Her words caused him to tremble.

"What are you saying?" he asked. "I don't understand what you're saying."

"You have to let her go," Wanda insisted. "She's waiting for you to release her."

Dale jumped back. "She said that? No, I can't! I won't do it!" he protested. "I changed my mind. God can do miracles. His gifts are eternal!"

"Her gift was being loved all of these years by you. The miracle is in you," she explained.

"No; there has to be more," he argued. "We were supposed to last forever!"

She took his hand and squeezed it. "When you're ready," she contended. "You're going to be just fine, my brother. Just fine, I know it. You've been highly favored because God sets aside the godly man for himself."

She kissed him on the cheek, turned, and headed for the other room.

Dale stood there, completely lost. He knew what this meant. Lizzie was ready for her new life. Her body was no longer a suitable home for her beautiful soul and spirit. Their one-in-a-billion love story was fast coming to a not-so-perfect ending. It was time for him to say goodbye too.

"God help me!" he cried from his heart.

***

He didn't sleep at all that night. He was afraid she would be taken from him if he did. So he stood guard to prevent that from happening. That gave him a lot of time to think. He was both resentful and angry. Not at anyone in particular; instead, his contempt was directed at everybody and everything in general. When he looked around and saw other people laughing and smiling, he realized that the soundtrack of his life was much different than what many others were composing. He felt cheated.

However, the real problem was that lately, he was doing a lot of philosophizing about "God's will" in his suffering. If there were unseen and uncontrollable forces at play in the world besides God, then that meant that people were nothing more than pawns in a brutal game of life where tragedy and destruction are inevitable because they are literally lurking around every corner. The one question that kept running over and over in the back of his mind was, *What good is a God who doesn't help us when we need him the most?*

Dale knew that there was a chance that he was overthinking everything, so he wasn't taking himself too seriously. Most adults understand that bad things, unbearable things, can happen in anybody's life. Hearts are broken every day.

But he was just being honest that oversimplified or hyper-spiritual answers hailing the goodness of God were not working for him. Maybe he would come to see it differently at some point in the future, but he even had his doubts about the likelihood of that happening. All pretense was gone now, especially between him and God.

His mother wanted to stay at the house with them as time was getting short. He gave in to her request even though he really didn't want her there. Nothing against her, but he wanted as much alone time with Lizzie as he could get.

Altogether, it was just the five of them now, counting Lisa. Michael had pretty much retreated back into his cave, although he would check in on his mother every so often. Dale didn't want any more prayer-group people hovering over them. He didn't want the pastor there either.

Michael was lying on his bed with the door to his room open when Dale walked by.

"Hey, Daddy?"

"Yeah."

"Can I ask you a question?" Michael inquired.

Dale stopped in stride, backed up, and stood in the doorway.

"What is it?" he asked.

"What do you know about Job?" Michael questioned.

"Who?"

"Job, you know, in the Bible?"

"Um, I know that he was a godly man whose faith was tested by the devil when he lost everything he had," Dale responded.

"Do you think he was a real man, or is the story fiction?" Michael pressed.

"Well…my position on that has changed over time. Now I tend to believe the stories in the Bible, even the ones in the Old Testament," Dale acknowledged.

"Me too," Michael said. "So, what do you think is the point of the story?"

"Um…that we need to trust in God, and not in our material possessions," Dale asserted.

"Yeah, that's partly it, but I don't know…I think it might be bigger than that," Michael suggested.

"Bigger how?" Dale engaged.

"I think it's mostly about who God is."

"How do you know about Job?" Dale wondered.

"I've been reading about him in this Bible," Michael revealed. He held up a medium-sized Bible with a blue cover.

"Where did you get that?" Dale asked.

"I bought it," Michael replied.

"What made you do that?"

"I had some questions about some stuff," Michael said. "I was asking Aunt Wanda. She told me about Job."

"Really?" Dale queried. "You read the story?"

"Yeah," Michael affirmed. "I remember it a little from before, but I had forgotten about it."

"And what do you think the point of the story is again?" Dale questioned.

"I think that he needed to lose all the stuff he had so he could come to the end of himself and see God for who he really is."

"And who exactly is God?" Dale probed.

"He's the perfect father," Michael declared.

He sounded confident.

"If God is so perfect, then why is there so much pain in the world?" Dale contended. He was shaking inside and cleared his throat several times because his voice was filled with emotion, and he didn't want Michael to hear it.

"Satan thought that Job's trials would break his spirit. But they only made him stronger, and so they were good for him in the end. Life is both pain and joy. The joy comes from God."

"You read all that?" Dale asked.

"Yeah. Like I said, I wanted to know. I've been really confused."

"Do you feel less confused now?" Dale wondered.

"I don't know, maybe a little, Michael reported. "But I really like the story. I think that it would make a great movie or something because the message in it is more relevant to us today than all of the same old stuff that they keep making movies about, you know, like the Ten Commandments and stuff."

Dale was confounded, and he was caught entirely off guard. He never thought he would ever find himself discussing Old Testament theology with Michael.

"I never really thought about it that way," he admitted. "You might be right."

"I am right," Michael insisted. "I feel like this is the stuff that people really need to know today, you know. The point is that no one should live their life without hope and in despair every day because we can always go home to father's house."

Dale smiled as his heart wept within him. He felt unsteady on his feet, and he fought hard to constrain himself.

"You sounded just like your Uncle Louis when you said that," he finally expressed.

"I did?" Michael questioned.

"Yes, it's not just what you said, but more the way that you said it... I'm sorry, it just took me back for a moment..." he trailed off.

"I wish I could have met him," Michael commented.

"Me too," Dale said. "So, you're a Christian?"

Michael looked startled by the question.

"Yes, at least I think I am...Why? Did you think I wasn't?"

"I just never heard you say it," Dale explained.

"I assumed we were all Christians in this house," Michael stated.

"I guess I just never thought you guys were paying attention," Dale confessed.

"Are you kidding?" Michael asked. "We heard everything you said...Well, I take that back. I don't know about Christopher."

Dale was slightly amused despite himself.

"Well, thanks for telling me. It means a lot to me to hear you say that."

"You know, mom is worried about you, don't you?"

"I gathered that," Dale conceded.

"She says you don't really know how to grieve."

"Is that right? Because I didn't know there was a right way and a wrong way to react when your whole world is crumbling at your feet," Dale defended.

"But there really is," Michael replied. "Everybody's world gets rocked sometimes. I remember when you told Christopher one time when he was crying because his team lost a game that sometimes losing is better than winning because when you lose, you can see your weaknesses better. Do you remember that?"

"Yeah, I remember…I'm doing the best I can," Dale stated softly.

"She knows that," Michael conveyed. "She just wants me to keep an eye on you."

"On me? Well, what did you tell her?" Dale questioned.

"What?" Michael asked.

"What did you say?"

"Yes," Michael advised. "I told her yes, I will do it."

"Good," Dale said firmly. "Because I have a feeling that I am going to need you to help me with that."

Dale tried to smile, but he only managed a slight curl and quiver of his upper lip.

"Okay," Michael replied and exhaled deeply.

Dale was relieved too, and he paused there a couple of seconds longer and stared at his son, the one who never wanted to leave his dad's house.

When he got to his room, Dale closed the door behind him and threw himself full force, face-down, across the bed.

Lizzie's scent lingered in the air. He was addicted to her fragrance, which he had inhaled daily as if it were oxygen. In the beginning, all he wanted was to love and to be loved by her. As a result, he found his life in her because it was her love that led him to the greatest love of all. And God's love not only never dies, but it also never fails.

He laid there for several minutes and cried a river. His misery was buried down deep, and the pangs of despair erupting within were trying to overtake him completely. His entire body ached, from the hair on the top of his head to the nails on his big toes. He was convinced that no human alive could ignore or deny this kind of trauma and grief.

But he also recognized that we don't know the entire story. Therefore, he was willing to consider that, like it was for Job, the key for him was learning to endure without sinning against God or cursing him because we know without a doubt that God really is good.

Indeed, he could accept now that serving God meant continuing to trust him in a dry and parched land where there is no water. Hopefully, his strength will grow in time—a commodity that he would soon have much more of than he knew what to do with. But it was still okay with him if he died this way. That's all the faith that he had left—a dribble. He was almost empty.

Spontaneously, he gave thanks to God for giving him Lizzie to have and to hold for this part of his journey. She was well worth the heartbreak. And at that moment, he was about as grateful as a man could be. That is, a man who was about to be crushed and buried alive.

Chapter 33

Dale was startled by the knock at the door. It was Wanda. Lizzie was awake. He had no idea how long he had drifted there, lost in space. The only reason he came upstairs in the first place was to freshen up a little as he had stayed awake most of the night watching Lizzie sleep. Although he was tired, the last thing he wanted to do was take a nap. He was at war with himself in every way. The Bible says that the body is weak, even when the will to do something is not.

"Okay, I'll be right there," he shouted through the door.

By the time that he made it downstairs, Lizzie had fallen back asleep. Dale was terribly disappointed. He desperately needed to talk to her before it was too late. Even after his conversation with Tracy, he had spent so much time running here and there trying to make sure that everyone else had a chance to get closure that he had not given any thought at all to what he wanted to say to her. They had discussed her final wishes several months back. She had been very clear about everything. He knew what to do.

The real issue for him was that Lizzie already knew how much he loved her and that she was the light of his life. He really couldn't think of anything else that he could say to her that she hadn't already heard. And he knew her, there simply was no need for him to say those things again. She never liked it when he was too sappy. It was an urge that he had learned over time that he needed to resist.

Nevertheless, there still was something heavy on his heart to tell her. He could feel the weight of it. He just didn't know what it was. As he watched her sleep, he realized that all he really wanted was for her to be free. True love is supposed to endure all things, even death. So if it was really over, then his prayer was for her to dream away in peace. He never meant to be a problem for her.

She ended up sleeping for most of the day. Whenever she opened her eyes a little, it seemed like she didn't really know where she was or fully recognize him. She also appeared to be hallucinating some. He thought he heard her mumble her way through a conversation with her mother or somebody. Lisa said that it was normal as her body was slowing down. Dale was suddenly terrified that he had missed his chance for one last goodbye after everything that they had been through.

It was just before midnight when he heard her stirring. He was sitting in his chair just meditating. Wanda was in the kitchen with Simon, her husband, and his mother had gone up to Christopher's room to get a couple of hours of sleep. Lizzie's breathing had changed considerably over the last several hours, and it had become more interrupted.

"Hi," he said through bated breath.

"Hi," she whispered back.

He stared intently into her eyes and could see the difference. The light was nearly gone.

"You know, I'm gonna miss you," he said. He swallowed hard.

"Me too," she replied. "You should probably get married again."

"You think?" he asked suspiciously.

"Yeah, I do…You're not that bad…But you've let yourself go a bit, so you should go work out at the gym."

"I'm sorry, but there's nothing wrong with my body," he rebuked.

"You gotta work the abs, brother!" she mocked.

"I don't ever remember hearing you complain before."

"I didn't want to hurt your feelings," she said with shallow breath.

She kept closing her eyes and then fighting to reopen them. Her lips looked dry and parched. He dabbed them with the little moist sponge that was in the cup next to the bed.

"I'll have you know that I already have several hook-ups lined up," Dale teased. "And that's not counting Chuck, my new friend from the prison."

"That's…not funny," she said and coughed.

"All I'm saying is that this brother still got game. So, don't you worry about me."

"Hmm. Okay, I won't …but you might wanna get some new clothes…"

"Enough already," he interrupted and kissed her on the lips.

"Are you cold? You seem cold. Here let me pull up this blanket around you…there, is that better?"

"Uh-huh," she said and nodded. Her eyes were closed again. Her breathing was more labored.

There was a surreal feeling about the moment. He stood there holding her hand.

Intuitively, he closed his eyes and forced his own body to settle down enough so that he could hear her. He was no longer aware of his surroundings as he pushed his way through.

He somehow found himself on hallowed ground where he was able to speak directly from his heart to hers and from his spirit to her spirit. Unrestrained, he told her everything that he had been unable to say with words spoken. She responded in kind.

And from that place, he poured out his love upon her like oil and blessed her.

It was bittersweet, like the last dance to the most beautiful love song ever written.

She wanted another pledge.

He felt rushed.

They held on tight.

He could feel her love slipping away.

"You just go to sleep now," he directed. "I can see how tired you are. Run to the father. I'll fight, I will...I promise."

We were crushed and overwhelmed beyond our ability to endure, and we thought we would never live through it. In fact, we expected to die. But as a result, we stopped relying on ourselves and learned to rely only on God, who raises the dead. (2 Corinthians 1:8b-9 NLT)

About the Author

Ed Thompson is a lay minister in Syracuse, New York. He is also a trial attorney in New York, having practiced law in Syracuse for more than twenty-five years. He is a former federal prosecutor and a former assistant public defender. Additionally, Ed received a master's degree in biblical studies from Alliance Theological Seminary in 2020. Previously, Ed received a BA degree from Ohio Northern University in 1982 and a JD degree from Albany Law School in 1985. Presently, he resides in Baldwinsville, New York, with his wife and daughter.

Ed can be contacted at ethompson.esq@gmail.com.

Other books by Ed Thompson

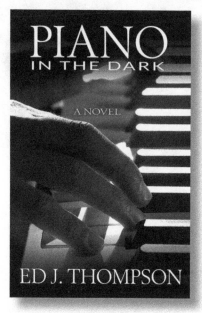

Sandy Coleman loved God his whole life. The only son of a Baptist minister, he grew up in the church playing the piano and leading worship every Sunday. His musical gifts are undeniable, and the people at Mount Moriah Baptist Church in Syracuse, New York, adore him. However, a chance meeting with Tony Moreno, a handsome, young legal aid lawyer would change his life forever. As their forbidden romance unfolds, Sandy's secret life is exposed and he is distraught when he is suddenly and mercilessly forced to leave the church. With virtually no friends and limited support from his family, his world slowly spirals out of control as he is painfully torn between his physical passions and his love for God. Nothing makes sense to Sandy. Doesn't he deserve to find love and be happy just like everyone else? Sexuality is not a choice, right? Could anything be worse than when the heart desires something that God might not want it to have? More than a love story, Piano in the Dark is a raw and honest look at the unresolved conflict between the church and homosexuality.